Unpacking Secrets

Rachel Fitzjames

ISBN: 978-1-967700-00-4 (Paperback)
ISBN: 978-1-967700-01-1 (Ebook)

Library of Congress Control Number: 2025906406

The story, all names, characters, and incidents portrayed in this production are fictitious. No identification with actual persons (living or deceased), places, buildings, and products is intended or should be inferred.

Book Cover by Maldo Designs

Editing by Melissa Rotert – Wordplay Copy & Line Edits

A note to readers

Each book in the Spruce Hill series features on-page, open-door steamy scenes, along with swearing and some degree of suspense. There may be a limited amount of on-page physical violence as well as the threat of peril facing one or more characters. Specific content in this story that might be of concern to readers includes death of a parent/grandparent (historical/off-page). As a general reassurance, no animals or children are ever harmed in my books.

For more details, please visit https://rachelfitzjames.com/ or use the QR code below.

*To my husband, who fell in love
with the Lakeside Inn
maybe even before I did.*

Contents

1. One — 1

2. Two — 16

3. Three — 23

4. Four — 32

5. Five — 40

6. Six — 48

7. Seven — 62

8. Eight — 76

9. Nine — 87

10. Ten — 94

11. Eleven — 106

12. Twelve — 115

13.	Thirteen	125
14.	Fourteen	139
15.	Fifteen	147
16.	Sixteen	161
17.	Seventeen	172
18.	Eighteen	180
19.	Nineteen	188
20.	Twenty	197
21.	Twenty-One	205
22.	Twenty-Two	212
23.	Twenty-Three	227
24.	Twenty-Four	240
25.	Twenty-Five	246
26.	Twenty-Six	251
27.	Twenty-Seven	260
28.	Twenty-Eight	268
29.	Twenty-Nine	284
30.	Thirty	295
31.	Thirty-One	304
32.	Thirty-Two	309
33.	Thirty-Three	320
Epilogue		326

Also by............338

Acknowledgements............340

About the author............342

One

*T*HIS CANNOT BE REAL, I thought as I studied the building in front of me.

A family legacy I'd never heard of, an inheritance from a grandmother I'd never known. That initial sense of disbelief still hadn't quite worn off, even as I stood before the charming Tudor-style inn. My gaze traveled from the steep, gabled roof down to the perfectly landscaped flower beds on either side of an arching wooden door.

This building—this business—was now mine.

After a phone call changed the course of my life, I was the new owner of the Lakeside Inn, a bustling bed and breakfast in the middle of Nowhere, New York.

Scratch that.

Once rated one of the safest towns in America, Spruce Hill lay tucked away between Lake Ontario to the north and the Finger Lakes to the south. My internet search the week before had produced little more than a few wineries outside of town, the inn itself, and a conspiracy site about a string of unsolved murders in the surrounding area back in the eighties and nineties.

Since the safe town rating was more recent, I decided to ignore that bit of trivia.

After two long days of driving and an overnight stay at a creepy motel outside of Chicago, I was tired, hungry, and quite possibly delirious. The inn, with its white stucco exterior and dark exposed beams, made me feel like I'd crossed an ocean rather than a handful of states.

It was cute and quaint and, mind-bogglingly, it belonged to me.

I pressed my hand hard over my mother's ring where it rested against my sternum, drawing a deep breath that lifted the opal into my palm. Missing her was like missing a limb. It had always been us against the world, but now it was just me and the aftermath of a truth she'd kept hidden my entire life.

Her ring and the unexpected, strangely cryptic note she'd left for me to find in a nightstand drawer, telling me to contact the owner of this inn, were the only tangible proof that this wasn't a dream.

Unfortunately, when I did as she directed, I learned the owner—my grandmother, who I'd thought long dead—had passed away only a matter of months after my mom.

My childhood home, tucked in a quiet suburb outside of Minneapolis, was officially sold to a young couple expecting their first child. Most of my worldly possessions were crammed into suitcases in my car, with only the most sentimental items taking up space in my best friend's guest room closet until I was settled and ready for her to ship them to me.

My gaze turned to Lake Ontario, nestled right up against the pretty gardens behind the inn. Sunlight glittered across the gently waving surface, accentuating each ripple drawn by the spring breeze.

I took a step down the path to explore further, but I was interrupted by a sudden jingling of keys and a robust laugh.

"Well now, you must be our long lost friend. I'm Gerard Walker, caretaker here at the inn."

A portly older man appeared from behind the corner of the building. His English accent was soft, faded after what I imagined must be decades far from home and remarkably soothing to my nerves. He was the perfect caricature of a grandfather, with his twinkling eyes and a shock of white hair.

When he held out a hand, I felt like a child, playacting at business ownership. I forced down the uncertainty to shake his hand with as much confidence as I could muster.

"Yes, I'm Juliet Morrison."

"Juliet," he repeated, his voice heavy with emotion. "It's a delight to finally make your acquaintance. By heavens, you do look like Nan. That wild red hair, those freckles. And you have her eyes, blue as the morning sky over the lake."

It was strange, hearing my unknown grandmother referred to in such a familiar fashion. Until my mother's letter set off this chain of events, I hadn't even known Nan existed. Though I pasted what I hoped was a polite smile on my face and wracked my brain for an appropriate response, the awkward silence stretched.

Finally, Gerard cleared his throat and gestured toward the inn. "Why don't I show you around?"

"Sure, that sounds great," I said with relief.

I followed his stout frame to the inn's heavy wooden door. It looked practically medieval, I thought, expecting a dim interior filled with long oak tables and serving wenches. Instead, the door opened into a sunny, cozy sitting room. The patterned wallpaper was a bit old-fashioned, but then, so was the floral upholstery. It could have been straight out of a country living magazine.

"Nan and our housekeeper, Gemma Gregson, decorated the place themselves," he told me as we walked into the room. "They wanted it to feel like a family home, rather than an impersonal hotel."

"It's beautiful." I touched a petal in the bouquet of silk flowers on a side table.

"I, ah, assume the lawyer explained the management situation to you?" he ventured. His hands were clasped tightly together as he watched my perusal of the room, as though my opinion of the place actually mattered.

The lawyer. Right. After calling the inn and being informed the owner had died, I received a call from a lawyer the next day. I still hadn't wrapped my head around it.

"Yes," I said slowly. "Mr. Escobar said that the inn practically runs itself and I'm basically the owner in name only. He promised that all of the employees would be staying on, which I hope is true, because I have no idea what I'm doing here."

Clearly relieved, Gerard said, "Yes, yes, that's exactly so. Nothing to worry about, dear girl, we all know what we're doing. I act as caretaker of the grounds and the building itself, then there's Sally, our chef, and Mrs. Gregson, the housekeeper. My grandson, Henry, took over the reservations and accounting for Nan when she got sick, but she ran the place singlehanded for years, until bringing Mrs. Gregson onboard just before your mother was born."

"That's the entire staff?" I asked, surprised.

"We pull in additional waitstaff and an extra maid or two as needed, depending on the season. Soon enough, we'll need a new groundskeeper, but these old knees haven't let me down yet. Henry is out running an errand, but he'll be back soon. I'll introduce you. The others are around here somewhere."

I nodded, more overwhelmed by the small, intimate staffing than I would've been by a large crew. My status as the outsider cemented then and there.

"Henry has a head for numbers. I'm sure he'd be happy to show you the revenues, in case you'd like to step into Nan's shoes down the road."

My mouth dropped open before I could stop it. "Oh. I mean, that'd be fine," I stammered.

I had zero interest in learning about profit margins or managing the inn. The lawyer made it sound like I would essentially act as a figurehead in this operation. I was an artist with zero experience running a business—somehow, I doubted cashing out customers or reshelving books at my last job would translate to useful skills for the owner of a bed and breakfast. I'd enjoyed the job for the freedom it gave me to pursue art in my spare time while still paying my bills.

Never in my life had I been so unprepared for anything.

Gerard smiled reassuringly. "Of course, dear, whatever you wish. Everyone is very excited to meet you."

"Great," I replied, trying to smile back. I followed him down a hallway, studying the old photos hanging there along the way.

"The inn was built in 1850, though it was a private residence until Nan purchased the property in 1971 to convert it to a bed and breakfast. She and her husband lived in the owner's quarters until she got pregnant with your mother, then they made an offer on the adjoining property where the cottage sits. Sally lives in the owner's quarters now, so there's always someone on site for emergencies."

I hadn't thought to research the history of the place, not when my own history was so up in the air, but now I wanted to know everything. "So you offer breakfast to guests, and they're on their own for lunch and dinner?"

"That's how we've done it for years, but we recently started offering dinner service for guests, by reservation only, in addition to our usual breakfast. Sally is very talented and Nan hoped to eventually expand to offering a full dinner menu. Her illness delayed those plans a bit, but we're working hard to get them rolling again."

A gray-haired woman in a floral dress hurried toward us and grasped my hands in hers as she gave me a full once over. "Oh, goodness, you must be Juliet. I'm Gemma Gregson. We spoke on the phone the other day. Well, if you aren't just the spitting image of Nan!"

The comment struck me speechless for a second time.

"Ah," I began, searching for something to say in response.

I needed to brainstorm a better way to react to those exclamations. Fortunately, my reticence didn't slow Mrs. Gregson down one bit. The older woman reached out to touch a lock of my hair, though she caught herself and dropped her hand before making contact.

"That red doesn't lie," she said, clucking her tongue. "Melissa was blonde as blonde could be, but she had a temperament that was better suited to a redhead, as I'm sure you must know."

How bizarre it was to hear strangers refer to my mother by name. I still didn't know how to respond, so I simply smiled. Fortunately, Mrs. Gregson overlooked my silence and turned to Gerard.

"The doorknob in the pantry is loose. Sally asked me to send you to fix it, if you have the time? I can show Juliet around."

"You're in capable hands," the older man said with a wink. "I'll take you over to the cottage when Gemma is satisfied you've seen every nook and cranny of the inn."

I mumbled my thanks as he ambled away.

Mrs. Gregson beamed at me. "Well, then. This is the dining room, of course. Breakfast is served from seven to eleven each morning. Sally likes to put out some buffet items when we have a full house, but she also has a standard made-to-order menu, as well as a daily special."

A dozen or so tables dotted the hardwood floor, each decorated with a lace tablecloth and a small candle in the center. The dark paneling on the walls gave way to a stretch of tall windows overlooking the gardens and the lake, bringing in a fantastic amount of light even as afternoon faded to evening.

"This view is really something," I said softly.

"Isn't it? Even in the winter, our guests love it. We encourage them to spend time wherever they wish, and we keep that cupboard stocked with board games and books for them to enjoy." She gestured toward an armoire tucked into a corner. "It's not unusual for the tables to be taken up outside of breakfast hours. Shall we continue the tour?"

Just as I turned to follow her toward the door, my gaze stalled on the artwork scattered throughout the room. Mrs. Gregson noticed my interest and guided me toward the wall opposite the windows.

"These are all local landmarks," she said, gesturing to a small watercolor. "Most of them are Nan's contributions, like this one, but we have a handful of work from other local artists as well."

For a long moment, I studied the painting, each daub of color calling to me like a whispered voice, familiar but foreign. I'd never developed any talent for watercolors myself, but I loved them, the gentle power of every soft stroke.

Tearing my gaze away, I managed a smile for Mrs. Gregson. "Can I see some of the rooms, if any are free?"

With a tender look, Mrs. Gregson led me out of the dining room and continued the tour. We stopped briefly in the impressively modern kitchen at the back of the inn to meet Sally, then headed upstairs to peek into one of the unoccupied bedrooms on the second floor.

"The inn has ten suites in total," my tour guide informed me, "each with its own full bath. We get a good number of honeymooners, anniversary trips, that sort of thing. Our busiest seasons are spring and summer, but we do quite well throughout the entire year."

Making a noncommittal noise in my throat, I followed her silently throughout the interior of the inn. Everything was lovingly decorated; I had yet to spot a single thing that looked mass produced.

My grandmother had clearly put her heart and soul into this place.

For the first time since learning about Nan's existence, I was struck by a deep, penetrating sorrow. Part of me felt like I had no right to grieve for someone I'd never met, but the timing of it all seemed so tragic.

Mrs. Gregson glanced out a window at the top of the stairs. "Oh, good. Henry is back. I'll bring you by the office to meet him, then Gerard will take you over to the cottage."

The cottage. My new home. A flutter of anticipation rose up inside of me through the shadow of grief. My throat was still too tight for speech, so I just nodded.

Against that eager flutter, I tried to ignore the ball of dread in my belly at the thought of meeting Henry, though whether because Gerard had mentioned me taking over the job or because he must be closer to my age than the rest of them, I wasn't sure.

Maybe he was a sweet, nerdy type who liked numbers more than people. Maybe he was older than I envisioned, a middle-aged dad who valued family above all else.

Those images didn't reassure me as much as I would've liked.

Mrs. Gregson ushered me down the stairs and toward a little office tucked away across the hall.

"Good afternoon, Henry," she called, peeking around the doorframe.

I sucked in a steadying breath and followed her into the room.

"This is Juliet Morrison. Juliet, this is Henry Walker, our general manager."

The man behind the desk was not at all what I expected. He was absurdly handsome, with deep olive skin. Locks of hair so dark it bordered on black hung just long enough to fall over a brooding brow. His beautiful hazel eyes were a rich shade of green flecked with amber, but they regarded me with a coolness that ratcheted my anxiety to the next level.

I guessed he was somewhere in his mid-thirties, give or take a few years. He wore a white dress shirt with the sleeves rolled up to reveal sculpted forearms. This guy was definitely neither a geek nor a middle-aged dad. In truth, he looked polished and elegant, which made me feel frumpy and intensely unsuited to owning a business of any kind.

Mrs. Gregson, still lingering in the doorway, remained blissfully oblivious to his frosty gaze. She cheerfully called out something about leaving the young folks to it and disappeared before I could beg her to stay.

"Hi, it's nice to meet you," I said, offering my hand as I summoned a polite smile.

When he leaned back in the chair instead of clasping my palm, increasing the distance between us, I let the hand drop and clenched it into a fist.

"Right," Henry replied shortly.

His pointed scrutiny traveled over my haphazard road trip outfit. Embarrassment welled inside me as he surveyed the paint-splattered jeans and old college sweatshirt I'd thrown on that morning. The clothes were casual and comfortable for driving hours on end, but not exactly the height of sophistication.

When his gaze returned to my face, I was taken aback by the open hostility in his expression.

"The long lost heiress comes to claim her rightful place," he bit out. "Aren't we fortunate you're here to save us?"

My jaw dropped at his audacity. His deep voice was sharp, lending an aristocratic edge to his derision, even though he didn't share his grandfather's posh accent.

"I beg your pardon?" I sputtered.

"I'm sure you must have plenty of experience running a business," he went on, his tone brittle and condescending.

What the hell?

I scowled at him as my temper flared. It was one thing for me to doubt my own ability to take this on, but this jerk was *not* going to question my qualifications. He didn't even know me. Nan's will, as far as I understood, prevented me from actually running the place anyway, but if Henry Walker wasn't aware of that, I wasn't going to tell him—not while he was being an asshole, at least.

I forced my features to relax, though it took a gargantuan effort.

"Oh, I'm sorry," I replied, dripping sweetness. "I didn't realize you had a degree in hospitality. Maybe a refund is in order—you don't seem to have learned much from it."

Something in his expression shifted toward amusement, then the flash was gone. He slid a thick ledger onto the desk and his manner turned business-like as he stood, spun the chair around, and gestured for me to sit.

"My background is in accounting, actually. Here are the records for the past five months, starting January first. The books for previous years are over there on the shelf. The computer system is fairly straightforward, showing reservations and openings for each date. Nan upgraded a couple years ago to accept credit cards, the machine can be a bit finicky but the manual is in the drawer below it. Maybe the heiress will invest in a tablet-based POS system."

I continued to stand, ignoring the chair, and allowed myself to glare at him while I tried to control my response.

"I'm not here to steal your job," I snapped.

"No, you're just here to take over a family business you know nothing about," he fired back.

"I didn't ask for this," I ground out. "I didn't even know I *had* a family, nevermind a business to inherit. What exactly is your problem?"

The longer I stood there, the closer my fury got to boiling over. What right did this jerk have to question me? With a sudden, devastating smile, Henry's bad attitude evaporated into...well, I wasn't quite sure what, but I didn't trust for a second that it was sincere.

"Nothing at all," he answered. "Some of us have actual work to do. I guess we're finished here, then?"

"I guess we are," I replied tartly.

One corner of his mouth curved up again, ever so slightly, and I clenched my hands at my sides to keep from knocking the smile off his stupid, handsome face. With a final scowl, I whirled away from him, catching a whiff of some subtle cologne in the process.

He smells amazing. Too bad he's such a dickhead.

"Have a nice day," Henry called as I strode out of the office.

This was not how I imagined my introduction to the Lakeside Inn, not even a little. I was so fired up, I didn't pay attention to where I was going and ended up in the hallway filled with old photos. Without Gerard or Mrs. Gregson there to distract me, I moved closer to the framed pictures, seeking solace in the unfamiliar faces.

Except...they weren't all unfamiliar.

There was Nan, unmistakable with hair the same flaming red as mine, though she was slender and petite. Beside her was my mother, a teenager at the time, her blonde hair teased and crimped. Her curves were more like my own, even back then, and that resemblance soothed me.

Just as I lifted my hand to touch a finger to the image, Gerard stepped out from a door at the end of the hallway. His face broke into a smile when he saw me, but it faded quickly.

"Is everything all right? Did Henry do something to upset you?"

For a split second, I considered throwing Henry Walker under the bus, but that wouldn't win me any favor around here. I was the stranger, the newcomer, the—what had he called me? Right, the long lost heiress.

As if I'd been appointed queen of this kingdom rather than its floundering, clueless owner.

"Everything is fine, I'm just tired after the drive. Can you show me to the cottage now?" I asked, forcing a smile that hopefully looked more sincere than it felt.

"Of course, dear," Gerard replied. "Let's get you settled so you can relax. I hope you'll come for breakfast tomorrow, though. There's nothing like it. You have to experience Sally's genius for yourself."

I mumbled an answer that sounded like agreement, wondering if there'd be any way to get out of that particular commitment, and followed along behind him as we left through the heavy front door—fortunately without passing Henry's office along the way.

Well, Gerard's grandson was right about one thing. I *was* here to claim my rightful place. He'd just have to deal with it.

Two

Henry

WHAT THE FUCK JUST happened?

After Juliet stormed out of my office, I stared blankly at the computer screen for a good half hour. My grandfather would have my head if she went running to inform him how I treated her. And I wouldn't blame her one bit if she told him about that little shitshow.

I didn't even want to think about what Mrs. Gregson would do if she found out.

The housekeeper might be softer at heart than Nan ever was, but given her excitement about Juliet's arrival, I was sure an insult to the heiress would earn me a stern lecture, at the very least.

At worst? It'd be like a tidal wave of *Disappointed in You* lectures from every grandparent figure in my life.

"You're an idiot," I whispered to myself.

With a sigh, I sat back in the chair and rubbed my hands over my face. Not only was I not sure how to fix the situation, I wasn't even sure I *could*. Juliet didn't seem like the forgiving type with that short fuse, and setting a match to the embers had been altogether too thrilling to keep me from doing it again.

When she was standing there in front of me, I'd watched her bristle under my intentionally cold perusal—and I'd been perversely pleased by it. The woman was indeed a dead ringer for a much younger Nan Montgomery, though Nan had been so slender as to almost seem fragile for as long as I could re-member.

Juliet was nothing of the sort. Fragile wouldn't make it into a list of the top hundred adjectives I'd use to describe her.

I doubted she was any taller than Nan, whose presence always seemed far bigger than her few inches over five feet, but Juliet was all soft curves and rounded limbs. At first, she'd seemed almost timid, at least before the flames started leaping off her.

The kind of flames that indicated something I didn't want to notice about this woman. Not yet, not ever.

Passion.

It shouldn't have annoyed me, the echo of Nan so clear in her riot of blazing curls and those fierce blue eyes behind a sprinkling of freckles, but it did. It drummed up more emo-tion than I'd had in my system in a long time—emotion, and something more.

The flare of attraction that sparked through my body irritated me even further. Instead of warning me away, the fury radiating from her had only made me wonder what it'd be like to kiss her.

I got the impression it wouldn't be as soft and sweet as she looked. Underneath, this woman had a backbone of steel.

Another thing she and Nan had in common.

Regardless, that lapse in concentration had nearly knocked the wind from my sails, so I'd plopped my ass back down in the chair and smirked at her to cover my momentary flash of curiosity. The smirk had only pissed her off further, stoking those flames of aggravation higher.

For me? The attraction hadn't faded, nor had the curiosity. I still wanted to know, but there would be no kissing.

She might be beautiful, but I sincerely doubted she'd be sticking around.

Even if she wasn't Nan's granddaughter, my own stupidity had effectively obliterated any chance I might have had to win her over. Hell, I wouldn't be surprised if she'd marched straight out of here to demand they hire a new manager immediately. I'd be lucky to still have a job once word got around about how I'd spoken to her. Even if none of the old guard came right out and said it, the guilt-tripping alone might weigh on my soul heavily enough to send me packing.

Why couldn't I have just kept my mouth shut?

Juliet Morrison had spirit, that was for damn sure, and once I was ready to be honest with myself, I would have to admit that the quick comebacks and those blazing blue eyes had been a refreshing reminder of Nan.

Sally popped her head through the doorway, her eyebrows drawn down in a glare. "I just saw our new employer storm out of here like she was ready to punch someone, Henry. What did you do?"

"Do? Why does her bad mood mean I did something?"

"Because everyone else here is happy to welcome Nan's flesh and blood back into the fold. Whatever your issue is with Juliet, you better sort it out fast."

"Why?" I demanded, recognizing full well that I sounded like a petulant brat.

"Because Nan wanted this for her, Henry. You know she did."

I rubbed a hand over my eyes. "I know. Would you believe me if I said I didn't mean to rile her up like that?"

"Probably not," Sally replied.

"It's true. She's got Nan's temper."

"And you're just sweet as pie, huh?"

"Usually," I muttered.

It was half true—I was normally pretty even-keeled, but Juliet Morrison ignited something that had lain dormant inside me for a long time.

Interest.

"Usually doesn't matter when you're picking fights with the boss, Henry. What did you say to her?"

Regret thrummed through me. I couldn't tell Sally the things I'd said to Juliet—the chef already thought I was the asshole here, and I didn't disagree. I stared back at her, wishing I could rewind the day and start again.

"You should be happy she's here," Sally said, still glaring. "This place could use some young blood, especially while you're trying to bring us into the new millennium."

"Yeah, as long as she doesn't run it all into the ground."

She gave me an exasperated look. "Give her a chance, Henry. She's family. You need to fix this before anyone else finds out you picked a fight. If she decides to hightail it back to Minnesota, we could all be out of a job. She's coming back for breakfast tomorrow. That's your chance to make a better impression for a change."

"When have I ever *not* made a good impression?" I replied, lifting a brow.

"Every time you've ever opened your mouth?"

I rolled my eyes but kept my mouth shut, because she might have been right. Today had definitely *not* been a good impression, not when I couldn't contain myself in front of our new boss.

Sally studied me for a minute, then shook her head. "Get yourself under control, Walker. She's here to stay and you're going to make things difficult for everyone if you can't accept that. You're lucky I'm the only one who saw her storm out of here."

"I know," I repeated. "I'll take care of it. I'll apologize, smooth things over."

"You better." With that dire parting shot, she left me alone in the silent office.

Sally was right.

I should apologize. Juliet hadn't even been in Spruce Hill for a full day, and I'd acted like a spoiled child. None of this was her fault, but knowing that didn't make it any easier to deal with her arrival, with the constant reminder of Nan's death. Even my own grandmother's passing hadn't hit me so hard, but I was only in elementary school at the time.

Though I knew Juliet was somewhere around thirty based on all the gossip in town regarding her mother's abrupt departure, she looked like a college kid. Fresh-faced and pretty, but sharp.

Damn, was she sharp.

Nan's temper had been legendary, but she'd rarely let it fly in front of the inn's staff. I couldn't remember ever bearing witness to it, but now that I'd met the granddaughter, I could certainly picture it.

Juliet.

I forced myself to think of her by name, though I wasn't entirely sure it suited her. It sounded too dainty, too delicate for someone whose deep blue eyes could spit fire the way hers had, but at the same time, it evoked a certain essence of drama that suited her quite well.

Maybe it was a better fit than I'd first imagined.

Even as I resigned myself to having to apologize to her, I decided I would wait for the right opportunity rather than seeking her out. If she wasn't willing to fight for her rightful place at the inn, then she damn well didn't deserve it.

Nanette Montgomery had been as close to me as my own grandparents, and her legacy deserved someone who wasn't scared off by a single encounter.

I was a patient man. I could wait.

When the time was right, I would apologize for being an asshole.

Hopefully, by then the woman—*Juliet,* I reminded myself firmly—would have decided exactly what she was looking for in Spruce Hill so that I didn't have to waste my energy on someone who didn't give a shit.

Three

JULIET

THE LAKE I WAS dying to explore came into full view as we circled around the inn, revealing an expanse of deep, breathtaking blue under a cloudless sky.

"Oh, it's beautiful," I whispered.

I was no stranger to smaller bodies of water, coming from Minnesota, but my hometown wasn't very close to the Great Lakes. The water here stretched as far as the eye could see. Gentle waves rolled against the rocky shoreline, lapping at the far edge of the exquisite garden.

"Nan chose this property because of that view," Gerard replied, smiling over at me. "The inn was her lifeblood, but these gardens were her pride and joy. She spent much of her free time out here."

I knew very little about gardening, but the blossoms bursting from each carefully tended bed were bright and cheerful. Some quote about the earth laughing in flowers sprang to mind; I could almost imagine my grandmother working along the little pathways between beds, weeding or painting among the colorful blooms.

My mother had loved flowers, despite her self-professed black thumb. I pictured her playing in these gardens as a little girl—it seemed a perfect wonderland for a young child's imagination.

The cottage wasn't visible as we followed the narrow path out of the garden, but it came into view just after we passed a tiny stand of fruit trees.

My heart leapt straight into my throat.

If the inn itself looked like something from a Renaissance faire, the cottage was straight out of a fairy tale. Its gray stone walls were accented by climbing green vines and topped with a sloping shingled roof. Though the garden flower beds we'd passed were neat and linear, the cottage was surrounded by a sea of wildflowers. We were barely a hundred yards from the inn, but the apple and pear trees blocking the view made it like another world back here.

Gerard handed me a keychain, smiling a bit mistily. "Here you are, my dear. You'll find everything you need inside. I pinned a list of phone numbers beside the fridge. The main number for the inn and my cell phone are on there. If you have any questions, just give me a ring."

I nodded. "Thank you."

"You can move your car from the parking lot into the drive-way," he said, pointing to the other side of the flower-filled yard. "Do you need help unloading your things?"

"No, I've got it. I appreciate the tour."

"Of course, dear. Hopefully I'll see you in the morning."

As he ambled back away, I soaked in the sight of the cottage, committing every stone, every curl of ivy to memory.

My mom's house had never felt like *mine,* not even after she died six months ago. It was too big, too full of memories for me to bear staying there on my own, so I'd focused my energy on packing it up to sell instead of letting grief swamp me. It needed new life, and so did I.

As of a week ago, we'd both been given just that.

The prospect of running an inn was too huge to take in just yet, but this little house? It was making everything feel very real. Even the sharp fury Henry had provoked was dimmer now, like this place was working its magic on me already.

With a deep breath, I walked up the cobblestone path to the front door, which was surrounded by beds of purple and white violets. The dark wood was weathered, worn to a beauti-ful sheen. A wreath of dried flowers encircled the hand-painted welcome sign hanging over a bronze door knocker.

I looked down at the keys in my hand. One bronze key was engraved with the initials L.I.—I took that to stand for Lakeside Inn. There was a similarly sized silver key that must belong to the door in front of me, then a tiny gold key beside it, too small to fit into a regular lock. All three hung from a single ring, accompanied by a silver compass rose keychain.

I closed my fist tightly around the keys, squeezing until the edges bit into my palm, then I forced my hand to relax, unlocked the door, and swung it open.

For several long moments, I stood there in the doorway, taking in the sight of my new home. Sunlight danced through the windows, glimmering off of stray flecks of dust in the air. The effect was magical, like tiny fairies dancing in the beams of light.

I turned and surveyed the rest of the living room. Like the inn, it had been decorated with love, each trinket and piece of art positioned just so.

Drawn to the small selection of photos perched along the mantle, I moved toward the stone fireplace and ran a careful finger along the edge of one silver filigree frame, studying the little girl in the photo. She wore a frilly little party dress and a lace-trimmed bonnet with pale golden ringlets peeking out.

With a pang, I realized it must be my mother.

"Mom," I whispered into the silent room, "why didn't you tell me the truth? Why would you keep this from me? Keep me from my family?"

I felt like a voyeur as the word *family* echoed in my mind like a gong. Another photograph showed a tall, skinny man in a dark suit holding hands with a woman who could only have been my grandmother. The colors were faded, but there was no mistaking the red hair under her lacy veil. They stood in front of a stone lighthouse with the lake stretching out behind them.

Is this what everyone sees when they look at me? The ghost of Nan?

We might share a face and a head of unruly red curls, but the rest of me was all my mom—wide hips, strong shoulders, soft belly, muscled legs that we put to good use each summer of my childhood for bike rides and paddle boats. For a moment, I was overwhelmed with gratitude that I'd inherited all that from her. It was like a layer of armor against the discomfort of resembling someone I'd never met.

As I let my gaze wander across the other photos, I realized the man who must be my grandfather was only in a handful of them before he was gone. Dead? Divorced? I was struck by the pattern in this family—single daughters raised by single mothers. It seemed like an odd coincidence. I'd never known my father, because my mom always said he died before I was born.

I now realized it was an eerily similar story to what I'd been told about my grandmother, the famous innkeep of Spruce Hill, who had actually been very much alive until recently.

My train of thought was interrupted by an emphatic buzz from the phone in my pocket. I tugged it free and couldn't hold back a laugh when I saw that I'd missed half a dozen texts from my best friend Sarah, who was now in Prague with her husband.

It had taken all my powers of persuasion to convince her not to rush back home after I told her the news about my mysterious grandmother and this surprise inheritance, but I knew my friend too well to think she wouldn't spend a great deal of time wondering what was happening here.

I read through each text with a smile, imagining Sarah surreptitiously typing as they toured cathedrals and historical monuments. She wanted to know if I'd arrived safely, how the drive had been, what the inn was like, if I'd learned anything yet about Nan.

Sarah, you won't even believe this place. It's incredible. I can't wait for you to see it.

Her response was too quick for me to believe she'd been doing anything other than waiting for an update.

Already added a stop to our itinerary when we're back in the country!

With one last glance at the mantle photos, I slipped the phone back into my pocket and decided to explore the rest of the cottage before fetching my bags from the car. There was a cozy little kitchen through an archway off the living room, and while it was nowhere near as modern as the inn's, it was clean and bright. A tiny dragonfly suncatcher hung in the window over the sink. I drew a deep breath as I listened to the faint tinkle of wind chimes from somewhere outside the back door.

Off the kitchen was a short hallway leading to a bathroom—which, fortunately, was far more updated than the kitchen—and a decent sized master bedroom. Clean sheets and a colorful quilt were folded at the foot of the bed. The afternoon sunlight streamed through delicate lace curtains to illuminate a large framed painting of a landscape, but the rest of the walls were bare.

Waiting for me, maybe?

I moved closer to study the artwork, realizing that it was a picture of the lake behind the inn with the inn's gardens in the foreground. A tiny signature graced the lower right hand corner, the same one I'd found on the little watercolor painting at the inn.

I sucked in a breath of appreciation for Nan's skill. I'd often questioned where my artistic talents came from, given my mother's inability to draw much more than stick figures.

Right here, I realized, running my finger over the signature. This is where it came from. The knowledge that I shared more than just physical traits with Nan was both inspiring and heart-wrenching.

I stepped back from the painting, soaking in the sweeping curve of each careful stroke of paint until my phone buzzed again with a single line of text from Sarah.

Remember, we love you.

The simple sentiment soothed my travel-weary soul. I replied, echoing my best friend's words, and bid the artwork farewell as I went to explore the second story.

The upstairs portion of the house consisted of a single bedroom, empty except for a narrow mattress on a wooden frame and the same lace curtains as the master bedroom, plus a crawl space filled with dusty boxes and trunks of clothing. I decided to leave sorting through them for another day, especially when

I started sneezing within a few seconds of searching for the light switch, so I backed out of the crawl space and returned to the kitchen to start a pot of tea.

The view of the lake, even from this distance, calmed me. I stood for several minutes, gazing out at the shimmering surface until the knot in my chest slowly unraveled.

When the kettle finally uttered a shrill whistle, I rifled through the cabinets for a mug, then set my tea to steep while I went to move and unload my car. The small parking area at the end of the driveway was cleverly disguised from view, tucked away in a little grove of trees off to one side of the cottage. I grabbed my laptop and the biggest of my suitcases out of the car and began the long process of unloading and unpacking.

On my third trip, the ancient suitcase I'd found in my mother's closet split open, spilling underwear and socks all over the gravel path. While I struggled to control my frustration, I spotted something colorful in the grass.

"What the hell?" I muttered, reaching for it.

The object was a small painted rock, covered in daisies. My breath left my lungs in a whoosh when I turned it over in my palm and saw my mother's name in a childish scrawl on the bottom of it. For a moment, I could only stare at it, eyes burning, but six months ago I'd cried every tear inside me until my eyes were as dusty as the boxes Nan left behind.

Then, beneath the ache of loneliness in my chest, a tiny curl of warmth kindled, spreading outward into my limbs, like my mom was standing right beside me again, encouraging me to go on.

Maybe this wasn't a mistake, after all. Maybe this was where I was meant to be.

I tucked the painted rock into my pocket, gathered up the items that had burst from the suitcase, and got back to work unloading the car.

Several trips and one aching back later, I collapsed across the bed and declared myself officially moved in. I was more exhausted than I could remember ever having been, but it was tempered by a euphoric sense of accomplishment.

Though I was tempted to go for a walk along the lake, exhaustion seeped into my limbs and I decided it could wait one more day. I got ready for bed, sorted out the pile of sheets and quilts to make the bed in the downstairs bedroom, and fell swiftly into a deep, dreamless sleep.

Four

Juliet

T HE NEXT MORNING DAWNED with a bright, cheerful sunrise. I woke up earlier than usual thanks to the dainty curtains hanging in my new bedroom, so I decided to take advantage of the unexpected early start.

With a good night's sleep behind me, I could almost forget what happened with Henry.

Almost.

Still, my temper had cooled enough to shake him from my mind. Everyone else had been wonderfully kind, even the lawyer on the phone. I glanced at the kitchen counter, where I'd set my mother's letter as I unloaded the car. It looked harmless enough, written on thick paper from her favorite stationary set and tucked into a matching floral envelope, but its contents were far from innocuous.

I didn't even need to read it to know exactly what it said.

My dearest Juliet,

If you're reading this, I'm gone and can no longer protect you, so you must protect yourself. Trust your instincts and know that every choice I made, I made for you. It was a matter of life and death. I can't bear the thought of leaving you alone in the world. Contact the owner of the Lakeside Inn in Spruce Hill, New York. She'll explain everything I was too selfish to tell you in my final months.

Love,
Mom

I found it while packing up her bedroom, the task I'd avoided as long as I possibly could before the sale of the house was finalized last week. The envelope lay tucked in the drawer of her bedside table, the handwritten letter and my mom's beloved opal ring sealed inside.

At first, I thought maybe it was a gift, like she'd booked me a stay at some random inn so I could escape the oppressive weight of my grief. What exactly I needed protection from, I still didn't know, but I'd found the phone number for the inn on an incredibly outdated website and made the phone call.

The woman who answered the phone—I now knew it was Mrs. Gregson—had regretfully informed me that the owner passed away only months ago, not long after my mother. Struck numb by the dead end, I'd given her my phone number when she asked for it and assumed that was the end of the road.

The next day, Nan's lawyer called and changed the course of my life.

Shaking myself from the memories, I smoothed out my hair and studied the options in my closet. Much as I didn't want to give anyone, least of all Henry, the power to make me self-conscious about my clothes, I dressed in dark jeans and a nice lavender camisole under a slouchy oatmeal sweater. It might not scream consummate professional, but it looked nice.

As I stepped out the front door, I let go of all the turmoil, breathed in the sweet scent of the flowers in the yard, and whispered, "I could get used to this."

The only response was a chorus of birdsong from the treetops nearby.

I strolled around the side of the cottage and followed a small footpath leading down to Lake Ontario. The sky overhead was a fresh, brilliant turquoise, dotted with wispy white clouds. I squinted against the morning sun, cupping a hand over my eyes to try to see across the water, but all I could make out was an endless stretch of gleaming gray-blue. Even when I peered to either side of where I stood, the curving shoreline prevented me from seeing any other houses nearby.

Where I came from, lakes were plentiful, but they were nothing like this, not without driving for hours to reach the shore of Lake Superior. This was like gazing out from the edge of the world.

For a long time, I simply stood there, listening to the song of the birds overhead and the soft lap of the waves. This place seemed custom made for me, peaceful and quiet and so beautiful that my hands itched for a pencil and paper.

"I could *really* get used to this," I repeated, a little louder this time. A startled robin burst into flight from a few yards away.

Though the maps had shown a small sandy beach nearby, somewhere along the lake, this section was outlined by large rocks and boulders. I wandered aimlessly along the shore, enjoying the solitude. It was a different world out here, like I was all alone with the water and sky and breeze.

I paused where the path ended, just at the edge of a forested area.

The urge to spread my arms wide and close my eyes to soak in this moment was too strong to resist. Afterward, I breathed deep, opened my eyes, and pulled out my phone to snap a picture of the incredible view. I sent it to Sarah, along with a reminder to enjoy her trip instead of worrying.

The phone rang almost immediately with an incoming video call. I had no idea what time it was there, but I should have known she'd jump on the opportunity to check in again.

"What part of 'enjoy your vacation and stop worrying about what's happening in New York' did you not understand?" I grumbled, trying to hide a smile, but seeing her face settled something in my chest.

Sarah's unrepentant grin filled my screen. "I need details, Jules. How is it? Is the inn as cute as the photos on the website?"

"It's cuter," I admitted. "I didn't expect to feel anything for the building or the property, but it's like something was pulling me here. Like me coming to Spruce Hill was meant to be, if that makes sense."

"Of course it makes sense. A family member you didn't know about left you a legacy. How could you not be drawn to it?"

"I don't even have to pay rent for this adorable cottage. It's part of the inheritance, so I can live off the proceeds from selling Mom's house for months. Years, maybe. Aside from leaving you halfway across the country, there was nothing keeping me back home. Nothing to rival a chance to make art without worrying about how I'm going to afford groceries."

"You're not leaving me anywhere, Jules. No matter how far away you are, you've got me."

Quietly, Sarah's husband Andre called, "And me!"

I laughed, but the warmth building inside me was almost overwhelming. "I miss you."

"I miss you, too. Has the shock worn off yet?"

"No," I laughed. "A mysterious inheritance, along with the realization that my mother lied to me for my entire life?"

The prospect of it still left me feeling mildly numb, even in light of the low pulse of excitement in my veins.

"You know, I always thought I'd be the one with a mystery inheritance," she teased. "Maybe some distant uncle would leave me a creepy old house in Minneapolis or something. I didn't expect you to end up living a fairy tale while I'm across the ocean!"

"Like traveling all over Europe for months is some kind of punishment." I grinned and held the phone up to show her the rest of my surroundings. "I'll send you some pictures of the gardens behind the inn, they're phenomenal."

"Have you met your *staff* yet?" she asked, saying the word like she was the Queen of England. "Any young hotties, perhaps? It's about time you had some fun, girl."

"They're not *my* staff, they're the inn's staff. I met them yesterday when I got in, they're very nice. Mostly."

Of course my best friend picked up on the qualification. "Mostly? Someone I need to throw down with?"

"No, I can take care of things myself. The manager is just...not very excited that I'm here. His grandfather has been the caretaker at the inn longer than either of us have been alive, though, so I don't want to ruffle any feathers. Not more than I have already, at least."

"Feathers have been ruffled, hmm? Let me guess—your temper got the best of you?"

I made a face at the phone. "Let's just say if you'd been in my shoes, you probably would've broken his nose. When his grandfather said Henry could show me the books, I imagined he'd be a middle-aged math nerd."

Sarah burst out laughing. "Show you the books? Guess you didn't share your distaste of math with the guy, huh?"

"I figured it wasn't smart to explain just how unqualified I am for any of this. I'm heading over for breakfast soon. Hopefully today will be a fresh start." I paused to look out over the water before saying, "I'm really nervous. I wish my mom was here to explain all of this."

"Oh, honey, I know. I'm sure she had her reasons, though. You were her whole world, Jules."

Tears threatened, so I took a deep breath to get a handle on them. "I know. Look, I should go, and *you* should enjoy your trip. I don't want Andre holding a grudge against me for the rest of our lives because I interrupted your vacation so many times."

"You know he doesn't mind. Go on, but I expect regular updates, especially if nerd boy messes you with again. I'll need to know who to ship the glitter bomb to. Love you, girl. Kisses!"

I blew her a kiss and ended the call, then slipped the phone back in my pocket and stood at the edge of the water for several long minutes, mentally converting segments of the beautiful landscape into paintings, until my stomach grumbled.

Next time, I'd definitely have to sit down out here with my sketchbook, I decided as I started back toward the inn. The hardest part would be deciding what to draw first.

As I crossed through the gardens, I turned back toward the lake, wondering just where my grandmother had positioned herself to complete the artwork hanging in my new bedroom.

The flowers were different now, but I meandered back and forth a bit along the path until I thought I'd found the right spot.

I lifted my head to stare out at the water beyond as I tried to memorize the view. I wanted to compare it to the painting when I returned to the cottage.

Finally satisfied that I would remember the image clearly enough, I headed in for breakfast. And while I steeled myself for another possible confrontation with Henry, I couldn't bite back a smile at the image of him covered in purple glitter once Sarah got a lock on his location.

It was good to have friends, even if they were halfway across the world.

Five

HENRY

I WAS FINISHING THE last bite of my breakfast in the dining room when I saw Juliet meander into the gardens. The college art student ensemble was gone, replaced by dark denim that hugged every curve, a cream-colored sweater that fell off one shoulder as she shifted her position between the flower beds to look out toward the lake, and a wild tumble of red curls cascading down her back.

Shit. I had zero interest in exploring the battle of emotions waging in my chest.

Throwing back the rest of my coffee, I carried my dishes into the kitchen, stubbornly avoiding Sally's eyes. I should have known better than to expect that to work.

"You should say good morning like a civilized human being," she hissed at me when I passed behind her.

"Yes, yes. I'm perfectly civil."

A cough that sounded a lot like *"bullshit"* echoed after me as I left the kitchen and entered the side hall instead of the dining room. I shook out my arms like a boxer preparing for a match and bounced on my toes a few times, hoping loosening my muscles would bring a cloak of calm over me, then listened quietly as Mrs. Gregson greeted Juliet at the door.

While their conversation drifted toward the dining room, I stayed hidden in the hallway dotted with the photos Nan had hung, each one carefully framed and positioned just so. I shifted to the left and paused in front of one of my favorites.

It was Nan and my Gram, dressed in florals and wearing big straw hats with ribbons streaming from them. Their arms were wrapped around one another and they were both smiling broadly for the camera, but there was a certain sadness lurking in Nan's eyes. It was visible in every photo taken after her daughter left town.

"Why?" I whispered, touching one fingertip to the corner of the frame. "Why would you work so hard to build all of this, only to leave it to someone you never met?"

As though Nan would give me an answer, I stared hard at the photo until I no longer heard Juliet and Mrs. Gregson, then I closed my eyes and let my head fall forward.

"I hope she's got half of your brain, Nan. We need someone like you at the helm, not some clueless stranger. Everyone says you knew what you were doing with this. I want to believe they're right, that this is a good thing."

I dropped my hand, taking one last look at the photo before making my way to my office.

Months had passed since Nan found news of her granddaughter after nearly three decades of searching, and I could still see the delight on her face, that radiant glow under the age-spotted, papery skin. Of course, that was only the beginning. One article led to another, and news of her own daughter's recent death knocked Nan flat, literally and figuratively. The old lady had been tough as nails for as long as I could remember, but at that point her health, her very will to live, started to corrode.

After my grandmother died, Nan became family, taking care of me and my brother after school, loving us like we were her own grandkids. In the last few years, the inn became almost as much my own labor of love as it was Nan's.

No, I wasn't going to celebrate bringing in a newcomer with no experience in this business. I'd taken a chance in coming to work at the inn, made a career change that turned out to be fulfilling even if it had its moments of frustration.

"There you are."

The voice jolted me from my thoughts and I turned to face my grandfather. "Hey, Gramps."

"I hoped I might find you here. Juliet is having breakfast in the dining room. Alone," he said pointedly.

"I already ate."

His usually jovial expression darkened. "She's a sweet girl, Henry. I might be an old man, but I'm not clueless. I saw the look on her face when she came out of your office yesterday.

Whatever happened, you need to remedy it. You will be kind and courteous and welcoming, because that girl has no family left in this world. Nan would be beside herself if she knew anyone or anything was keeping *this* family from her."

I pinched the bridge of my nose, a mixture of shame and frustration simmering under my skin. "I'll sort it out. You can all stop harping on me."

"Nan loved you, you know."

The statement was firm, irrefutable. It lodged in my chest like a bowling ball, crowding out everything else with a swift wave of grief.

"I know," I whispered.

"She didn't do this to hurt you, Henry. It wasn't guilt or vengeance or some kind of lark. Juliet is her only living relative, and Nan wanted this for her."

I looked up at him and a flood of other memories, good memories, washed over me. Running wild through the inn's gardens with my brother, having tea and cookies with Nan and Gram after school, learning to wield a hammer at my grandfather's side to make a birdhouse for Nan's birthday.

This place *was* a family, and I was old enough to recognize that forcing Juliet out of it was an asshole move.

"I'll fix it. Just...it might take some time. She's got a temper on her."

Gramps flashed a brilliant grin at me and nodded. "That doesn't surprise me in the least. She's her mother's daughter, after all, and Melissa got that straight from Nan."

With a wink and a flick of his fingers, he left the office and I forced myself to my feet. I figured there was a good chance she'd tell me to get lost the minute I entered the dining room, but for the sake of harmony here at the inn—and to prevent future guilt trips—I'd play nice.

My steps faltered when I caught sight of Juliet sitting by the windows in the otherwise empty dining room. She had a tiny sketchbook next to her plate and I watched for a moment while her pencil danced across the page. Every so often, she paused to take a sip of coffee or a bite of French toast, but her gaze never left the paper.

Get on with it. I puffed out my cheeks on a long exhale and approached her table.

"Good morning."

She didn't even glance in my direction when she replied. "Morning."

"Look, we didn't get off on the right foot—" I broke off when her furious blue eyes lifted from the paper and locked on mine. Beneath the anger, something else hovered, something heartbreakingly sad, but it evaporated so quickly I thought I might have imagined it.

"You were perfectly clear yesterday in expressing how you see me. There's no need to discuss it further," she said, the words dripping with ice despite the burning sapphire of her gaze. "I don't see any need for us to interact outside of what's required for the sake of the inn."

That coldness grated on my already sparking nerves. "How magnanimous of you to deign to speak with the manager of *your* business about such decisions."

The pencil creaked as her grip tightened around it, drawing my gaze down to the sketchbook. There on the page was a perfectly recognizable drawing of the dining room, but the tables were reconfigured.

"You've been here less than a day and you're making changes already?" I asked, my voice low and nearly vibrating with anger.

"No," she snapped. "But this view is phenomenal and if we're going to offer dinner service, we should take advantage of that."

"This is a small town. It's generally frowned upon to *take advantage* of our customers."

"Oh, for fuck's sake, that's not what I meant," she muttered under her breath, jaw clenched as she slammed the sketchbook shut and shoved the chair back so she could rise.

Hearing her curse was almost enough to make me smile, but I fought it back down. "Isn't this a business decision affecting the inn, like *you* said we should discuss?"

"There's nothing to discuss. You want the inn to stay exactly as it was until the end of time, be my guest. Message received, loud and clear. I'll stay in my lane, you stay in yours."

"What a productive discussion."

I waited for whatever tirade she was about to unleash, but she simply nodded at me before gathering up her dishes and pushing past me, her shoulder jamming hard against my chest.

"Have a lovely day," I called after her.

Had her hands not been full, I was sure she would've flipped me off on her way to the kitchen. As soon as she cleared the doorway, I bolted toward my office—between Sally and my grandfather, I didn't need another lecture. I'd tried, hadn't I?

The olive branch had been extended. Juliet Morrison caught that sucker in her bare hands, froze it into an ice spear, and threw it back in my face.

I sank down into my chair and groaned, trying very hard not to think about the redheaded firecracker who was probably plotting my demise with Sally right this minute. I didn't want to see those red curls or that fierce blue gaze every time I closed my eyes, but the image persisted, a reminder that my grandfather was absolutely right.

She belonged here. She was Nan's legacy. There was no denying it.

Still, Juliet might *look* like Nan, but what good would that do us? We needed someone who could *think* like Nan, someone clever and cunning and able to keep things moving around here.

Until she proved she had a brain in her head, had the intelligence to match Nan and not run this place into the ground with her lack of experience, I would attempt to withhold judgment.

From where I was standing, the greatest threat to the inn's success wasn't the death of its founder. It wasn't even the archaic website or lack of any kind of online reservation system, as I'd lamented plenty of times since I came on board a few years ago.

It was a young, clueless artist from Minnesota.

Six

Juliet

I MUTTERED A FEW choice words under my breath as I left the inn, grateful that I didn't pass Gerard or Mrs. Gregson on the way out. As I shoved my way through the heavy front door, I imagined it was Henry's broad chest.

Not that I'd noticed the firm muscles beneath his dress shirt when I shouldered past him in the dining room. Or noticed again how damn *good* he smelled.

This was definitely not how I'd imagined the morning going.

As I stalked through the gardens, I cursed Henry for obliterating every shred of peace the walk along the lake had instilled in me. Every doubt I'd about coming here bubbled rapidly back to the surface.

Maybe he's right, I thought glumly. *Why the hell did I ever think this was going to work?*

I kicked a rock along the path to the cottage, wincing as my toe connected with it. To my surprise, it struck something with a metallic clang when it rolled into the grass. I bent down to see what it was, wondering if I'd find another painted rock.

There, in the lawn at the edge of a flower bed, lay a heavy brass circle about the size of my palm.

I brushed the blades of grass aside and saw that it was engraved with a dragonfly, my grandmother's name, and the dates of Nan's birth and death. I laid my hand over the plaque, closed my eyes, and took a few deep breaths.

This is why you're here. Because of family, not business.

Inheritance or no, discovering I had this family history would have brought me to Spruce Hill to learn more.

Hopefully the lawyer would be able to find some loophole regarding the ownership of the inn so I wouldn't have to interact with Henry Walker ever again, then I could focus on learning more about Nan, my own mother's life here, and what had caused such a rift between them.

With a sigh, I stood and forced myself to shake off Henry's negativity. This was my legacy, dammit, whether it was a complete surprise or not. I would not let some nasty accountant ruin it for me.

I straightened my shoulders, lifted my chin, and continued on to the cottage.

To my new home. A refuge, a reprieve from the constant barrage of memories in my mother's house, a sanctuary against the overwhelming reality of owning an inn.

Now that my crisis of faith was over and my blood pressure had settled from the rollicking boil Henry inspired, my mind raced with the things I still needed to do. Most importantly, I had to go into town for groceries, make a list of questions for the lawyer, and sort through the boxes that were stored upstairs.

"And while doing all of these things," I grumbled, scowling, "I will avoid Henry Walker at all cost."

With a sigh, I forced him from my thoughts and wondered instead how many people around here remembered my mother from back before she left town and severed all ties with this place.

Would anyone be willing to talk about it? Would anyone know why she went away?

I grabbed my purse and used my phone to map directions to the nearest grocery store. Despite the secluded atmosphere around the inn and the cottage, it was only twelve minutes to the center of town.

As I traveled down the road to Spruce Hill, houses and storefronts popped up with increasing frequency. I made a mental note of some of the adorable little shops I wanted to check out, but within another few minutes, I reached the grocery store.

While I strolled the aisles, getting the lay of the land, I tried to think objectively about my encounter with Henry. His grandfather and Mrs. Gregson had been welcoming, but maybe they *did* all resent my presence here. I didn't know what would've happened to the inn upon my grandmother's death if I hadn't been there to take ownership of it—would it have gone to one of them? Or all of them, even?

If so, I couldn't blame them for being unhappy with the situation. Nan seemed like an unorthodox lady, so it was impossible to guess what her contingency plan might have been if the lawyer hadn't found me.

"It's a lovely day, isn't it?" said an older gentleman with a full beard, wrenching me from my thoughts in the cereal aisle.

"Yes," I replied, adding a box to my cart, "it is a beautiful day."

"Forgive me for asking, but do I know you?"

The man was studying me with pale blue eyes and an odd little smile on his face. My eyebrows shot up as a thread of unease twisted in my chest. I was used to the "Minnesota nice" stereotype, but there was an intensity in the man's demeanor that made me uncomfortable.

"No, I don't think so. I'm new in town."

"You remind me of someone. It'll come to me, I'm sure. Enjoy your day, miss."

His face folded into a smile, though it was nearly lost under the beard, and he gave a small salute as he wandered off. I took a deep breath, forcing my muscles to relax. My reaction was probably just the aftereffect of my confrontation with Henry Walker—or my mother's warning about trusting my instincts.

Trying to reconcile this sweet little town with her ominous note was fraying my usually steady nerves.

Mrs. Gregson's words about having Nan's red hair echoed in my head. The spitting image of Nan, she'd said. Was that really enough to give random men pause in the supermarket over the similarities?

The cashier was a young woman who offered a polite smile and some small talk without any references to Nan, my appearance, or the inn. I accepted the reprieve gratefully, hoping it was a sign that my presence in town wouldn't throw the entire population into a tizzy.

When I got back to the cottage, I grabbed a bag of pretzels and plopped down on the couch. In an anachronistic twist of fate, this sweet little fairy tale cottage was equipped with high speed wifi as well as a hundred cable channels, though the television was small and hidden inside an antique-looking armoire to the left of the fireplace.

I rifled through my art bag until I found a small notebook. Between pretzels, I jotted down questions to ask the lawyer.

First and foremost, I needed to know the logistics of this whole arrangement. Did I *want* to stay here forever? If I could get out of owning the inn eventually, without jeopardizing staying in the cottage, would I?

This location seemed like it would be wonderful for my art, but beyond that, I wasn't sure if this was the kind of place where I could happily spend forever.

On the other hand, I couldn't imagine spending the rest of my life in a Minnesota suburb, either, so maybe Spruce Hill had greater potential than I'd originally thought. Selling my mother's house and leaving my job at the bookstore had cut the last true ties to my hometown, apart from Sarah.

Tired of so many questions and so few answers, I grabbed a sketchbook out of the bag and closed my eyes to conjure up some of the paintings from the inn. I made a basic sketch of as many as I could recall, figuring I could ask Gerard or Mrs. Gregson where to find each location—at a time when Henry wasn't around, preferably.

The thought of him was enough to set my temper rising. Stupid, smirking, handsome son of a...

I sucked in a deep, calming breath. If he wanted to resent me for something beyond my control, fine. Whether I stayed here or not, the two of us didn't have to be friends. I was fully capable of being civil—icy, maybe, but civil nonetheless. I wouldn't let him influence my decisions about staying here.

With that resolution made, I closed my eyes, let inspiration saturate my mind, and trusted the pencil to lead the way.

T HOUGH I AVOIDED STEPPING foot into the inn itself over the next few days, I visited the gardens for hours at a time to lose myself in a sketchbook. I managed to catch Gerard out there one day as he fixed a loose piece of trellis and jumped on the opportunity to ask him about the inn's artwork.

"Good morning, Juliet," he greeted me.

"Good morning," I called back as I strode toward him. "I wondered if I could ask you where to find the places in some of the paintings around the inn, especially from the dining room?"

His smile widened. "Absolutely. I'll make you a list, would that suit?"

"That'd be great, thank you."

"We'd love to hang some of your artwork in the inn, you know," he said softly.

The words lodged hard in my chest. No matter what happened, I was part of the inn's history now. That knowledge turned into a leaden ball in my stomach, but I managed to force a smile and a nod.

"Sure. I'm heading home, but have a good afternoon, Gerard."

The older man smiled and lifted a hand in farewell. He didn't say a single word about Henry, fortunately for us both.

On Friday morning, just a few hours before my appointment with the lawyer, Gerard appeared in the garden where I was playing with oil pastels, trying to capture the beautiful chaos of color that surrounded me. He passed me a handwritten list.

"Here you are," he said with a friendly smile. "They're all local landmarks. I jotted down some basic directions for each one, but ask anyone in town and they'll help you if you need it."

"Thank you so much, Gerard. This is perfect."

I accepted the piece of paper with a rush of gratitude. A knowing look came across his face and I wondered if he was already aware of what had transpired the other day. It seemed unlikely that Henry would confess his sins so readily, but I wasn't going to tattle to the man's grandfather about his rude behavior.

"Of course, my dear. Don't be a stranger at the inn, hmm?"

"Sure."

The lie slipped easily enough from my tongue, though it filled me with guilt. I smiled as benignly as I could to cover it up.

Gerard went on his way and I studied the list. Hiking through the woods and painting for the next few months sounded infinitely better than studying accounting ledgers under the tutelage of the town jerk.

As the sun rose higher in the sky, I packed up my supplies and walked back to the cottage, breathing in the sweet perfume of the flowers. It wasn't until I came through the front door that my stomach began tying itself in knots.

Though I didn't think there was anything to be anxious about, I couldn't quell the butterflies. I tucked the painted daisy rock in my purse for good luck, then headed out to the lawyer's office to face my future.

The address wasn't far from the grocery store, so I spent the first portion of the drive imagining the area was all part of an enchanted wood.

What a beautiful place Spruce Hill would've been to grow up in.

The thought made me wonder if people like Henry Walker took it all for granted, but I scowled and forced the image of him out of my mind. I would not allow him to darken my mood.

I reached the office with several minutes to spare. With a deep, steadying breath, I unbuckled my seatbelt and went inside. A smiling secretary greeted me and told me to have a seat. I'd barely settled into the chair when a handsome middle-aged man in a pristine suit appeared in the doorway.

"Miss Morrison, I presume? I'm Daniel Escobar, your grandmother's attorney," he said with a smile.

His voice was like velvet, rich and soothing against my fraying nerves. I stood quickly and shook his hand.

"Yes, thank you for meeting with me."

He gestured toward his office and we entered. I sat in an absurdly overstuffed chair in front of the huge desk as Mr. Escobar slid a red file folder toward me.

"I'm sure this is all very unsettling for you, Miss Morrison. Learning you had a family member you knew nothing about is surprising enough, but inheriting such an estate is doubly so."

"That's for sure," I replied with a short laugh, "and please, call me Juliet."

"Nanette Montgomery was like a grandmother to everyone around Spruce Hill. You've inherited a legacy that reaches far beyond the inn, as I'm sure you'll learn." He smiled warmly at me.

"Oh, I'm beginning to see that," I said dryly, and the lawyer laughed. "What I don't understand is why I'd never heard of her before a few weeks ago?"

His dark eyes filled with regret. "Nan never stopped searching for your mother. They parted on bad terms. Melissa succeeded admirably in cutting every tie to her mother and to Spruce Hill when she left town. Nan hired private investigators, one after another, and nothing much came of it. She'd all but given up years ago."

"Why did my mother leave Spruce Hill? She told me my grandmother died before I was born. I don't understand why she lied. The note she left me was...cryptic, to say the least."

The lawyer shook his head. "That I don't know, I'm afraid. I moved to the area long after your mother left and didn't get to know Nan until several years later. Nan never went into detail, but I got the impression she didn't know exactly why Melissa went away, only that she'd been acting strangely in the weeks before her departure, shortly after Nan found out Melissa was pregnant."

I knew in that moment that I wouldn't be leaving town anytime soon, Henry Walker be damned. The truth might take a lifetime to unravel, but I owed it to myself—and to my mother and Nan—to find it.

"If she gave up on finding my mother," I said slowly, "then why did she leave the inn to me?"

"You can thank social media for that, actually."

"Nan found me through social media?"

At my incredulity, his lips twitched. "Three months ago, you won an award for your artwork."

"Yeah, it was just a little community art show, but my friend Sarah convinced me to enter, since she knew I was struggling after my mom died. Sarah is one of my biggest fans," I said with a smile, despite the brief twinge of homesickness. "She announced it far and wide after I won."

Mr. Escobar smiled back. "Well, Nan happened to scroll past a photo of you with your painting. According to Mrs. Gregson, Nan said, and I quote, 'There is no chance in hell that is not my granddaughter.' The resemblance is really quite startling."

"But she didn't contact me then," I said slowly.

It would still have been too late for Nan to reconnect with her only child, but I could've been there for her in the end. A look of pain crossed the lawyer's face, mirroring my own.

"She'd been ill for quite some time, Juliet. As delighted as she was to have found you, that was also when she learned of your mother's death. Nan took a turn for the worse soon afterward."

I squeezed my eyes shut. "I wish she'd contacted me right away. I would rather have had that time than any inheritance."

"Her condition deteriorated too rapidly for her to reach out, I'm afraid. I didn't even know she'd located you until after she passed, when the staff at the inn informed me. Nan never gave up hope, Juliet. Her will was written in such a way that the inn was to go to her direct family members, with a specific account designated to pay for further investigations if necessary."

My heart clenched painfully when I thought about how close Nan had come to finding me, only to have her body betray her at the very end.

"After Mrs. Gregson mentioned the photo to me, I tried to track you down. We spent weeks scouring social media, trying to locate the picture. Henry managed to get into Nan's phone and personal laptop, but there was no sign of it. All the staff remembered was your first name, which was mentioned in the post, and Nan's excitement. We had no leads until you called the inn."

"And I missed the funeral," I said quietly. Another blow. I rubbed at my sternum.

Mr. Escobar smiled gently. "Knowing you were out there, the staff made some arrangements in the hopes that you'd be found. At the end of the summer, there will be a memorial celebration held in Nan's honor at the gardens of the inn. They wanted you to get to know her by going through what she left behind, then to have a chance to say hello and goodbye in your own time."

All of my questions about getting out of this surprise obligation evaporated into the realm of unimportance as more pressing concerns floated in to take their place.

"What about my grandfather? I saw pictures at the cottage from a wedding, some when my mom was a baby, but then he was gone. Is he still alive?"

"Unfortunately, no," Mr. Escobar replied, looking for all the world as though this were a completely normal conversation. "Nan married her high school sweetheart not long after graduation. His name was Philip Montgomery, a banker from a very prominent family nearby. He died only a few years after your mother was born. I believe it was a boating accident out on the lake."

Mr. Escobar ran through each condition of the will with me, answering every one of my questions before they were even asked.

The cottage belonged to me, free of stipulations. I could live in it, rent it out, or sell it at any time. As long as I maintained residency in Spruce Hill for twelve months, I could then choose to sell the inn and walk away with enough money to support me for years to come based on the estimated value of the property. During that time, I could learn the ropes at the inn if I wanted to, but there was no requirement that I take over Nan's job.

The business was successful and despite my breakfast blowup with Henry, I had no interest in making any changes to what appeared to be a cornerstone of the community, so that was fine with me.

Basically, in exchange for a single year of my life spent in the town where my mother had grown up, I could move on to whatever I wanted with a level of financial security I'd never dreamed of before.

It didn't make up for losing Nan before I even got the chance to meet her, didn't make up for knowing my mother had lied for all those years, but it was quite a consolation prize.

The decision was made. Even without the inn and the money, the mystery surrounding my mother's departure from Spruce Hill probably would've been enough to convince me to stay for a year. Everything else was icing on the cake.

After what seemed like another hour spent signing paperwork, I shook hands with Mr. Escobar and walked out into brilliant afternoon sunshine. Somehow, this meeting had forged a link to Nan in a way even taking up residence in her home had not been able to do.

This *was* where I belonged.

Nan wanted to find me, right up to the very end. All of my earlier anxiety flew right out the window. I was—relieved? Free?

Whatever it was, it was light and buoyant, fizzing up inside me. Instead of being bound to this place by obligation, I was now drawn to it, connected by something deeper than I'd ever anticipated. I rolled down the windows and drove back to the cottage, singing along with the radio at the top of my lungs.

This next year might very well be a beautiful new beginning.

Seven

JULIET

THE FIRST THING I did upon returning to the cottage was lug boxes down from storage and create neat rows on the living room floor.

By the time everything was moved, I was sweaty, aching, and completely covered in dust.

Now that the literal heavy lifting was done, the rest would require more in the way of focus. I surveyed the impressive spread of boxes and bins, then decided my success called for a bath.

The claw-foot tub was massive and the linen closet boasted a wide array of bath products. I chose a particularly fragrant lavender bubble bath, then spent the next hour soaking away my aches and pains.

When the bath water grew cold, I drained the decadent tub and wandered into the kitchen, rifling half-heartedly through the cupboards. Despite my grocery trip, nothing looked appealing enough for dinner. I flipped open the laptop I'd left on the counter, did a quick search for local restaurants, and stumbled upon a place called The Mermaid.

The photos were adorable, the reviews glowing, and the website allowed for online orders, so I perused the menu and made my selections.

Spending a Friday night alone eating takeout while sorting through boxes of dusty artifacts wasn't a thrilling prospect, but I was used to it after dealing with my mom's attic back home.

The Mermaid was a cute family-owned place located a bit farther into town than I had previously ventured, its entrance flanked by two golden mermaid statues. This section of Main Street was full of character. I decided then and there that I would come back another day to explore on foot. I spotted a stationary shop, a quaint little bookstore, a yoga studio, and an arched entrance gate to Spruce Hill's Town Park.

If I was going to make this place my home, I wanted to familiarize myself with everything it had to offer.

After holding the door for an older couple who were leaving with a stack of boxed leftovers, I stopped short just as I entered the restaurant.

Standing in front of me was none other than Henry Walker, looking even more stupidly attractive than he had at the inn.

He wore a close-fitting white t-shirt and jeans, and his hazel eyes sparked to life when he spotted me.

"Juliet," he said, inclining his head with mock civility.

"Henry." My voice was cool, despite a simmer of annoyance at encountering him again.

I wished I'd done more than throw my wet, tangled curls into a ponytail. My cheeks were still flushed from the heat of the bath and I hadn't bothered with anything but a swipe of lip gloss before leaving the house. Casual looked amazing on Henry, of course, since I could now see all the lean muscles he'd been hiding under his dress clothes.

It didn't seem fair that someone so nasty could be so good-looking, especially when I always looked like a slouch in comparison.

"Haven't seen you around the inn," he mused, lifting a dark brow. "Bored with playing the boss lady already?"

I forced myself to silently count to ten, but I only made it to four before firing back, "Oh no, I'm here to stay. I just didn't realize you needed so much supervision to do your job properly."

The spark in his hazel eyes blossomed into a flame, then the peppy blonde behind the hostess stand called his name and I offered a sweet smile as he turned away. Henry paid for his dinner and stalked out of the restaurant, glowering at me as he passed.

Jackass.

I fought the urge to stick my tongue out at him, applauding myself for my restraint, then smiled at the cashier, paid, and hoped that Henry had left the parking lot by the time I walked out.

No such luck.

There he was, leaning against the hood of the white pickup I'd parked next to, talking to a couple of guys who directed friendly smiles at me as I headed toward my car.

My steps faltered, but there was no way to avoid walking past them. I lifted my chin and went the long way around, behind the cars, setting the bag of takeout on my back seat as the two strangers strolled away from Henry's truck.

Before I could open my door to get in, he strode toward me. I gritted my teeth and braced for a blowout.

"Are you going to fire me?" he demanded, stopping two feet away.

"Because of your little temper tantrum? No," I shot back, glaring at him. "Are you going to quit because you think I'm some spoiled princess who doesn't belong here?"

It would be bad for business to lose him. No matter how much I disliked him, with Gerard also on the inn's payroll, I knew such a move would have a ripple effect that no one would be pleased with.

Henry studied me, his expression fierce, though it looked like he was struggling to stay calm.

"No," he said finally.

I threw up my hands. "Fine, that's settled. Can I go now?"

When he didn't answer, I moved to open my door.

"Juliet, wait."

His hand caught my wrist before I could slide into the seat, those long fingers wrapping easily around the delicate bones. For an instant, my attention was caught on the sight of his tan skin against my freckles, then just as quickly, my patience evaporated.

I jerked my arm from his grasp. Part of me noted the shocked expression on his face, but I was too angry to care, so I let the words fly from my mouth.

"From what I can tell, you're doing a good job at the inn and Nan clearly wanted you there, so I will do my best to tolerate you. But if you *ever* touch me again, Henry Walker, I will break every bone in your hand. Do you understand me?"

His eyes flew wide at the threat. For a heartbeat, I thought I saw a flash of admiration in them, then he flexed his fingers as though my skin had burned him.

"Message received, loud and clear."

He backed away from the car, both hands raised. I wasn't sure if the gesture was meant to calm me down or to protect himself in case I attacked like some kind of feral animal—which was exactly what I felt like at that moment.

I experienced a momentary twinge of guilt for losing my cool as I watched him stomp toward his truck and pull out of the parking lot. When I slid into my seat, I folded my arms on the steering wheel, laying my head down against them.

All of my anger dissipated as quickly as it had flared. Henry could have been a great source of information, but our tempers had now burned that bridge.

I swallowed my regret as I tried to focus on the task at hand. The food smelled amazing and I still had a living room full of boxes to sort through, after all. I drove home in silence, distracted from my earlier enthusiasm by the confrontation with Henry. This was a small town—there would be no chance of avoiding him completely, not even if he did leave his job at the inn.

If I was perfectly honest with myself, I didn't even want him to quit. Now that I had a plan for the next year, I had no interest in taking over the bookkeeping, nor did I want the hassle of finding a replacement for a job I knew so little about.

Dammit.

All I wanted was to focus on the mystery surrounding my family. The last thing I needed was the hot accountant throwing drama my way.

Once I got back to the cottage, I juggled the takeout in one hand and my keys in the other, hoping dinner would soothe my temper. I reached out to unlock the front door only to realize it was unlatched, a bare half inch gap between the frame and the open door.

Had I forgotten to close it all the way? I could've sworn I locked it when I left, but my mind had been swirling with information even after the bath.

My fingers tightened around the key as I pushed the door open and peered into the cottage as though someone might jump out from behind the couch.

Silence greeted me, so I stepped inside and set the food on the kitchen counter. I considered calling the police, or even Gerard, but did I really want to invite even more drama into my life here? The last thing I needed was to be known as the silly little woman who forgot to pull her door fully shut and panicked.

No, I could handle this. I methodically checked every room of the cottage with the keys caught between my fingers like claws, in case I stumbled upon an intruder. Nothing looked out of place or tampered with, no one lurked in the shadows. Everything was exactly as I'd left it.

Between my mom's warning and my irritating run-ins with Henry Walker, my nerves were getting the best of me. I'd just have to be more careful about locking the door in the future.

Reassured, I sat at the kitchen table and finished the first half of my panini with embarrassing speed. I leaned my head back and closed my eyes for a moment, then put the other half on my plate and moved to the living room.

I was staring at the sea of boxes, wondering where to start, when my phone rang.

"You are supposed to be enjoying your long-awaited opportunity to travel," I scolded as I answered the call. "How many times do I need to say this?"

"Andre rolled his ankle on a cobblestone street, so we're taking a day of rest tomorrow and I'm allowed to stay up late. How's it going across the pond?"

"Well, the manager of the inn despises me and I might have threatened to break his hand when I picked up my dinner tonight, but other than that, things are swell. I'm surrounded by boxes, *again,* and I'm not sure I'm going to find any more answers here than I did from my mom's stuff."

Sarah was silent for a few seconds before she said, "Uh, can we backtrack to threatening to break his hand?"

Around bites of sandwich, I caved and told her in full detail about my disastrous meetings with Henry at the inn, including a too-thorough description of his good looks, then about this evening's altercation. As my best friend, Sarah was righteously indignant on my behalf, though she muffled her laughter over my violent reaction to him touching me outside The Mermaid.

"Girl, you better get a grip on that temper," she warned, then her tone turned serious. "His grandfather works at the inn, too?"

I sighed heavily. "Yeah."

"So it's a pretty small operation, right? Tight knit? Maybe Henry is jealous, but it sounds more likely that he's still grieving."

I didn't want to feel it, but a twinge of sympathy filtered through me. Sarah had an annoying habit of being right, which forced me to consider that her read of the situation might be more accurate than my own, even from across the Atlantic. If the staff at the inn was like one big family, then all of them were probably still hurting after Nan's death.

"Look, I should get to bed, but I expect updates regularly, especially about Henry the Hottie. Do try not to get arrested for breaking his bones, though. It'll be a bitch to wire bail money from here. Love you, Jules."

"Love you, too," I said softly, then tossed the phone aside as I returned to the boxes before me.

Though some of the lids were labeled with an indication as to their contents, others had no such helpful notations. I slid the boxes around like a giant game of Tetris, until all of those with labels were to my left and the unknowns to the right.

As daylight faded and the remainder of my fries congealed into a limp, cold pile, I questioned whether I would ever find actual answers in any of this junk. If Nan hadn't wanted to confide in anyone about her daughter's departure from town, was it likely she'd left any clue as to the reason in these boxes?

What am I even looking for?

Frustration got the better of me and I shoved aside the box nearest to the kitchen with my foot. The lid toppled off to reveal a pile of small leather journals, each marked with the year in embossed gold letters. On top lay a bundle of letters, tied with a ribbon.

My mouth dropped, then I lifted a skeptical eye toward the ceiling and called, "Thanks, Nan," only half-joking.

I sat on the edge of the sofa and lifted the bundle, my chest constricting at the rush of déjà vu. Would these be as life-changing as finding my mother's letter?

Though each envelope was sealed as though to be mailed, the only thing written on the outside of each was, *"To my dearest grandchild."* Briefly, I closed my eyes against a wash of sorrow, then I opened each envelope and spread the contents across my lap.

Letters, cards, a delicate cluster of pressed violets, a tiny watercolor painting of the cottage. Nothing ominous, no warnings or cryptic messages within, only...love.

Love for a grandchild she'd never met, whose name she didn't even know.

I read over each one half a dozen times, stroking my fingertips over the handwriting that was so similar to my mother's but with a unique swirl to the capital letters. My eyes filled with tears as I studied the little painting, imagining myself as a child, receiving these treasures in the mail.

God, I would've loved that. Even if we'd never met, I would have rejoiced in knowing there was someone else out there in the world who cared.

Maybe I wouldn't have felt so very lost when my mom died.

Eventually, I forced myself to set the bundle aside, more than a little bereft at severing that thread of connection, and turned my focus to the box of journals.

My mother was pregnant when she left town, Mr. Escobar had told me that much. I thumbed through the journals until I found the right year, then put the rest into chronological order. The rainbow of journals made an arc across the floor.

It was almost nine o'clock when I finished sorting, but my heart pounded wildly in my chest and I knew I wouldn't sleep until I read through at least one journal. As I opened it to the first entry, a wave of anticipation crashed over me.

That was, perhaps, a bit premature. The elegant handwriting appeared to describe relatively mundane events as they occurred at the inn.

> *Martha Jennings wants a June wedding in the gardens. I told her we're booked solid but she will not stop jabbering about it. Bridget O'Hennessy snuck a flask of vodka into the Women's Board Tea this afternoon, I thought Chairwoman Hasslebeck was going to have a fit.*

The sense of humor evident in even these innocuous entries reminded me so much of my mother that my heart clenched. I couldn't help but laugh at some of Nan's snarky commentary—from what I could tell, she had been a tough old bird, unafraid of speaking her mind.

I continued reading, handling the pages carefully, until I finally caught sight of a familiar name.

> *Officer Jameson brought Melissa home last night after a ruckus outside the school dance. I sent her up

ial cheerful sarcasm veered a bit clos-

urnals continued for many years after
, the final entry in this one was dated
ther would have been very newly preg-

y even before I read the words.

t the inn last night, drunk as a
anding to see Melissa. They fought,
banshees for nearly an hour, then
is not herself this morning, but I'm
e inn to prepare for the Women's
eon.

thing.
g pages were empty. Was that the day Mom ran
much as a word to anyone in town?
the next journal and thumbed through it, but
short and to the point, and there was no men-
mother. Gazing down at the row of journals on
ndered if any of them would detail Nan's search
.

e decided to separate her personal life from busi-

tting late, and as much as I wanted to throw open
zen boxes to search for other notebooks or diaries,

I sat on the edge of the sofa and lifted the bundle, my chest constricting at the rush of déjà vu. Would these be as life-changing as finding my mother's letter?

Though each envelope was sealed as though to be mailed, the only thing written on the outside of each was, *"To my dearest grandchild."* Briefly, I closed my eyes against a wash of sorrow, then I opened each envelope and spread the contents across my lap.

Letters, cards, a delicate cluster of pressed violets, a tiny watercolor painting of the cottage. Nothing ominous, no warnings or cryptic messages within, only...love.

Love for a grandchild she'd never met, whose name she didn't even know.

I read over each one half a dozen times, stroking my fingertips over the handwriting that was so similar to my mother's but with a unique swirl to the capital letters. My eyes filled with tears as I studied the little painting, imagining myself as a child, receiving these treasures in the mail.

God, I would've loved that. Even if we'd never met, I would have rejoiced in knowing there was someone else out there in the world who cared.

Maybe I wouldn't have felt so very lost when my mom died.

Eventually, I forced myself to set the bundle aside, more than a little bereft at severing that thread of connection, and turned my focus to the box of journals.

My mother was pregnant when she left town, Mr. Escobar had told me that much. I thumbed through the journals until I found the right year, then put the rest into chronological order. The rainbow of journals made an arc across the floor.

It was almost nine o'clock when I finished sorting, but my heart pounded wildly in my chest and I knew I wouldn't sleep until I read through at least one journal. As I opened it to the first entry, a wave of anticipation crashed over me.

That was, perhaps, a bit premature. The elegant handwriting appeared to describe relatively mundane events as they occurred at the inn.

Martha Jennings wants a June wedding in the gardens. I told her we're booked solid but she will not stop jabbering about it. Bridget O'Hennessy snuck a flask of vodka into the Women's Board Tea this afternoon, I thought Chairwoman Hasslebeck was going to have a fit.

The sense of humor evident in even these innocuous entries reminded me so much of my mother that my heart clenched. I couldn't help but laugh at some of Nan's snarky commentary—from what I could tell, she had been a tough old bird, unafraid of speaking her mind.

I continued reading, handling the pages carefully, until I finally caught sight of a familiar name.

Officer Jameson brought Melissa home last night after a ruckus outside the school dance. I sent her up

I didn't think I could keep my eyes open long enough for the hunt.

With a heavy sigh, I set the journals aside. It would be a lengthy process, sorting through all of Nan's stuff—I couldn't expect to find all the answers right away, no matter how badly I wanted to.

This was a journey, a marathon rather than a sprint. I resigned myself to the fact that I would need to take things slow and not let myself get lost in the past.

After all, the past had already taken so much from me—surely I deserved to spend some time dealing with the present, too.

Eight

JULIET

THE MORNING SUN WAS blinding once again, so I buried my face in the pillow and vowed to pick up darker curtains sometime soon. Lace was pretty, sure, but who the hell used it for bedroom curtains?

Artistic old lady innkeepers, that's who. I preferred to sleep in cave-like darkness—maybe I wasn't so much like my grandmother, after all.

For a few minutes, I debated what to do with my day. Though I'd already filled an entire sketchbook with drawings, I had yet to break out my painting supplies. I could start work on an actual painting, spend more time searching through the dusty boxes in the other room, or venture out to one of the places on Gerard's list.

The promise of adventure won out.

*to bed and he said it was T who started it all, and
that he'd seen Missy and T together around town,
even though she and Lewis have been an item for
years. My heart tells me this will not end well, but
she refuses to listen to reason. Lewis is a good boy
and simply mad about her.*

Nan clearly had no reservations about using full names in any other entry, but for some reason, the initial was the only identification for this mystery troublemaker. Could he be my father?

I bit my lip, staring blindly down at the page. If the boyfriend had gotten my mother pregnant, then there wasn't much of a mystery to be solved—but why would she have left town and refused to look back? If her fight was with my father, it made no sense for her to cut contact with Nan, to change her name and virtually disappear.

Unless she was in danger.

There had to be a good reason behind my mother's extreme choices, I was sure of it.

I flipped through the pages, scanning for pertinent information, but the journal didn't have much more to offer.

Missy is becoming more distant, read one entry, and another simply said, *Had a big fight with Missy tonight. Just can't get through to her.*

Most of the other entries were about residents of the town or guests at the inn, but I got the sense that Nan was growing

The day was going to be warm, so I threw on a pair of denim shorts and knotted a dark blue t-shirt at one hip. After shoving my hair into a ponytail, I laced up the hiking boots I'd packed, purchased years ago for a spring break trip to the Grand Canyon with Sarah, and loaded my backpack with a sketchbook, camera, snacks, and a water bottle.

I grabbed the bundle of letters from Nan off the couch and moved to the kitchen to add my mother's to it, but the countertop was bare. For a long, silent moment, I stared at the spot where I'd set it down during my trips to and from the car, but it didn't appear. A quick look in the recycle bin, in case it'd gotten stuck to the takeout boxes last night, revealed nothing.

Had I been so distracted by my run-in with Henry that I moved it and forgot where I put it?

Cursing the man under my breath, I brought Nan's letters to the bedroom and tucked them under the mattress, safe from errant breezes and absentminded artists. I'd probably find Mom's letter a week from now, tucked "someplace safe" that I'd convinced myself I'd remember and had immediately forgotten.

Back in the kitchen, I traced my fingertip down Gerard's list, landing on a place called Cooper's Point. His note mentioned a short hike from the parking lot to the lookout point. I was more the type to enjoy nature from a comfortable perch with a sketchbook in hand, but I was sure I could handle a few miles roundtrip.

Piece of cake. Hopefully the fresh air would clear my head.

The drive was short and simple, a straight shot past the turn leading into Spruce Hill. I pulled into the tiny lot and found a spot in the shade, grabbed my bag, and set off to find Cooper's Point. At the edge of the trees, I located the path, which was well-worn and wide enough to walk two or three abreast in most spots. Birds sang in the trees overhead as I breathed in the scent of pine and soil and life.

Why didn't I do this more often? Moving to Spruce Hill was the perfect opportunity to pick up a hobby like hiking, and the fresh air was intoxicating. The woods were so peaceful, everything around me coming to life as spring inched toward summer.

When the path slanted upward at an incline, my calves started burning with the exertion and my euphoria quickly faded.

This was why I didn't hike. Right.

Pausing to catch my breath, I braced my hands on my knees and listened to a bird trilling overhead. Just before I continued trudging up the hill, a twig snapped somewhere to my right.

The tiny hairs at the back of my neck prickled like I could feel someone staring at me. I straightened slowly, fighting the urge to spin around and run back to the car. Though I glanced into the thick forest butting up against the path, I didn't see anything unusual, certainly nothing to warrant the sudden rush of fear through my veins.

There was nothing except the quiet sounds of nature surrounding me, the rustle of wind and my own uneven breaths mixing with birdsong, but the feeling of being watched didn't quite subside.

Forcing myself to start moving again, I hiked until muscle strain and the sweat beading across my forehead distracted me from my unease.

I could see nothing but trees and the worn path in front of me up until the final curve. Then, suddenly, the trail opened into a clearing. Before me lay a breathtaking view of the lake and surrounding forest. A rustic wooden rail lined the cliffside, which dropped down a distance far enough to make me dizzy when I peered over the edge.

Though the forest crept right up to one side of the clearing, to my left was a steep incline down toward the creek—not quite as terrifying as the cliff straight ahead, but I edged closer to the trees, just in case.

My muscle fatigue was quickly forgotten as I snapped dozens of pictures from a variety of angles and spent the next hour and a half sketching. The day heated up quickly as the sun rose high over the expanse of trees, but the changing light revealed new wonders for me to capture.

When I stood from where I'd been kneeling, I left the sketchbook on the ground to stretch out my back and arms. Then, with my eyes on the horizon, I took one step back away from the rail, then another, holding my thumbs and forefingers up to try to frame the view just right.

Almost there.

A sharp crack broke through the quiet of the forest, far louder than the snapping twig from my ascent and significantly closer.

My body jerked in surprise—was that a gunshot?

Before I could determine the source of the sound, the sickening realization that I'd stepped back too far broke past the rush of adrenaline, and I lost my footing.

For a heartbeat, I was frozen mid-air, trying desperately to catch my balance, then I tumbled down the hillside toward the creek bed.

Branches and roots clawed at me as I fell, snagging my hair and skin like talons. I tried to cover my face with my arms, but I could barely tell up from down, bouncing painfully over rocks and fallen tree limbs. When I finally rolled to a groaning stop at the bottom, I held perfectly still, afraid I'd broken every bone in my body.

The pain was all-encompassing. I couldn't even tell where it was coming from.

The world spun drunkenly overhead in a dizzying blur of tree limbs, leaves, and clouds. I could hear nothing over my own ragged breathing, as though the birds had stopped singing upon seeing some idiot rolling down a hill.

"Oh my god," I rasped, then reality hit.

I'm going to die out here, alone. No one will come looking for me.

I hadn't told anyone where I was going, not even Sarah. Surely that was the most basic rule of hiking, and I hadn't even thought about it.

Who was there to tell, anyway? The guy who hated me, or the old people who worked at the inn?

A strangled sob burst from my throat as I fought down the panic rising inside me.

Slowly, as my eyes focused again on my surroundings, I was better able to gauge the extent of my injuries. Every inch of exposed skin on my arms and legs was scraped raw. I lifted each arm carefully into the air, bending and flexing my elbows and wrists.

A sharp twinge in my left wrist seemed like cause for concern, but I could still open and close my hand. Nothing broken, which was a relief. The scratches on my arms weren't deep, though they stung like hell.

When I attempted to bend my knees, I flinched. My right kneecap must have struck a rock or a log on the way down, and the resulting bruise blooming under my skin was already dark and angry. Both ankles seemed uninjured, a fact for which I was supremely grateful. The hike back to the car wasn't going to be fun no matter what, but it would have been an awful lot worse on a broken or sprained ankle.

I turned my head slowly back toward Cooper's Point, realizing my sketchbook and backpack were still up there.

Even on my best day, I wouldn't have been able to climb back up the steep hill from this spot. I'd have to find the base of the path in order to make the ascent again, *then* hike all the way back to the car.

Forget it—I'd just hope my stuff was safe up there until I could handle the trek. Again.

I was still staring toward the Point when a flash of movement up at the edge of the clearing made my heart lurch in my chest, but it was gone before I could determine what it was. Human? Animal? After plummeting all the way down that hill, I couldn't trust that I wasn't imagining it.

The pain, that twig snapping in the forest along the path, the gunshot...it all melded into the perfect storm for a prime freakout.

I needed to keep it together.

Focusing back on my current predicament, I touched the pocket of my shorts, looking for my phone, but it had been knocked loose during the fall. With a gasp, I groped at my neck, terrified I might have lost my mother's ring. Its reassuring weight still lay against my sternum, trapped between the t-shirt and my skin. I muttered a swift thank you to the universe for watching out for me on that front.

As I stared numbly back up the hillside, a droplet of something ran into my eye. I wiped at it, thinking my eye was watering, then I gaped at the back of my hand in horror. It was blood, smeared now across both my hand and my forehead. Though I counted my blessings that no bones were broken after that fall, the sight of those scarlet streaks caused me to whimper aloud.

"It's okay, you're okay," I whispered, repeating the words in a pathetic attempt at coaxing myself to stand. "Just get up, you'll be okay."

Some internal portion of me screamed back, *This is definitely not okay!*

I was caught between full out panic and the knowledge that no one was coming to help me out of this. If I didn't get to my feet and start making my way back to the car, well, the alternative wasn't something I wanted to explore.

Slowly, I sat up and looked around for any sign of my phone. Sunlight glinted off something buried in the dead leaves of the forest floor a few yards away.

With a sigh of relief that morphed swiftly into a groan, I rose to my feet. The phone was miraculously undamaged, but I had no signal out here. Out of options, I pocketed the phone, fixed the ponytail that had come halfway out of my hair elastic, and began walking.

A few painful steps later, I was already limping.

The trees were thick down here and my confidence in which direction I was traveling faltered embarrassingly soon into the journey. The soft babble of the creek kept me company, so I decided to follow it, hopefully back to the path I'd taken out to the Point.

My knee throbbed and, soon enough, the sweat beading across my forehead caused blood to drip into my eye again. I was barely managing to hold it together, stumbling along until the thin stream of water beside me joined up with the main body of the creek.

Once there, I doubled over and fought back the tears. If I started crying now, I was afraid I might never stop. It might have been melodramatic of me, but there was a certainty deep in my gut that my survival depended on me not falling apart out here.

"You can do this," I said aloud. "You *have* to do this. Buck up, Jules."

The words were not as reassuring as I might have hoped.

I rested a few minutes longer while I debated whether it was safe to use the creek water to wash the cut on my forehead or wet my suddenly dry mouth. Headlines about flesh-eating bacteria and sewage runoff flashed through my mind, so I decided against it. With a deep breath, I started hobbling along beside the creek, hoping I would soon find the original trail.

Even once I was sure I must have traveled far enough, I still hadn't found it. The trees seemed to be closing in around me instead of spreading out, until I could barely see more than a few feet on either side.

Over the gentle trickle of the creek and the birdsong above came a different sort of sound and I froze.

Are there bears in these woods? Mountain lions?

What kind of moron went traipsing into the forest without researching local predators?

The sound, if there had been one outside of my overburdened imagination, was gone by the time I stopped berating myself. I checked the phone again for a signal, though whether I was hoping to call for help or research the local bear population, I wasn't entirely sure. It didn't matter anyway, since I still had no service.

I wiped at my left eyebrow with the back of my hand, relieved to see there was no resulting streak of fresh blood on my skin, and forced myself to start walking again.

A few minutes later, the sound came again—a distinct rustle of leaves, louder this time. I glanced wildly around for something to defend myself with and found a large branch, perfect for use as a walking stick. I gripped it in my right hand, trying to quiet the harsh sound of my own breathing.

At least I'd go down swinging.

The creature that popped out of the underbrush several feet in front of me was neither bear nor mountain lion. It was, strangely enough, an inquisitive-looking Border Collie wearing a red bandana around its neck.

I stayed right where I was, stick in hand in case the dog was rabid, but it simply wagged its plumed tail and trotted toward me.

"Hi there," I said softly, lowering the weapon a smidge. The dog cocked its head at the words and padded closer.

"Blue!" The male voice sounded close. "Blue. Come here, girl!"

My head shot up. I shifted my grip on the branch again, wondering if some axe murderer had brought his dog along to track down lost women in the woods. When the owner of the voice appeared from between the trees, I was caught in a precarious balance between relief and dread, because I knew him.

It was Henry Walker.

Nine

HENRY

I surveyed the bloodied woman standing before me, trying to process exactly what I was seeing.

For that first second, I almost didn't recognize her.

With those flaming red curls pulled back in a pony-tail—even one with several locks falling loose and detritus from the forest floor tangled in it—her freckled face was streaked crimson on one side from temple to chin and she had a branch clutched before her like a staff. Nearly every inch of bare skin on her arms and legs was either criss-crossed with scratches, smeared with dirt, or darkened with bruising.

"Juliet?" I whispered, horrified by the state of her. "What the hell happened to you?"

Once I was able to drag my gaze away from her injuries, I looked sharply at the forest around us, wondering if there was an assailant somewhere that I needed to contend with.

"I'm fine," Juliet said finally, though it didn't answer my question.

I worried that she was already in shock. Her expression was curiously blank, those bright blue eyes startling against her bloody face.

"Fine? You look like you just walked off the set of a slasher flick. Juliet, did somebody hurt you? You're covered in blood."

I regretted the blunt words as soon as they were past my lips. The sound that burst from her throat was somewhere between a laugh and a sob, and I shoved my reaction down immediately, trying to keep the horror from my expression. Whatever had transpired, she was hurt and she was alone.

"Hey. Hey now, you're safe," I said softly, taking a few steps closer to her.

She hadn't dropped the branch yet, so I moved slowly and kept my voice soothing. It was up to me to convince her to accept my help. When she didn't take a swing at me, I took that as a good sign.

"Everything's going to be okay, Juliet. Can you tell me what happened?"

"I fell."

I glanced skeptically at the even landscape behind her. "Fell? Fell where?"

"Not here," she replied, but the words were flat, with no trace of her usual sarcasm.

"Juliet," I said as gently as possible, concern flooding me at both her robotic response and the faint sway of her body while I approached. "I think you might have a concussion. Do you know where you are?"

"I was at Cooper's Point. I heard...I don't know. A gunshot, I think. I stepped back and fell down the hill."

I was close enough now to reach out and touch her, but I refrained, the memory of our altercation outside The Mermaid still fresh in my mind. Cautiously, expecting she might strike me at any moment, I stretched my arm to take the stick from her hands and set it against the trunk of a tree. Then I held her gaze as my brain caught on what she'd said.

"A gunshot?"

"Yes." She sounded so sure, so clear despite the hazy look in her eyes.

"There aren't many hunters out at this time of year. Are you telling me you fell down the *ravine*?" I asked, thinking maybe I'd misunderstood.

I hoped so. If that was what happened, she was lucky she hadn't broken her damn neck.

"Is that the hill off to the side of Cooper's Point?"

Juliet's breath hitched on the words and she looked like she might start crying at any second. My heart twisted painfully at the contrast between her current state and the spitting fury of our previous meetings. With one wrong word on my part, it was distinctly possible she would finally break down.

Though I didn't know exactly how to reassure her, I kept my tone light as I took another half step toward her.

"I think the word 'hill' implies a gentle slope that kids might sled down in the winter," I replied, "while a ravine is steep as hell and full of rocks and sharp sticks. It looks like you made the acquaintance of quite a few of them on your way down."

Juliet gave a wobbly smile, but the sheen of tears in her eyes broke my heart. My gaze traveled over her again, this time to assess the severity of her injuries. When my inspection ended back at her forehead, I pursed my lips.

"Why don't you sit down," I suggested gently, gesturing to a boulder beside the creek. "Let's have a look at you. I can take care of that cut, at the very least."

Juliet nodded, but she stood rooted to the spot. I let out a slow, patient breath. This would have been a whole lot easier if we hadn't gotten off to such a rocky start. I acknowledged my own culpability in that and would do whatever it took to get past it if she'd let me take care of her now.

"Look, I know you don't like me, but you're injured. Please let me help you."

At my careful tone, the tears she'd been fighting spilled over, rolling down her cheeks. She didn't protest, though, just nodded again and lowered herself onto the rock. Blue stuck close to her side and I could tell her presence was a comfort as she sat beside my unexpected patient. Juliet laid a hand on the dog's head, dropping her gaze to the ground.

"I didn't picture you as a dog person," she said after a moment.

"This fact probably won't surprise you, but I find dogs less complicated than humans."

When she met my eyes, I smiled gently before I knelt down beside her and rummaged through the small black bag strapped to my waist, sorting through my stash of first aid supplies. I didn't carry much with me, but it would be enough to clean the blood from her face, at least.

"Is that...a fanny pack?" she asked faintly.

"It most certainly is not. This, Ms. Morrison, is a lumbar pack." I shot her a sharp look as I adopted an attitude of mock outrage. "Hikers wear lumbar packs. *Tourists* wear fanny packs. There's a very clear difference. I suggest you learn it if you're going to keep hiking around here."

Juliet snorted, momentarily distracted from her injuries by my teasing. "Clearly. I'll study up before my next hike. Which will probably be...never, after this."

When I found the packet of gauze, I glanced up and studied her face for another moment. She seemed steadier now, her responses more fluid, so I decided to stick with humor as the antidote to her shock.

"I have to ask this, for the sake of my own safety. If I touch you now, Juliet, are you actually going to break every bone in my hand?"

With a grimace of embarrassment, she managed a shrug and a tiny, apologetic smile as she said, "Ah, no. I'm sorry about that."

"Look, I'm sorry I was such a prick. You didn't deserve that."

Now was as good a time as any, even if this wasn't how I'd imagined my apology would go. I pulled out a bottle of water and poured some onto the gauze, but I paused to meet her eyes before I spoke.

"Outside the restaurant that night, what I was trying to do was apologize, not antagonize you further. Obviously my brain and my mouth work independently of each other sometimes. I have no excuse for my behavior, but I really am sorry. Change is hard, I guess."

"That's the understatement of the century," Juliet muttered under her breath, but I only grinned in response.

When I dabbed carefully at her temple with the wet gauze, she flinched. Blue laid her chin on Juliet's uninjured knee, so she turned her attention back to stroking the dog's ears while I cleaned up the streaks of blood. The cut didn't look serious, and though it had obviously bled freely for a while, the flow had stopped.

As I gently swiped at the dried blood and dirt on her cheek, Juliet resolutely avoided meeting my gaze. I couldn't blame her for that. She barely knew me, and what she did know was un-flattering, to say the least.

While I didn't want to take advantage of her current state, this might be my only chance before we butted heads again.

"Can you forgive me?" I asked quietly.

At last she met my eyes, that startling blue of hers standing out vividly against the smears I couldn't quite remove with one small square of gauze. For a moment, she looked so lost, so vulnerable, that hot shame burned inside me. This woman had lost her mother *and* her grandmother, and she still had the courage to pick up and move across the country on her own.

Asshole that I was, I'd only made things harder for her. I opened my mouth to apologize again, but she held up a hand to stop me.

"I'm sorry, too," she replied.

My shock must have been evident, because the damned woman laughed. The sound was low and musical, with a husky, breathless quality that I wasn't sure was characteristic of her laughter or simply a result of all she'd just been through.

Either way, it sent a bolt of warmth tumbling through me, curling comfortably inside my chest. As her lips curved and her eyes brightened, I had the sinking suspicion that life in Spruce Hill was never going to be the same again.

Ten

JULIET

Henry looked so surprised by my apology that I started laughing, though maybe exhaustion, pain, and dehydration were taking their toll. It fizzed up inside me until I had to let go of the dog to clap a hand over my mouth.

All the while, he stared like he'd never seen me before.

I tried to bottle up the ridiculous giggles shooting out of me like champagne bubbles, but when his lips quirked, I let them run their course. To make the situation even more awkward, this all went down with his face mere inches from my own.

"Look, Henry, I don't...dislike you," I said when I finally caught my breath.

There was something soft in the green and gold depths of his eyes, though I couldn't quite define it. Compassion? Pity? Forgiveness? Even when he snorted at my statement, that soft-ness remained.

"That was very diplomatically worded, but I realize I haven't given you much reason to like me just yet, so don't worry about it."

Henry pulled out his phone and slid his thumbs quickly across the screen before pocketing it again.

I'd have to find out what cell service he used.

His hands were large and capable, his strong forearms dusted with dark hair. There was nothing about him to indicate a life spent crunching numbers behind a desk—the woods seemed more like his natural environment.

It was strange I'd noticed so little about him before now, but aside from my initial impression of his romance novel attractiveness that first morning in his office, my focus had quickly shifted to his attitude.

"What brought you out to Cooper's Point?" he asked.

The question dragged my attention back to his face, which was drawn in concentration as he wiped a spot of blood from my jaw. His touch was gentle, almost tender. The man was a study in contrasts. Whether it was the artist in me or just my semi-dormant libido, the stirrings of inter-est grew into a distant rumble.

"I went up there to draw. I've been planning to get sketches of all the locations Nan used for the paintings at the inn." I frowned, the movement sending a streak of pain across my eyebrow. "My sketchbook is still up there, and my backpack. I have to go back to get them."

Henry gave a startled laugh. "Not right now, you don't. I'll take care of it, after we get you sorted out. Did you lose consciousness at all after the fall? Any nausea?" he asked, studying me closely as he covered each of my eyes with his hand to check my pupils.

"No, I was just dizzy from rolling when I got to the bottom." I looked at him quizzically. "Were you a Boy Scout or something?"

He grinned, that same devastating expression he'd flashed all too briefly at the inn. I wanted to blame my tumble down the hill for how my belly dipped, but I knew the fall wasn't responsible.

It was all Henry.

"Or something," he replied. "I was a bit of a daredevil as a kid, so I've had my share of concussion checks."

An image of him as a child, climbing trees and swinging from monkey bars, popped unbidden into my head and I realized I wanted to learn more about him. When I opened my mouth to ask him to tell me, though, the words caught in my throat. I didn't know what made me feel so awkward around him—if I had to guess, at that precise moment, it was probably his proximity.

I wondered idly what kind of cologne he wore that smelled so damn good, like salty sea air and ocean waves, but asking him now was definitely not going to reduce the tension between us.

Ultimately, I decided to keep my mouth shut.

Henry rummaged through his pouch for another gauze pad and squeezed some ointment onto it, then smeared it across my temple.

"There," he said, finally satisfied. "That should hold you until we get into town. Where else are you hurt?"

He set his palms lightly on my shoulders and began squeezing in gentle pulses down my arms. I blinked at him, trying to ignore the shiver his hands activated along my spine.

"Um," I said, then silently cursed myself for sounding like a moron. "My left wrist hurts but I don't think it's broken, and I banged my knee pretty hard on the way down. Everything else is just scratches and bruises, I think."

If he noticed the tremor, he graciously pretended not to. After gently checking my injured wrist, one of his hands moved to my knee and the other to my ankle, bending and straightening the leg like I was a doll. The heat of his palm against my bare skin drew a gasp from my lips, which he must have mistaken for pain.

"Sorry, sorry. That's one hell of a bruise, but I don't think anything's busted," he said, flashing a quick, encouraging smile. "Do you think you can keep walking? We're about a mile from my truck."

"A mile? I've been walking forever. I thought the trail to the Point was only a mile, start to finish."

"Oh, it is." He leaned back on his heels as he studied me, then offered another disarming grin. "However, you followed the creek—which was smart, by the way, or you could've ended up anywhere in these woods—and the water meanders back and forth. You veered a good distance away from the trail. Fortunately for you, I know a shortcut."

Thank god. I puffed out my cheeks on a long exhalation.

"Fantastic," I muttered, attempting to rise gracefully to my feet as he did the same. My maneuver was a failure, though, so I had to catch my balance by grabbing his biceps even as I squeaked out, "Sorry."

Was it possible to humiliate myself any more today than I already had?

His response was another slow curve of his lips, and when I snatched my hand back, he slid his arm around my waist to support the weight off of my injured knee.

From town jerk to knight in shining armor. The shift gave me whiplash.

I was still unsettled by the transformation, even if I had to admit that I enjoyed his smiles far more than his scowls.

As we walked, I focused so hard on not collapsing into him that I couldn't manage small talk. Henry didn't seem to mind the silence, though. He simply took as much of my weight as possible, given that I was determined to keep myself from relying too heavily on him, and kept quiet.

Blue started out padding along beside us, as though she needed to make sure I was okay, but eventually, Henry told her to go ahead and the dog took off. Every few minutes, she would retrace her steps to cock her head at us, then trot away again.

"She likes you," Henry told me after the fourth or fifth time.

"Or she thinks I'm a clumsy idiot who can't keep up," I joked, a bit weakly. "Which, unfortunately, seems to be true."

He shook his head, patiently helping me to hobble over a fallen branch. "She must've known you were up ahead. She took off like a bat out of hell. It's lucky she didn't obey my commands to come back or I never would've found you."

The thought sent another shiver down my spine and, though I might have imagined it, it felt like his arm tightened around me ever so slightly. My sense of time was distorted, like the fall had jumbled my brain a bit, but maybe it was just that the sun was barely visible beyond the thick canopy of green leaves above us.

Every step sent sharp pain radiating outward from my kneecap. I didn't want Henry to think I was any more helpless than he already must, but before long, the pain started making me dizzy. I swayed suddenly and Henry swore under his breath. When I tried to apologize, my mouth couldn't quite form the words.

It didn't matter anyway, because his next move shocked me into silence.

He swept an arm under my knees and lifted me easily against his chest before I could even consider a protest. The world spun like a kaleidoscope before my eyes, so I squeezed them shut, breathing in the fresh scent of him.

"I'm too heavy. You don't have to . . ." I trailed off, realizing he probably did, in fact, have to. Otherwise, we'd be out there until nightfall.

"Relax," he said, his voice low and gentle again. "I've got you. I grew up in these woods, but even I don't want to be out here after the sun goes down. We're almost there, anyway."

My eyes were closed tight against the waves of dizziness crashing over me, so I could only hope he was right.

Good lord, he was even stronger than he looked, though I'd noticed his impressive biceps when I grabbed onto him before. Carrying me didn't seem to slow him down one bit—in fact, when I cracked an eye open to see if the forest had stopped spinning, it was obvious he was moving faster while holding me than he had while helping me limp onward.

Before long, we were at the edge of the trees with Blue running in excited circles around us. This was not the paved parking lot where I'd left my car, but a narrow gravel pull-off along the road. Henry's white truck was the only vehicle in sight.

"You can put me down," I croaked.

Henry merely snorted in response. I wanted to argue, but I was drained, both physically and emotionally. He set me carefully to my feet only once we reached the passenger side of his truck, but he kept his arm around my waist to hold me upright while he opened the door. Blue jumped in and wagged her tail at us.

"Move over," he told her, and she promptly got behind the wheel.

I laughed but looked at the pristine interior of the truck's cab, then down at the dirt and blood adorning my outfit.

"I'm going to get your seat all dirty," I warned him.

Henry nodded, his hazel eyes creasing at the corners as he smiled. They were a deep, mossy jade today, thanks to the green t-shirt that showed off every muscle in his arms, and that earlier softness still lingered.

"Yes, that does seem likely. Can you get in by yourself or do you need me to lift you?"

Very carefully, I hoisted myself onto the seat, trying to ignore the sudden heat of his hand on my hip as he helped me up.

"Thank you, Henry," I said quietly, feeling like there was a whole lot more I needed to convey. The rest of it caught in my chest and my mouth snapped shut.

"You're welcome, Juliet."

The sound of my name from his lips hung in the air for a heartbeat before he closed the door and strode to the driver's side. Blue wagged her tail and happily scooted into the narrow space between us when he got in. Henry ruffled the fur between her ears before shifting the truck into gear.

"First stop, medical attention."

"I really don't need medical attention," I argued. "I'm fine."

I frowned at his skeptical look, then flinched at the movement, and I could practically hear his eyes rolling back in his head.

"Look, I appreciate your hardy constitution, but I found you wandering in the woods, bleeding from the head. My ex is a doctor. She'll meet us at the clinic in town and check you over before I take you home."

With a sigh of resignation, I buckled my seatbelt and let him chauffeur me into Spruce Hill. My curiosity was piqued by the mention of an ex, as though it might shed light on his personal life. Blue swayed between our shoulders with each bump in the road and I closed my eyes to keep the blur of the passing trees from bringing on a fresh spell of dizziness.

The radio was set to some kind of alternative rock, and I made a mental note of it—one of the few things I knew about Henry. The list was painfully short.

Always prepared. Good with numbers. Kind to animals. Really freaking strong. Then, after a moment, I added, *Smells like absolute heaven.*

Aside from the whole clash of tempers upon our first meeting—and our second, and third—he was actually a pretty decent guy. He was tall, nearly a foot taller than me, and a bit on the lanky side. But damn...the way he had swept me into his arms.

If only I hadn't been coated in crumpled leaves and bloodstains, it would've been a truly impressive image.

Before the truck even slowed, Blue's whole rear end started wagging along with her tail, leading me to assume we were approaching the clinic. As if being found limping through the woods like that wasn't enough humiliation for the day, now I would have to meet some stranger looking like—what had he said? An actor from a horror movie?

I reached up to surreptitiously smooth my hair back, plucking a leaf and a small twig from my disastrous curls in the process.

Henry pulled up in front of the clinic, a modern little building right on the main road through town. Blue jumped out the driver's side door after him, but before I could even unbuckle my seatbelt, Henry opened the door and reached in to help me.

"My arms are fully functional," I snapped at him, though my fingers were moving too sluggishly to press the release button before he got to it.

"So is your mouth," he shot back, using the same sarcastic tone I recalled from our first meeting.

Flecks of gold mingled with the green cast in his eyes as he paused, our faces only a few inches apart. We glared at each other for the space of a few breaths, then a grudging smile tugged at his lips.

"If I don't get you inside, Libby is going to march out here and demand to know what's taking so long. You don't want to get on her bad side, trust me."

I conceded, allowing him to slip his arm around my lower back so I could slide down to solid ground. A dull throb had formed beneath the cut on my temple and, though I would never admit it to him, I was grateful for his support as we made our way slowly toward the giant glass door of the building.

Blue let out an excited woof and circled us several times, then sat in front of the door with an expectant look on her face. Even in a small town like this, I couldn't imagine the dog would be allowed inside a medical office, but Blue seemed to know the drill better than I would.

Just before we reached the door, it slid open to reveal an exquisitely beautiful woman with dark, upswept curls. Her eyes were a deep, warm brown that glinted with good humor.

"Well then, what have you brought me this time, Henry?" she asked.

Surveying the two of us, she slipped her hand into the pocket of her lab coat and tossed some kind of treat to Blue, who snatched it expertly from the air. The doctor's scrutiny was as intense as Henry's, scouring me from head to toe. With immense effort, I managed not to squirm.

"Found this lost waif wandering in the woods. She took a spill down the ravine at Cooper's Point," he told her. "She must have been bleeding pretty good from the cut on her forehead, but it had stopped by the time I found her. No nausea or loss of consciousness, though she got dizzy during the hike back to the truck. Banged up the right knee, sore left wrist. Damn lot of scratches but I ran out of gauze before I could clean anything except her forehead."

I didn't miss the swift look of shock that crossed Libby's face when he mentioned the ravine. It wasn't quite the horror of Henry's reaction, but as a doctor, Libby probably had more practice schooling her expression.

Ahh, what a way to make a reputation for myself.

I fought a grimace. The woman who tumbled down the ravine—just lovely. So much better than being known as the unexpected heiress.

"It's a good thing you found her, then," Libby said after a beat of silence, her lips curving into a smile. She held out a hand. "I'm Henry's ex-wife, Dr. Elizabeth Bardot, but please, call me Libby."

"Juliet Morrison. Nice to meet you."

I took her hand with a weak smile. Libby's grip was warm and strong. One of her dark brows quirked upward.

"I imagine it might have been nicer to meet under better circumstances, but welcome to Spruce Hill, nevertheless."

Henry told Blue to stay put—and, to my surprise, the dog promptly obeyed—while he helped me inside. The clinic was bright and cheery, decorated in vibrant colors, but clearly closed for the night. We made a slow procession to an exam room.

Before I could protest, Henry placed his hands on either side of my waist to lift me onto the exam table. I glared at him, but his only response was a wink and that adorable half smile.

"I'll take Blue home while you two, ah . . ." He trailed off, waving his hand vaguely in the air toward my injuries. "I'll be back soon."

Libby kissed his cheek, causing him to roll his eyes goodnaturedly. I lifted my hand in a brief wave and Henry inclined his head in my direction before swiftly exiting the room.

"All right then," Libby said, smiling brightly. "Let's have a look, shall we?"

Eleven

JULIET

THOUGH I FELT LIKE a kindergartner with a skinned knee, I submitted to Libby's very thorough inspection as graciously as I could. She wrapped my injured wrist in an elastic bandage, swabbed what must have been a few dozen scratches with antiseptic, checked a number of bruises across my back and shoulders, and probed the area around my aching kneecap as gently as possible.

"Henry's text said you walked pretty far from where you fell," she said, setting an ice pack on my knee. "You'll need to take it easy for a few days, maybe a week, but I think you'll heal up just fine if you rest it. Doctor's orders. Please, for the love of god, be a better patient than Henry Walker."

I couldn't hold back a grin at the doctor's admonition—I could just imagine what a pain in the ass Henry would be if he were the one all banged up.

"I promise I will not go hiking again anytime soon. Or ever again, really. The shine has definitely worn off. I'm thinking about taking up needlepoint instead."

Libby laughed. When she moved to inspect my forehead, she hummed in approval at Henry's first aid work. Her concussion check was a bit more in-depth than his, but she seemed fairly confident that I would survive. After applying two butterfly bandages to close the wound, she stepped back to study her handiwork.

"I would really like to run some more tests to be sure you don't have a concussion," she said, dark eyes locking on mine, "but that would involve heading over to the hospital."

My entire body tensed at the words. I would never forget the hospital room where my mother spent her final days, that antiseptic smell and the buzz and beep of machinery. If Sarah found out I was hospitalized, she would probably jump on the next flight back to the States—and I wasn't sure I'd even try to stop her. Being alone in a hospital was one of my worst nightmares.

"I'd rather not," I said quietly.

Libby smiled as though she understood completely, though I wasn't sure if it was because she knew about my mother's illness or just because she was a perceptive woman.

"I didn't think so. Is there anyone you can stay with? It'd be best if someone could keep an eye on you throughout the night, at least."

Oh, shit.

"Um. I don't really know anybody in Spruce Hill all that well," I admitted.

Much like my realization that no one in town would mourn me if I'd never come out of those woods, the words threatened to lodge hard in the center of my chest.

"I'll stay with her," Henry said from the doorway.

My gaze shot toward him, my lips parting in surprise as his offer sank in. He was leaning one hip against the frame, looking handsome and utterly at ease. Clearly traipsing through the woods hadn't damaged his aesthetic as much as it had mine.

"I don't think that's necessary," I began, but Libby shot me a stern look, so I mumbled, "The spare bedroom isn't really set up for company yet."

Henry's mouth quirked at the corners and my pulse kicked up right along with it.

"I can take the couch. Or you're more than welcome to stay at my place, if you'd prefer," he added, blinking innocently back at me.

I tried to think of a good excuse—hell, *any* excuse—but nothing came to mind. Libby smiled brightly, blatantly ignoring the swift rise of tension between us.

"Well, that's settled then. I'll get you some things to take home," she said, stepping aside as Henry moved forward to help me down.

With me still seated on the exam table, we were nearly eye to eye, close enough for me to count the golden flecks in his irises. His body radiated warmth, along with a hint of that damn scent again, and it seeped into my own limbs. As he waited for me to make the first move, he studied me as intently as I was studying him—searching for weakness, maybe, or for confirmation that our uneasy truce was still in effect.

After a moment of silence, I laid the ice pack aside and grudgingly set my palms on his shoulders so he could lift me down. The uncomfortable silence stretched as my left side slid slowly down the length of Henry's body before my feet hit the floor.

"Um," I said, avoiding his gaze as long as possible.

When I finally glanced up at him, that same little smile was playing across his lips and a lock of dark hair had fallen across his forehead. I couldn't remember ever being so tongue-tied around a man in my entire life and was somewhat disgusted with myself over it.

"What about Blue?" I asked weakly.

"I dropped her off with Libby's husband, Mark. They'll keep her for the night, she'll be fine. We picked up your car, too, and parked it back at the cottage. I brought something for you," he said, his hand firm under my elbow as we exited the room. My backpack sat on a chair near the front door. "I found the camera, it's inside the bag. I searched all over the clearing but I didn't see a sketchbook anywhere, I'm afraid. It might have fallen into the underbrush somewhere. I hope it didn't contain anything irreplaceable?"

"Nothing I can't recreate from the photos. How on earth did you get out there and back so quickly?" I asked, baffled.

Henry gave me a strange look. "You've been here for over an hour, Juliet. It's almost six."

"Damn," I breathed. The clock on the lobby wall confirmed it. "Time flies when you've got a head wound, I guess. No wonder I'm starving."

Henry laughed. "I think we can remedy that. I ordered a pizza, we can pick it up on the way to your place. Unless you'd rather spend the night at my house?"

My nose scrunched at the casual way he said it and he responded with another wide-eyed look of innocence.

"Or I can drop you at the hospital, if you're that opposed to having company."

I smiled sweetly in response. "Oh no, you can be my honored guest. Of course, the couch is probably as old as your grandfather, but I'm sure it's quite comfortable."

A wicked gleam entered his eye. "If you'd prefer to—" He broke off, snapping his mouth shut as Libby reappeared.

I was desperately curious about what he was going to say, but I forced myself to pay attention to Libby as she went over instructions for changing bandages and taking painkillers. Henry was tasked with ensuring I stayed awake for the next several hours and Libby ordered him to check in on me throughout the night, which made me cringe.

Finally, the good doctor patted my shoulder, handed Henry the paper bag of supplies, and smiled approvingly as he looped the backpack over one shoulder and slid his arm around me once more.

This was getting to be a bad habit, but that warning didn't keep me from appreciating his support. It was a little too easy to lean on him, to trust his strong limbs to keep me upright in case I stumbled. I attempted to bear a bit more weight on my own two feet, grimacing in the process, but Henry's grip stayed firm.

I would have rolled my eyes, but I was afraid I'd get dizzy and collapse against him.

Once we were situated in the truck, I leaned my head back against the seat and closed my eyes. Henry sang along with the radio, the deep timbre of his voice lulling me nearly to sleep, but every so often, he'd murmur my name or squeeze my uninjured knee to keep me awake.

Until a few hours ago, the mere thought of him was enough to send my blood pressure sky high. Now, I found myself comfortable enough with him to give up on all semblance of polite conversation.

If I ever had to defend that feeling, I would blame my injuries.

Drowsing in the passenger seat, I barely even noticed when he shifted the vehicle into park and ran in to pick up the pizza.

The smell of it was enough to bring me back to my senses, though. My stomach rumbled loudly and I cracked open one eye to peek over at him.

"Almost home," he said, grinning at me.

I closed my eyes again, embarrassed. Though Henry made sure I never dozed off, before I knew it, the truck had stopped again and the rush of cool evening air swept over me as he opened my door. When his arm slid under my knees, I peeled my eyes open as quickly as I could.

"I can walk," I insisted. The words came out a little too shrill for my liking.

"Sorry, just trying to help. By all means," he said, gesturing toward the cottage.

Henry plastered a benign smile on his face. He had my backpack slung over his shoulder again, leaving me with only my battered body to contend with.

I took a deep breath, hoping the painkillers Libby gave me at the clinic had kicked in already, and slid off the seat, landing with my weight on my good leg. Henry waited patiently while I tested out my injured knee and I found myself able to limp along a little less pathetically than before.

"The key is in the front pocket of my bag," I told him.

"Huh." The way he said it made it clear it was an observation rather than a question.

"What?" I demanded.

I risked a quick glance at his pensive expression before returning my gaze to the path leading up to the cottage. The last thing I needed was another fall, especially right in front of him, so I picked my way carefully along.

He was quiet for a moment, then replied, "I don't think Nan ever locked the front door, that's all."

"I forgot to, the other night," I admitted. "Then I had to search the house with my keys between my fingers, in case someone broke in."

"If you were afraid there was someone inside the cottage, you shouldn't have gone in at all." When I glanced at his face again, he looked horrified at the prospect of me trying to fend off an intruder with only my keys for a weapon.

Flustered, I shrugged. "I didn't want to overreact by calling 911, and I wasn't going to ask your grandfather to check my closets for the boogeyman."

With a disgruntled scowl, he said, "Next time, you can call me."

I nodded, unwilling to argue after this hellscape of a day, and watched him fish the key from my backpack before I recognized the familiarity in his earlier statement.

"You knew Nan well, then?" I asked, curiosity chipping away at the fog in my brain.

Henry paused to unlock the front door before he answered.

"Nan was my Gram's best friend. They used to meet for tea every afternoon when I was little. My parents were both working, so after school, my brother and I would go to my grandmother's house for a couple hours. After she died, Nan arranged for us to come here after school until we were old enough to be home alone. She'd bake cookies or snag some desserts from the inn for us to snack on. She was like family."

His wistful smile made my heart ache for him. It was strange how things worked out. My first nemesis in town turned out to be my first source of real insight into Nan's life.

Instead of being jealous that he'd gotten to experience a childhood with Nan in such a vital role, I was touched, pleased to know Nan hadn't gone without young children to dote on in the absence of her only grandchild.

"I'm sorry," I said, wishing I could think of something more eloquent to offer.

Losing a grandparent you hadn't known existed wasn't quite the same as losing one who'd helped to raise you. Suddenly, I doubted Henry would make such a distinction—he seemed to have a good heart. I wished I'd been able to sense that when we first met, to see beyond the antagonism caused by my arrival and my risk to not only his livelihood, but to Nan's legacy, as well.

I couldn't blame him for lashing out under those circumstances. It wasn't the first time my temper got the better of me and I was sure it wouldn't be the last, but I hoped Henry and I had turned a corner.

And maybe, if I stopped fighting it, a friend with a good heart was exactly what I needed in my life right now.

Twelve

HENRY

I GAVE MYSELF A moment to miss them both, Gram and Nan, but tonight wasn't about what I'd lost. Juliet needed someone in her corner, and now that we were on speaking terms, why shouldn't it be me? Hopefully finding her and bringing her home safely would win me some points on the redemption scale.

Some distant part of my brain chanted *finder's keepers*, like she was a treasure I'd stumbled upon in the woods, but I tried not to dwell on that thought.

My eyes locked on Juliet's face. "You really do look like her, you know."

"So I've been told," she replied.

I forced my gaze away as we entered the cottage, moving slowly until she was able to flip on one of the lamps near the door. When I saw the sea of boxes on the living room floor, I gave a startled laugh. Nan had been something of a neat freak; I could just imagine her opinion of this chaos.

"What is all this?"

"Most of what Nan had in storage upstairs," she told me, watching my face for a reaction. "I thought maybe I could find some details about why my mother left town...or why she lied about us having no other family, or who my father was. You don't happen to know any of those answers, do you?"

I looked skeptically at the spread. "I'm afraid not. I can't remember ever hearing any speculation, really, but most people knew better than to gossip about Nan's family. Do you think Nan even knew who your father was?"

"Maybe not," she admitted. "My mom must have been only a couple months pregnant when she left. I just thought maybe somewhere, there might be some clue about it. I guess I was hoping to get lucky while going through this stuff. I didn't even know Nan existed until it was too late. What if I have other family out there that I don't know about?"

It might have just been exhaustion, but I could hear her voice rising in pitch and watched as she bit back any further outbursts. I saw the conflict in her cornflower eyes and guided her to the cozy recliner that had been shoved into a corner of the room.

"Easy," I said, my voice and hands gentle despite the teasing words. "That's a battle for another day. For right now, you just need to relax. I'm going to run back out and get the pizza."

She nodded, closing her eyes while I fetched our dinner. When she moved to get up from the chair upon my return, I stopped her before she could rise.

"Don't even think about it," I warned as I pulled dishes from the kitchen cupboards.

Thankfully, I was familiar with the cottage, because she was in no shape to assist. I handed her a plate of food and a water bottle from the fridge, then grabbed my own and plopped down on the sofa. We ate in silence, then I put the remainder in the fridge and went to rummage through a closet in the downstairs hallway.

Juliet frowned in confusion when I returned with a pile of neatly folded blankets and a spare pillow.

"I didn't even realize that stuff was in there. I feel like a moron, not knowing my way around a cottage this small," she said glumly.

"I'd be happy to give you a tour tomorrow," I joked, tossing the bedding onto the couch. When she narrowed her eyes at me, I grinned and added, "Look, it's a good thing for both of us that I'm familiar with the place. Libby would annihilate me if she heard that I expected an injured woman to wait on me."

Juliet gave a reluctant smile. Now that her skin was no longer streaked with blood, I was able to appreciate that expression more fully. I sat down beside the blankets and stretched my legs out in front of me.

"I guess that's true. Just feels a little weird," she admitted. "This whole move has been kind of surreal."

"Where did you live before?"

A few hours ago, I hadn't had any interest in knowing more about this woman, but now I was invested, eager to learn all I could. She'd clearly inherited more than just Nan's red hair and heartstopping blue eyes. It took a damned lot of strength to get up after the kind of spill she'd taken, then walk for miles in an unfamiliar forest, all alone.

A swift wave of relief that I'd been the one to find her filled me as I waited for her response.

"Just outside of Minneapolis."

I didn't think I was imagining the flash of homesickness in her eyes. "Do you have any family out there?"

Juliet was silent so long that I opened my mouth to apologize for the question, but she waved it off before I could speak.

"My mom died six months ago. Pancreatic cancer. It was just me and her."

"I'm sorry," I said gently.

That loneliness I'd sensed earlier was written clearly across her freckled face. I wanted to say more, to offer some degree of comfort, but I couldn't find the words—and I still wasn't sure she'd even want them from me at this point.

Juliet apparently decided to seize the opportunity to learn something about me in return.

"What about your family? Aside from Gerard, obviously. You mentioned that you have a brother, does he live around here? What about your parents?"

"My brother Aaron is a nurse at Libby's clinic. He married his college sweetheart and moved to Oakville, just down the road. My parents bought an RV when they retired and are currently working their way across the country," I said with a grin.

My family was close, sometimes annoyingly so, but I loved them fiercely. Juliet didn't hesitate to smile back this time.

"My best friend, Sarah, is backpacking through Europe with her husband at the moment. She makes me feel like a homebody."

"You, a homebody? You just moved halfway across the country with a single week's notice, Red. That strikes me as pretty adventurous."

The comment caused a faint blush to rise in her cheeks, or maybe it was the nickname. Either way, I liked it. Maybe a little too much for my own good.

"Maybe. So...you've been married?"

"I wondered when you'd get around to that." I smiled at her expression, alight with curiosity. "Yes, Libby and I got married very young, realized we both had very different aspirations in life, and got divorced less than a year later. It was all very amicable. She married the love of her life a few years back, who happens to be one of our best friends, and now it's her life goal to find me someone to settle down with."

Juliet laughed. "Sounds like Sarah. I think wondering what's happening here is probably driving her up the wall right now. I'm positive it's making her poor husband crazy, having to deal with her worrying about me. They spent years planning this trip and saving up so they could spend as much time as they want over there, and here I am, distracting them from it all."

"At least you'll be keeping her entertained with your adventures," I teased.

Juliet threw a balled up napkin in my direction, but it fell short of actually hitting me. I laughed and laced my hands behind my head, watching Juliet's gaze drift to my chest. When I glanced down, I noticed that my shirt had stretched tight across my pecs, and I bit back a grin.

Even in her disheveled state, she was beautiful in a way that tempted me to hold onto her and never let go. I hadn't hesitated for even a second before volunteering to spend the night watching over her, though I fully anticipated the experience might be torturous for us both—for her, because she was clearly uncomfortable with the thought of me staying at the cottage, and for me, because she was in no condition for me to act on any of the less-than-chivalrous images I'd entertained while Libby patched her up.

Instead, I cocked a brow. "What about you? Did you leave a boyfriend back home, pining after you?"

"No," she said, grimacing. "My ex and I broke up when he proposed to me in my mother's hospital room, three days before she died."

"You have got to be shitting me."

"Nope. I managed to avoid him asking me to move in with him by moving back to my mom's house when she got sick, and I guess I thought that would slow things down. We barely saw each other during those months. I, uh, didn't handle the proposal scene very well."

"Who would? What a jackass."

With a glum nod, she shrugged and kept her gaze on her lap. "What's done is done, and that's *very* done after how I responded."

I wanted to ask for details, to get a clear picture of this fiery woman knocking her asshole ex down a peg, but we weren't there yet. Maybe someday. Instead, I turned the conversation back to safer subjects.

"Do you like it here? Spruce Hill, I mean?"

She finally forced her eyes back to my face. I grinned at her obvious reluctance, but then she wrinkled her nose and I was distracted by how adorable I found that particular expression.

"Well, the local hillsides are quite memorable." She smirked when I laughed. "But yes, I like the area. The town, the lake. It's beautiful here. I just feel like a total outsider, you know? Like I plunged into taking on this whole *life* involved with the inn and this house and I don't know anything about any of it."

"It's a lot to deal with," I said gently.

"My mom didn't even tell me. Not once in my entire life. All of this history, and she left me a note to find after she died."

No turning back now—apparently we were venturing into deeper topics. Later, maybe she'd blame the painkillers or ex-haustion for oversharing and letting me in, but at this exact moment, I couldn't deny the simple feeling of connection running like an invisible thread between us.

I *wanted* that connection, wanted to earn her trust, especially after I'd bungled so badly before, so I nodded sympathetically.

"Mrs. Gregson mentioned that after you called. What did it say?"

"That I needed to protect myself, that the choices she made were a matter of life and death, and that the owner of the inn would explain it all. It's here somewhere but I can't find the damn thing. The last thing she wrote to me, and I lost it."

Her voice wavered and I shook my head, hoping she wouldn't burst into tears. "Hey, we'll find it. Look at all this stuff—it's like a needle in a haystack right now, but it's gotta be somewhere. I'll help you."

After a shaky breath, she nodded. "Thank you. These boxes seemed less overwhelming than owning an inn at first, but now I feel like I'm drowning."

"I'll help," I reiterated firmly, waiting until she cracked a tiny smile before I continued. "And if Nan left it all to you...well, she was the shrewdest person I've ever met. She must have known what she was doing."

Juliet studied me, her eyebrows drawn together in consternation. "That sounded suspiciously like a compliment."

"It might have been. Don't tell anybody, though."

"What was she like?"

My lips tugged into a smile as I looked toward the photos on the mantle.

"Feisty," I said, cocking my head. "Smart. Canny, I think, is the word my grandfather used to use. She could be sweet as pie one minute and rip you a new one the next, without ever losing that twinkle in her eye. She knew practically everything about everyone in town, but she refused to gossip."

"I've been getting that impression. The commentary in her journals is hilarious," she said softly.

"I don't know if she had any kind of formal education after high school, but she knew everything there was to know about running that inn. She did almost everything entirely on her own for a long time, Gramps told me, until she finally hired the folks who work there now, most of them before I was even born. She was loyal and headstrong, tough as nails. She would have loved you, Juliet."

A visible tremor of emotion rocked her and she blinked back tears that turned her eyes a brilliant turquoise. For a moment, she avoided meeting my eyes, but I didn't take it personally, not when I could see she was struggling to control her reaction. When her gaze landed on the photos on the mantle, it seemed to steady her, so I ventured to speak.

"I know I apologized already, but I really am sorry about how I treated you at the beginning," I said quietly. "And if avoiding me is what kept you away from the inn, then I'm doubly sorry. I had no right to criticize you. I can't imagine how hard it was to lose your mother and leave everything you've ever known to come out here."

"I'm sorry too. Everything was just a bit overwhelming, and everyone else was so damn *nice,*" she said, leaning her head against the chair back.

She swallowed hard and risked a glance in my direction, catching me grinning at her disdain over the word before she went on.

"I needed something to pour my energy into and you certainly gave me that."

"Well, I'm glad I could help, then. If there was any doubt you were Nan's flesh and blood, it evaporated that morning. You're every bit as feisty as she ever was."

At that, Juliet couldn't hold back a smile. "You think so?"

"Hell yeah."

"Looking like someone you've never met isn't much of a connection, even if it finally explained the origin of my hair color."

"Possessing the same inner fire, though, that seems like something to cling to. Something to be proud of," I ventured. "You're exactly what she would have wanted in a granddaughter, Juliet."

From the radiant expression that dawned on her face, it was exactly what she needed to hear.

Thirteen

Juliet

Henry said Nan must have known what she was doing by leaving the inn and cottage to me; I would simply hope that he was right. Now that I knew what was at stake, there was no turning back.

After opening up to him, conversation flowed more easily between us. Henry told me more about the places on my sketch list—none of which were quite as remote as Cooper's Point, fortunately.

"If you ever want company when you're checking them out, I'm happy to go with you."

My breath caught in my chest at the sweetness of the offer, the earnest smile on his face when he made it, the fact that I'd judged him so very wrong.

"That's...really nice of you," I said after an awkward beat of silence.

His eyes were warm in the lamplight. "I'd rather be there to keep you from falling than worry you're out wandering the wilderness on your own."

I would've laughed at the thought he might worry about me, at least up until a few hours ago. Before I could settle into the intimacy of the exchange, Henry smoothly changed the subject, telling me about the inner workings of the Lakeside Inn and stories of his afternoons at the cottage with Nan when he was a child.

When I looked out the window sometime later and realized the evening had faded well into night, I blinked in confusion, surprised at how much time had passed. As if on cue, I yawned, covering my mouth with both hands. Henry stood and reached out to help me up.

"Come on, you managed to stay awake for four hours, now you need to get some rest. Doctor's orders."

He pulled me carefully to my feet and I let him help me limp to the bathroom. Though Libby had cleaned me up pretty well, my clothes were filthy and I was desperate for a hot shower. Even so, I couldn't bring myself to put forth the effort, nor was I sure I could stay upright that long on my own.

A sudden flash of embarrassment swept along my skin when I remembered Henry was standing there, watching my silent debate. Hopefully he wouldn't notice the pile of dirty laundry in the corner, because draped right on top of the heap was my favorite turquoise bra.

My cheeks flamed as I fought to keep myself from glancing over at it. "I can take it from here," I said.

Henry gave me a curious look but nodded. "If you need anything, just yell. I'll be right out here."

"I will," I said. "And Henry...thank you."

A slow smile spread across his handsome face. "You're very welcome, Juliet."

I latched the door with a soft click and leaned my cheek against it. New town, surprise inheritance, knight in shining armor. Whose life was I living, anyway?

Then again, most princesses probably wouldn't fall down a rocky hillside in the middle of nowhere. Maybe I should practice walking with a book on my head, once I could walk again without limping.

I tried hard not to think about him out there on the sofa as I grabbed my pajamas from where I'd left them on the radiator that morning. I was able to shove my shorts down over my hips without too much trouble before I carefully pulled on a well-worn pair of flannel pajama pants covered in unicorns. At least they were soft enough not to terrorize my raw skin.

After managing to pull my t-shirt off, I froze, staring into the mirror over the sink. Even if I unwrapped my wrist, I wasn't confident that I could twist it behind my back to unhook my bra.

Maybe I could do it one-handed—hadn't my college boyfriend bragged about having that talent? My battered muscles complained before I even got my hand level with the clasp, and whether it was fatigue, painkillers, or simple clumsiness, I couldn't get it undone.

I brushed my teeth, stalling for time, then pressed my ear against the door. Though Henry must've known about the hidden TV and cable channels, no sound came from the other room.

Frantically, I considered my options. Would I be able to slip into the bedroom without him seeing me half naked? Could I stand leaving the bloodstained bra on under my nice clean pajamas?

When I looked back at my reflection, my eyes were wide with panic and twin spots of brilliant scarlet highlighted my cheeks.

My knee was unbearably stiff by that point and every inch of my body ached with the reminder of the day's adventure. Trying to wriggle the bra down and over my hips with only one hand was almost too much to fathom. I clutched the oversized pajama shirt to my chest, unable to make a decision.

When Henry's voice came through the door, I jumped like a scalded cat.

"Juliet? Everything okay in there?"

Think! There had to be some way to put him off, but when I opened my mouth to reply, nothing came out. What would Sarah do in this situation?

His knuckles rapped lightly against the door. "Juliet, I'm going to open the door, all right?"

I beat him to it, hoping to salvage what little dignity I had left. After reassuring myself that I was covered as much as possible, I opened the door. Heat crept up my neck as I took in his look of concern. To his credit, his gaze stayed on my face, though I swore those eyes grew molten.

"I was afraid you might've passed out," he said, his tone light.

Trying hard to swallow my humiliation, I waved my bandaged wrist while the other hand held the shirt tightly against my bare skin.

"I can't unhook my . . ." I trailed off, wishing the floor would open up to swallow me.

Relief washed over his features. "Right. I can help with that."

The reality of letting him assist hit me like a freight train, but it was too late to refuse.

I turned, inadvertently facing the mirror above the sink. A long moment stretched before he stepped closer, then our eyes met in the mirror, blue against hazel. As desperately as I wanted to look away, I couldn't bring myself to break the connection.

When his knuckles brushed lightly against my skin, stroking over my spine, I sucked in a sharp breath. His gaze stayed locked on mine for another heartbeat, then he released the clasp and the spell was broken.

I swiftly turned back toward him, holding the shirt like a shield between us. Henry cleared his throat and took a step back.

"Thank you," I mumbled.

"Let me know if you need anything else," he said, his gentle tone at direct odds with the intensity of his expression. "Goodnight, Juliet."

"Goodnight, Henry."

I waited until he was back in the living room before pulling the shirt over my head and limping to the bedroom as quickly as I could. Safe in the quiet room, I closed the door and leaned against it.

Simmer down, Jules.

The chill of the wood against the back of my neck did nothing to erase the memory of his fingers, the lingering trail of heat along that section of my spine. After my skin finally cooled, I pushed away from the door and eased down onto the bed.

Hopefully sleep would help redirect my errant thoughts. Even if the prospect of Henry peeking in to make sure I was breathing throughout the night gave wing to a riot of butterflies in my stomach, I trusted him.

And since his willingness to stay here had been the only thing that kept Libby from pushing the hospital angle, I owed him a debt of gratitude.

Whether from sheer exhaustion or the painkillers, I crashed so hard that I didn't wake a single time during the night, even though I was sure Henry had obeyed his ex-wife's orders to the letter.

I AWOKE TO THE aroma of coffee brewing and something else, something I hadn't smelled since before my mother's illness.

Holy shit, was he making pancakes out there?

Henry cooking in my kitchen filled me with conflicting emotions. I hadn't been here long enough to make a huge mess, but the idea of him moving around in there, opening cupboards and pulling ingredients from my fridge, it felt strangely intimate. A certain warmth curled upward from my belly, wrapping around my insides.

For the first time in a long time, I felt almost pampered.

Then again, maybe he was bemoaning the pathetic state of my cupboards and trying to keep himself from starvation.

As I drew a deep breath, letting the inviting lure of pancakes bolster me, I turned my head to look at the clock on the bedside table. It was just past eight—for once, I'd slept through the rising sun sneaking past the curtains I had yet to replace.

Gingerly, I bent and straightened my knee a few times. It felt significantly better than the night before, even if it was a bit stiff. I moved slowly as I sat up at the edge of the bed, not willing to risk collapsing to the floor with bedhead.

Henry might be more of a gentleman than I'd given him credit for, but I could just imagine his expression if he saw me looking like Medusa when he had to rush to my rescue.

Again.

I grabbed my hairbrush off the bedside table, wrestled my hair up in a fresh ponytail without tweaking my wrist too badly, then stood—very carefully—and breathed a sigh of relief when no streak of pain shot through my leg. Curious, I pulled up the cuff of my pajama pants to inspect my knee. It was more of a dull twinge at this point, crowned by a remarkably ugly bruise radiating outward from the center of my kneecap.

Though I was determined to shower before putting on fresh clothes, I wasn't willing to walk out into the kitchen to greet Henry wearing just a thin t-shirt without a bra. In the end, I grabbed the biggest, softest hoodie I could find and pulled it on over my pajamas. It would do for now, so I slipped quietly into the bathroom to brush my teeth.

When I caught sight of my face in the mirror, I grimaced. The cut on my forehead still looked gruesome beneath the butterfly bandages and my cheeks were hideously pale.

I stuck out my tongue at my reflection, but the memory of Henry's expression in the mirror last night caused me to snap my mouth shut and turn away.

The sweet smell of breakfast drew me straight to the kitchen from there. Henry had his back to me as he stood in front of the stove, spatula in hand. He was flipping pancakes like a pro and had an apron tied around his waist. Out of respect for his efforts to feed me, I limited myself to a swift once-over, admiring the view of his strong shoulders moving beneath a white undershirt and the snug fit of his jeans over his ass and thighs, then focused hard on the back of his head.

While my hair frizzed like I'd stuck a finger in an electrical outlet first thing in the morning, his fell in enviable waves that brushed the back of his neck.

When he turned to place the pancakes on a plate, I stifled a snort. He was, in fact, wearing a frilly, flowered apron over his clothes. He looked unfairly attractive in this domestic setting, with his dark hair disheveled from sleep and threatening to fall into the warm hazel eyes that twinkled as they traveled over me from head to toe.

At least I wasn't alone in my perusal.

"Hi," he said. A soft smile curled his lips upward, though it was unclear whether it was because of how ridiculous I looked in unicorn pajamas and a hastily tied ponytail or because he was actually pleased to see me upright and steady on my feet.

"Hi," I replied, soaking in the warmth of his expression, no matter the cause.

I wished I'd thrown on jeans instead of staying in what I'd slept in. Then again, I'd spent the past few minutes reminding myself that I didn't need to impress him, so why did I feel so self-conscious now?

"How's your head?"

His gaze lingered on my forehead for a moment before he turned back to flip the next batch of pancakes. I sat carefully on one of the bar stools along the counter.

"It doesn't feel too bad, actually. Just looks terrible."

Henry didn't hold back an incredulous scoff in response to that. "Yes, you are truly hideous to look at, Juliet Morrison. How about your knee?"

"Ah," I mumbled, still basking in the glow of the unexpected compliment. "It's okay. Feels better than yesterday, at least, but pretty impressive bruising."

Henry lifted the pan and flipped a pancake high in the air. I applauded politely as he set the pan back down on the burner, gave an elegant bow, then slid a mug of coffee in front of me.

"Seemed like you must be a coffee drinker," he said, nodding to the bag of gourmet coffee I had left beside the coffee pot.

"So you're a detective," I mused. "And an accountant, and a good samaritan. *And* you cook? I should have visited this part of the country sooner."

He grinned. "What can I say? I'm a man of many talents."

I slipped awkwardly off the stool to grab a bottle of flavored creamer out of the fridge. When I sat back down, I turned my coffee to the perfect shade of beige.

"So, where'd you learn to cook?" I asked.

His brows quirked upward. "Why, Ms. Morrison, personal questions? You'd think we had spent the night under the same roof," he teased. I blushed and he added, "Nan taught me, actually. A chef to make breakfast at the inn was actually the first employee she added when she made the shift from a one-woman show, but she showed me a few tricks over the years."

"Oh." I studied him for a moment, picturing Nan and a very young Henry with their heads bent together in this very kitchen.

Henry grinned at my surprise and turned briefly to load the last of the pancakes onto a plate before responding. He slid his own plate over so he could hop onto the stool beside me.

"Anything else you want to know? Credit score, genetic markers?" he asked as he dug into his giant stack of pancakes.

"All in good time, Mr. Walker," I drawled as I took a deep swig of coffee.

This was the best breakfast I'd had in weeks—even better than the inn's, which shocked me. Maybe it tasted better because I was relaxing in my own environment, maybe it was Henry's easy camaraderie, but either way, I was happy.

Simply, wonderfully, stupidly happy.

Henry glanced up from his food to smile at me. "All in good time," he repeated. "Does that mean you're going to stop avoiding me?"

There was a certain gleam in his eyes that made it hard for me to tear my gaze away from this handsome stranger who'd saved the day, especially when he looked so damn adorable in that ruffled apron. I couldn't think of a way to change the subject smoothly, so I took a deep breath and turned back to the pancakes, clearing my throat.

Henry, on the other hand, seemed to have moved on from breakfast to playing twenty questions.

"Excellent, I'll take that as a yes. So, you're an artist?"

I hurried to swallow the giant bite I was chewing. "Yes."

"Paint? Pencil? Watercolor?"

"I like to sketch things out first, hence my overly dramatic hiking trip, but my true love is oil paints."

"I see," Henry said softly.

I lifted a brow. "Let me guess—just like Nan, huh?"

All he could offer was a helpless shrug, but his expression grew serious. I set down my fork and studied him for a moment. The interest in his eyes seemed genuine.

"What about your mother?" he asked gently. "Was she an artist too?"

A wave of grief rushed through me at the mention of her. I took a steadying breath, but Henry didn't push for a response.

"No, she was terrible at most forms of art," I replied, once I was sure I could do so without crying. "She was a seamstress. I shouldn't discount the artistic ability needed for that kind of work, though. She made really beautiful creations. Clothes, decorations, all sorts of stuff."

I didn't want to see the sympathy in his eyes, so I returned to my breakfast and, after a moment, he did the same. When we finished eating, Henry loaded the dishwasher, giving me a warning scowl to keep me from trying to assist. He pulled off the apron and hung it inside a narrow cupboard next to the pantry.

"Do you have any plans today?" he asked finally, looking at me intently.

"I don't plan to go hiking again, if that's what you're asking." When he grinned, I shrugged and said, "Normally I would get started on sketches today from the photos I took, but I feel like I deserve a few days off to recover."

He leaned a hip against the counter. "I wondered if I could take you for a drive?"

Surprise flooded my body and I echoed, "A drive?"

"There's a different place I'd really like to show you sometime, but we'll have to walk there. That one can wait until you've recovered fully. I know you've been out exploring, so I thought you might like a little tour of the area."

"Oh. That sounds great, actually."

The prospect of spending time with him was growing on me, too. When Henry's responding smile practically lit the room, I couldn't hold back one of my own.

"I'll run over and pick up Blue while you get dressed," he said, then his gaze intensified until I could feel the heat of it brushing my skin. "Unless you think you'll need some help?"

"Thank you, but I'm sure I can manage."

A flush crept up my neck and I tried my hardest to look dignified. He laughed as he helped me down from the stool, and I shivered at the same tingle of awareness that zipped along my skin every time he touched me.

"If you're sure," he teased.

My scowl only broadened his beautiful smile.

"I'll be back within the hour. I added my number to your list on the fridge. Now might be a good time to program it into your phone so I can rescue you next time you're in need."

"Very funny," I said dryly. "Go get your dog before I kick your ass out."

Henry clutched a fist to his chest and winked. "Straight to the heart, and after I made you breakfast. See you soon, Red."

Fourteen

JULIET

I WATCHED HIM STROLL back to his truck, then locked the front door and took a quick shower that made me feel almost human again. Despite my protest to the contrary, I did still question my ability to hook a damn bra, but I was absolutely *not* going to ask him to assist. Just remembering the look in his eyes when his knuckles grazed my skin made my entire body feel flushed and feverish.

Huffing out a breath, I dug through the dresser drawers until I found a sports bra I'd packed for the non-existent jogging pastime I thought I might take up here in Spruce Hill. I was more than ready to consign jogging to the same shallow grave as hiking, even if the sports bra was a bonus.

There would be no more dangerous adventures anytime soon—even if Henry offered to accompany me.

With a grimace, I stepped into the bra and shimmied it awkwardly up over my hips. It wasn't the most elegant process, nor the most comfortable, but in the end, I was victorious. After tracking down a pair of jeans with no paint splatters and a gauzy floral top that I judged cute enough to detract from the gnarly cut on my forehead, I studied my reflection in the mirror on the wall of the bedroom.

Without the bruise on my knee showing, I looked halfway decent.

As I rewrapped my wrist, though, I debated if there was anything I could do with my hair to disguise the bandages above my eyebrow. The sound of tires along the gravel drive interrupted my pondering, so I quickly clipped back the sides and left the rest loose to air dry.

I grabbed my purse and opened the door just as Henry strolled up the path. He'd changed into a black vintage band tee and, to my annoyance, he looked as handsome as ever. Blue rushed over to sit at my feet before I could study him further.

When the dog had gotten enough petting to satisfy her, I straightened. The expression on Henry's face wavered between shock and appreciation.

"What?" I asked.

I glanced down at my arms to be sure I hadn't inadvertently revealed some hideous wound, but most of the scratches had already faded to faint pink lines that dodged between my freckles. When I looked back at him, Henry shook his head slightly.

"Nothing, I just like your hair like this, all curly," he said. "You wore it this way the morning you came to the inn for breakfast, but things devolved before I could appreciate it. It suits you."

My eyes widened in surprise and he flashed that devastating grin. Despite the blush I knew was rising rapidly toward my face, I arched a brow.

"What, a little bit wild?" I joked.

His expression didn't change, so I rolled my eyes, ignoring the swift rush of pleasure the compliment invoked.

"Now, cut it out and let's get this show on the road."

He gave a dramatic bow and let his gaze sweep over the rest of me as we walked toward the truck. When he offered his arm, I shot him a dirty look, so he dropped it back to his side, smirking. I tried to ignore his proximity, but it was nearly impossible—every step was accompanied by his warm presence, looping around my body in the most tempting invitation.

"You're only limping a little. That's progress."

I snorted. Little did he know that I was only managing to not limp by walking at a snail's pace; I was determined not to stumble in front of him. The smile on his face didn't falter as he matched my slow trudge without looking annoyed or sarcastic. Blue was rolling ecstatically in the grass by the wildflowers but came galloping to the truck to jump in as soon as Henry opened the passenger door.

"She makes a good chaperone," I said without thinking.

My cheeks flushed even hotter when I realized I'd just im-plied this was a date. Henry simply closed the door after me and grinned through the open window, unfazed.

"She can ride in the back if you want to be closer to me. Just say the word, Red."

"You're hilarious."

That unruffled calm of his didn't break at all when I nar-rowed my eyes at him. His hand rested casually on the door and I forced myself to shut down the memory of his fingers against my back last night, even as the sight of his bronzed skin caused an expected flare of desire in my midsection.

Maybe I should have let Libby run more tests—my brain felt jumbled, my thoughts scattered. Would it be better or worse to blame a concussion rather than Henry's proximity?

One dark brow lifted ever so slightly as he watched me. I was sure he'd seen my reaction as clear as day, but he said no more, just smiled a little when he pushed away from my door to stride around to the driver's side. He winked at me over Blue's shaggy head as he started the engine and I turned my face to the window to hide my burning cheeks.

We drove the same route I'd taken to Cooper's Point, passing it and continuing onto a stretch of road I had yet to travel. I leaned my head back against the seat, enjoying the fresh spring breeze and absorbing the things Henry pointed out along the way.

When we passed a property with giant stone pillars and a wrought-iron gate, I said, "What's that, a castle?"

He laughed. "Might as well be. That's the Willoughby Mansion. Hot-shot defense attorney who doesn't appreciate trespassers, so try not to go tumbling onto the property."

"Ha. I'm hoping not to tumble anywhere ever again."

Interspersed among notable geographical landmarks and the area's history were stories about his family and childhood here. From the appreciation clear in his tone, a brief twinge of guilt struck me for thinking he probably took all of this for granted. I couldn't have been more wrong.

Henry was a natural storyteller. His deep voice was at once rich and soothing, animated and vibrant. I could happily listen to him all day.

Blue's tail had been thudding against my leg for the better part of the drive, but when the road angled left, it doubled in speed. We pulled past a stand of trees and suddenly the lake sprawled before us in all its glory.

"Oh," I breathed, earning a warm smile from my human companion and a frantic wiggle from the canine.

This had to be the beach I'd read about before coming to Spruce Hill. It wasn't a long stretch of coastline, made up of more rocks than sand, but it was secluded and breathtakingly beautiful.

Like Blue, I was practically bouncing in my seat with excitement. Henry eased off the road and parked the truck, revealing the broad expanse of calm blue water before us.

"I know you've seen the lake already, but this is my favorite spot along the shore."

I could see why. We were the only people here, nestled among the trees. It was like a private slice of paradise.

"Can we go down to the water?" I asked, already unbuckling my seatbelt.

"I figured you'd want to. Just be careful on the rocks. I don't want to have to fish you out of the lake," he teased, grinning at me.

I slid carefully out of the truck while Blue took off at a gallop toward a triangle of seagulls. They squawked at the dog and relocated farther down the beach, leaving Blue to pounce at the waves as they tumbled onto shore. Henry appeared at my elbow.

"Shall we?" he asked, offering his arm.

Though I was tempted to refuse on principle, the scene before me was so stunning that I couldn't find it in me to protest. Hell, I couldn't even drum up a snarky comment about not needing to lean on him anymore. Instead, I just slipped my hand around his elbow and let him lead me along the rocky path down to the edge of the water.

It was glorious in its simple beauty: earth, water, sky. Off to the right, I caught a glimpse of the lighthouse from Nan's wedding photo and I wondered if I'd be able to visit it myself.

Henry followed my gaze. "That's the Spruce Hill Lighthouse. It's open to the public certain days of the week. There are a lot of very scary stairs inside, though, so I suggest you wait until you're fully healed to tackle that one."

I made a face at him, but he only grinned and touched the tip of one finger to my nose.

With a reluctance that surprised me, I released his arm. To cover my reaction, I closed my eyes, throwing my head back and lifting my arms at my sides to let the breeze drift over me. It wasn't the ocean—which I'd only seen once, in any case, coming from the landlocked Midwest—but the smell of greenery and sunshine and water filled my soul to overflowing.

I was so grateful for this serenity, I had to swallow down the lump of emotion clogging my throat.

After several minutes, I opened my eyes to peek over at Henry. He was studying me with the same intent curiosity I recognized from when I planned a painting. I wanted to crack a joke, break the tension somehow, but I could only sigh softly and smile at him.

"Thank you," I mouthed.

It was stupid, given the loud cries of the seagulls and Blue's occasional bark, but I didn't want to disrupt the stillness of this place with speech.

His smile was beautiful. It spread slowly, as though each muscle made a conscious effort to join in the irrepressible pull of joy.

"You're welcome," he mouthed back.

I didn't know how long we stood there, close but not quite touching, watching the sunlight dance across the surface of the water. All I knew was that this place called to me in a way my hometown never had and that, somehow, Henry seemed to sense it.

Gratitude seeped through me, as warm as the sunshine on my face.

At least that's what I told myself. It seemed altogether too likely that the warmth was a side effect of my proximity to Henry Walker.

Fifteen

Henry

B LUE CAME TO LAY at our feet just as Juliet shifted her weight. I figured her knee was aching and nodded toward the boulders at the edge of the shore.

"Why don't we sit?" I suggested.

She gave a grateful nod, so I helped her over the rocky beach and lifted her onto one of the boulders, ignoring her scowl as I hopped up beside her. The rock's awkward shape forced her to sit right next to me, so close that our thighs were pressed firmly together from hip to knee.

I tried to convince myself that the sun-warmed surface of the rock was the only thing heating my skin through the dark denim of my jeans, but there was a faint pink to her cheeks that suggested she was feeling it, too.

Eventually, the peace of our surroundings melted away the awkwardness of our position. Juliet relaxed little by little, leaning ever so slightly against my side. In a tone just above a whisper, I pointed out a bald eagle soaring over the trees to our left. Her expression of wonder made me want to show her everything the area had to offer—everything I had to offer her.

Well, her expression and also the faintly floral, utterly intoxicating scent of her hair when I leaned close.

At the moment, it was difficult to tell what exactly drew me so intensely, but it was clear this woman was quickly getting under my skin. Though it wasn't what I'd expected, I was more than willing to accept it. Even if I wanted to, I wasn't sure I could resist the pull between us.

I was absolutely certain that I had no desire to try.

Blue trotted out into the water until it reached her belly, then pounced excitedly at a school of tiny fish. Juliet laughed when the dog returned to my side to shake herself off, sending a spray of lake water all over me. I yelped and shifted closer to use Juliet as a shield, dragging her partway across my lap in the process.

She shrieked when the cold droplets of water hit her skin. Laughter rumbled low in my chest and I grinned down at her.

"Hey! I'm injured!"

"Oh, I don't know, Red. You said you were *fine*," I replied, letting my gaze travel over her, lingering for the barest second at the lacy neckline of her shirt, "and I'm inclined to agree."

I reached up to brush a drop of water from her chin before settling her back into her spot beside me. Much to my delight, her cheeks flamed in response to the soft sweep of my fingers. That blush was something I was determined to invoke as frequently as possible when I noted the appealing shade of pink creeping along those delicate cheekbones.

Still, I was gracious enough to give her time to compose herself while I leaned away to grab a stick and hurl it down the shoreline. Blue chased after it with joyous bounds.

"Let me know if you get tired and want to head back," I said when I turned back to her. "Libby will rip me a new one if she thinks I'm delaying your recovery."

Juliet didn't look worn out, in my opinion, not in the slightest. With the breeze lifting curling tendrils away from her face and the sunlight brightening those turquoise eyes, she was absolutely breathtaking.

I had to force my gaze away before I did something stupid like lean in to kiss her, so I took advantage of Blue's return to throw the stick again.

"You agreed that I'm fine," she replied after a moment.

The hint of challenge in her tone had me grinning. In an attempt to resist touching her again, I eased back onto the rock until I was lying down with my arms folded behind my head.

"I did, indeed," I murmured, closing my eyes.

When I finally snuck a glance at Juliet beside me from under my mostly-closed lids, the serene expression on her face unleashed a strange flutter in my chest. Blue returned with the stick and Juliet had to lean across my body to reach it. I felt her shifting, so I opened my eyes fully, admiring the way her shirt lifted to reveal a smooth swath of skin at the small of her back when she launched the stick.

I'm such an idiot.

I'd thought to put a little distance between us by lying back on the rock, not to torment myself further. Last night had been a revelation—when I stepped into that bathroom, everything inside me coiled tight, desperate to drop my attention to those creamy bare shoulders hovering just at the edge of my field of vision. My entire body had gone tense with the effort of resisting that urge, and now? The feeling was only growing stronger.

If she hadn't been injured, if I hadn't been such an asshole in those early days, if I was sure she'd really forgiven me, I would have lifted a hand to trail my fingertips across her back. Hell, I might have even tugged at her arm just hard enough to send her sprawling atop me again.

It took every ounce of willpower I possessed to keep from reaching for her. This new pull between us was damn near irresistible, though I couldn't quite pinpoint why.

While I was focused on getting control of myself, Juliet sighed softly. The whisper of breath was barely audible over the sounds of the lake, but I sat up slowly and touched her shoulder, almost by reflex. Her skin was as soft as I remembered from the night before. Biting back a groan, I dropped my hand.

"You okay?" I asked.

She nodded, keeping her eyes on the water, but I could see her copper brows drawn together, a tiny dip between them.

"Just thinking. If it wasn't a gunshot I heard up there, what else could it have been?"

I puffed out my cheeks as I considered. "A tree branch breaking? We had some bad storms last winter, and sometimes trees get damaged enough to split a branch from the trunk. They don't always fall right away."

"It sounded close," she added softly. "Close enough and loud enough to startle me into stepping back too far at the edge of the ravine. I thought..."

"You thought what?"

She bit her lip and the crease between her eyebrows deepened. "It's stupid, but I thought I saw someone up there, right after I fell. I was still dizzy, though, then it was gone. It was probably just an animal."

Every minute of my hike with Blue, from hopping out of the truck to buckling Juliet into it, replayed behind my eyes. I'd seen nothing unusual, and the only thing Blue charged toward was Juliet, but those woods were huge. Definitely big enough to get lost in, intentionally or otherwise.

And her sketchbook was still missing.

She could have knocked it off the other side of the cliff when she fell, but Mark had gone back out with his hiking buddies the next morning to check the base of the ravine. There'd been no sign of it.

Someone might have picked it up between yesterday and today, but it seemed unlikely.

The surge of protectiveness rippling through my veins took me by surprise, but the last thing Juliet needed was to panic over what might amount to nothing.

I'd explore the possibility that someone else was out at Cooper's Point that day on my own, so she could focus on her recovery. Anything that threatened her safety, especially into what could have been a much more serious accident, needed to be dealt with.

"I thought I was the only enemy you've made in town," I teased, bumping her shoulder with my own to lighten the suddenly heavy atmosphere around us.

Juliet narrowed her eyes at me. "You could have hired a hitman. You certainly seemed pissed enough at me, between the inn and the incident at The Mermaid."

"This ain't the big city, Red. I'm just a small town boy, and believe me, I was more pissed at myself for not being able to control what came out of my mouth than I was at you." I cocked my head. "How do you know what a gunshot sounds like, anyway?"

"My ex-boyfriend was a hunter," she said, wrinkling her nose. "He insisted I go with him to the shooting range once. I hated it, but the sound is hard to forget."

"Well, I'll trust your expertise then. And I'll ask around town. Blue and I hike those woods a couple times a week. I don't want to risk running into some jackass shooting off-season out there."

"Thank you," she mumbled, looking a little flustered.

"What's that face for? Don't you want me to ask around?"

"No, I do," she insisted. "I just appreciate that you're willing to trust my judgment, even if I might be wrong."

It seemed like she was having a hard time reconciling the Henry Walker she was coming to know with the one she'd been desperately avoiding, which was something I had to take full responsibility for.

"Look, we got off on the wrong foot, Juliet, but this is your home now, too. I want you to feel safe here and I'll do what I can to make that happen."

Her pretty lips curved upward in a sweet, shy smile. "Right. Well, thank you, for all of it."

Frowning a little, I touched a finger to the tip of her nose. "You're getting sunburnt. We've barely been here an hour. That's got to be some kind of record."

She muttered something derogatory about her coloring beneath her breath, then grimaced at me. "As much as I'd like to never leave this spot, I should probably get back to the cottage before I fry. I should've thought to wear sunscreen."

I was also tempted to protest, but beneath the pink of her nose and cheeks, she looked a little tired. At her warning scowl, I offered a hand to help her off the boulder instead of lifting her down as I wanted to—anything to get my hands on her again.

Blue bounced toward us, tongue lolling happily from her open mouth.

"You stink," I told the dog. "You're riding in the back."

"Is that safe?" Juliet asked with a disapproving frown.

"You want to snuggle up to this smelly mutt in the truck?"

"It seems only fair," she replied, rubbing Blue's head with her uninjured hand. "We're the ones who brought her here."

When she looked back at me, I was still staring at her, dazzled. Libby had always been one of my best friends in the world and she was fair almost to a fault, but Juliet's sweet sense of justice simply bowled me over.

The woman in question rolled her eyes and said, "Look, do whatever you want with your own damn dog and your own damn truck."

"You're an unusual woman," I replied, my face breaking into a wide smile as I took her elbow to help her toward the truck. Then I leaned down so that my breath tickled her ear as I added, "And if you need help washing the smell of wet dog off of that flawless skin of yours later, you just let me know."

She blushed again as I ran my thumb gently along her bare arm. Blue leapt into the truck and Juliet slid in beside her, fighting a grimace at the smell now that they were in close quarters.

I had no such qualms. I made a face and nudged the dog closer to Juliet as I got behind the wheel.

"You're a big softy, Juliet Morrison," I said, shaking my head, "but you certainly do make life around here more interesting."

The drive back to the cottage, while pungent, was as peaceful as our time at the lake. Despite her insistence that she was perfectly capable of traversing twenty-some feet on her own, I walked Juliet to the front door. I didn't touch her, cognizant of the fact that I'd be sorely tempted to keep on touching her if I did, but when we reached the door, I gave her a smile that caused an audible hitch in her breathing.

"I'm sure I don't have to say this, but please take it easy. If you need anything else from upstairs, I'll bring it down for you. You've got my number. I'm just a text away."

She nodded. "Thank you, Henry. I had a really nice time today."

"I did, too. I appreciate you giving me a chance to prove I'm not a complete jerk."

"Well," Juliet mused, "you did want to make the dog ride in the back."

I laughed and said, "And when you see just how long the smell lingers, you might realize that was the wiser option."

The odor was much fainter now that we were outside of the truck, but as her cheeks blazed, I suspected Juliet was already fantasizing about a nice long soak in the bathtub—or maybe about my offer to help scrub the smell off her skin. When she finally forced herself to look over at me, I winked and gave a slight bow.

As far as I could tell, every thought in her head played clearly across her face, and damned if I didn't find that absolutely delightful, now that I was inspiring dirty thoughts instead of murderous ones.

"Once your knee is back up to snuff, I'll take you to my other favorite spot. You'll want to bring your camera and a sketchbook for that one, I think."

"I'm a quick healer," she said, flashing a grin.

"Uh-huh. We'll see, won't we? Go on, get some rest."

Without a word, Juliet smiled at me, those blue eyes filled with something warm and sweet, and slipped through the door to the cottage. I waited until she was safely inside before turning back to the truck.

Blue's ears drooped as though she missed Juliet already. I heaved a sigh as I got behind the wheel.

"Cheer up, girl," I told the dog as I shifted gears. "We'll see her again soon."

The reassurance did little for either of us, I noted with a tinge of frustration. What was it about her? Juliet radiated passion, as though that fiery spirit overflowed her enticingly curvaceous body and graced everyone nearby with the distinct sensation of basking in sunlight.

My original interpretation, crediting temper for that flame, had been dead wrong. It was something more innate, something that permeated her very essence. That spark colored all of her reactions, both good and bad, with those tiny licks of fire.

Though I was still ashamed of myself for picking a fight with her that first day at the inn, the memory of her threatening to break my hand outside The Mermaid made me grin as I drove home.

"She's something, all right," I said aloud.

Blue's tail thumped against the seat in agreement.

I pulled into my driveway and, before I even opened the front door, my phone started chiming madly with an influx of text messages from Libby. She and her husband, Mark, lived across the street and three houses down—I shouldn't have been surprised they were keeping an eye out for me to return.

Where did you take her?

How's she feeling?

Did you two make out yet?

I rolled my eyes and opened the front door. Blue sat herself down beside the couch, looking dejected.

"Don't give me that," I grumbled. "You just had the time of your life at the beach. You'll survive an afternoon without her. Besides, the first order of business is a bath for you, my smelly mongrel. Juliet might not mind the stench, but I do."

Blue, unfortunately, hated baths almost as much as she loved the lake. I sprayed her off in the downstairs shower stall, soaped her with some kind of dog shampoo that smelled inexplicably like blueberries, and toweled off as much water as I could before leaving her to dry in the sunshine on the back deck.

I decided to let Libby stew about my outing with Juliet and hopped in the shower without responding to her messages, though I set my phone by the sink in case Juliet needed to reach me.

As I scrubbed the tang of wet dog from my skin, I tried very hard not to imagine Juliet doing the same. In that, I failed most spectacularly. For a woman with such strength, she was perfectly soft, decadently sweet.

What I wouldn't give to run my soapy hands over each delectable inch of her.

Libby had teased me ever since junior high that I was ruled by two extremes—acting immediately on instinct or dissecting an idea into microscopic pieces before making a decision. If my track record with women was anything to go by, that was one area where I was prone to impulse.

And now? Every impulse in my body was hooked on Juliet Morrison.

Barely twenty-four hours ago, I couldn't stand the thought of her. No matter how many times I reminded myself of that, the memory of finding her in the woods yesterday streaked with blood and limping along kept flashing behind my eyes. Every time, it caused my heart to constrict with an echo of dread.

I grinned, though, when I recalled the fire in her eyes and the branch held before her like a weapon until she recognized me. She was a fighter, all right.

And the bra clasp—I actually groaned aloud at the thought of it. I saw every detail again clear as day when I closed my eyes: the flush in her freckled cheeks, the fine bones along her collar, the silken skin of her back beneath those pale pink straps, the way she shivered when my fingers brushed her spine.

I wouldn't be forgetting that anytime soon. I pressed my forehead against the smooth tiles of the shower wall until I could think calmly again.

"Don't get ahead of yourself," I muttered.

She hadn't been too keen on me before yesterday, either, but that tremor running up her spine...things had changed between us. I was sure of that much. This new spark of attraction was not one-sided. Whether she'd be open to exploring it, I had no idea, but I was eager to find out.

After dousing myself with cold water, I dried off and threw on jeans that didn't smell like lake-soaked dog. Libby had texted twice more, as had Mark, who begged me to respond so he could enjoy the afternoon with his wife. I grinned at that and replied as briefly as I could.

Injuries healing well. We hung out at the lake. No making out. Yet.

My finger hovered over the last word for a moment before finally deleting it and hitting send. Libby shot back a kissing emoji anyway. I was fairly certain she'd be playing wingman as often as she could in the coming weeks.

That begged the question of whether I planned to make a move, wingman or no. Juliet was technically my new boss, though in name only. A little light flirtation was one thing—throwing myself at her after our rocky start could be a mistake of epic proportions. It took barely the span of a heartbeat for me to come to a decision.

I would never forgive myself if I missed this opportunity.

What if she left town, went back to her old life, before I drummed up the courage to give it a try? If she shot me down, I'd figure out how to smooth things over, but in the meantime, I had to make a play. A subtle, careful play, and hopefully one that would convince her to engage instead of flee.

The next text came from Mark.

You gonna ask her out for real?

I kept my response short. *Yup.*

Rock on, man. Libby likes her.

I was grinning when I shot back, *I'm so glad I have her permission to proceed*, but Mark knew what I meant.

We want you to be happy. Can't wait to meet her, buddy.

Well, then. With my ex-wife's approval, what could go wrong?

Blue wagged her damp tail when I let her back inside to join me in the living room, apparently forgiving me for leaving her new best friend behind at the cottage. I ruffled her ears and plopped down on my favorite recliner.

As tempted as I was to close my eyes and reflect on the past twenty-four hours, I figured it was smarter to distract myself from the pretty new redhead in town. Blue settled at my side as I turned on the TV and flipped through the channels to find something that might hold my attention.

I needed all the help I could get to take my mind off of Juliet Morrison.

Sixteen

JULIET

I STOOD IN THE kitchen the next day, eating a sandwich as I stared out toward the lake. A fine veil of warm rain fell steadily over the landscape, giving everything the hazy quality of a half-remembered dream. The lake was a deep, murky gray beneath the troubled sky. Though I'd expected the rain to dim the colors outside the window, instead the grass turned to a rich, glittering emerald.

After so many beautiful spring days, the rain might have been a disappointment. In reality, I found it even more beautiful than the sunlight.

I spent the rest of the morning uploading photos of Cooper's Point from my camera and drawing in a fresh sketchbook, trying to recapture what I could recall from the one lost during my tumble.

All the while, I was still feeling guilty for how I responded to Henry that first day. This town was his whole life—his childhood, his family, his home. It wasn't difficult to imagine how I would have felt if some outsider burst unexpectedly into my world and put all of that at risk. He had a right to be unhappy, and I could have refused to rise to the bait.

How would things have turned out if he'd managed to apologize that night at the restaurant before I threatened him? Would I have accepted it and moved forward, or would I still be holding a grudge?

Knowing me, it was the latter.

Thankfully, he seemed like the type to be able to laugh at his mistakes instead of wallowing in them. How else would a man stay such good friends with his ex-wife?

After eating, I sat at the end of the couch where Henry had left his pillow and blanket neatly folded on the table, surreptitiously drawing a deep breath to see if his scent lingered.

Oh sweet lord, there it is, I realized, letting my eyes flutter closed for a moment as the barest hint of that intoxicating cologne met my nose. After indulging this folly for longer than was probably wise, I forced my eyes open.

"You have a problem," I told myself sternly.

The boxes cluttering the living room floor offered no response.

"You know who'd know what to do, boxes? Sarah."

The thought of my best friend brought on a pang of homesickness. I picked up the phone and fired off a text that didn't mention my hiking accident, the resulting injuries, or the terribly attractive inn manager who'd spent the night in my home. No sense freaking Sarah out over what probably wouldn't amount to anything.

Especially after I'd gotten her all riled up in my defense by describing our unfortunate first encounters.

As soon as it was sent, I froze, staring down at the screen. I was almost certain she'd be asleep by now with the time difference, but if she tried to video call, there'd be no way to hide my forehead from view, not without gazing off into the distance the entire time. Sarah would absolutely suspect something was up if I did that.

I waited a few tense minutes, then breathed a deep sigh of relief when she didn't respond to the text. I'd give her all the details eventually, preferably when there were no physical signs of my unfortunate fall.

For a brief moment, I allowed myself to imagine how my best friend would react to meeting Henry in person. Sarah's husband, Andre, was handsome in his fair-haired, Nordic way, but the contrast between the two men would tempt even a devoted landscape artist like myself to try to capture it on canvas.

With that in mind, I grabbed my sketchbook again in an attempt to distract myself from thoughts of Henry. I let the pencil lead while my mind wandered.

Some indeterminate amount of time later—minutes or hours, I wasn't sure—I stared down at the paper, bringing into focus a sketch of the lake from the day before, the lighthouse standing proudly in the background, Blue frolicking in the waves at the front. Seeing it, I realized I hadn't taken a single photo, not even on my phone.

Is he really that distracting?

I considered the question carefully, running one fingertip over the sketch.

Yes, as a matter of fact, he was. If only I could predict whether that was a good sign or a bad one, maybe I'd be able to put him out of my mind.

As if summoned by the question, my phone chimed with a text from Henry asking if I had plans for dinner. I bit my lip to keep from grinning like an idiot as I replied that I did not.

Are you up for company? Your choice of takeout, my treat. Chinese? Italian? Thai?

I gave him my preferred dishes from each option and told him to surprise me, then I set the phone aside and wandered into the bedroom. As I stood before my limited wardrobe, I wondered what the dress code was for this kind of non-date.

Nothing low cut, I decided that much right away, considering how his attention had drifted to my cleavage the day before. The memory of it was enough to quicken the blood in my veins and cause a slightly giddy feeling to rise up in my chest. A little flirtation at the beach was one thing, but brushing it off in the coziness of the cottage might be beyond my abilities right now.

There wasn't much to be done about my bruised forehead, though I'd removed the butterfly bandages that morning as Libby instructed, but there was no way I was greeting Henry in yoga pants and the shelf-bra cami I'd spent the morning in. In the end, I grabbed a simple teal t-shirt and a pair of jeans, managing to carefully clasp a regular bra without tweaking my wrist as I got dressed.

Would he think I'd done it for him if I left my hair down? I spent a ridiculous amount of time in front of the bathroom mirror as I debated hairstyles.

Finally, annoyed that I'd given his words so much power over my decision, I pulled my hair into a ponytail and forced myself to stop thinking about what Henry Walker liked. I was a grown woman who could make her own damn choices.

My last relationship had ended poorly during my mother's illness, but it wasn't as though I'd never spent time around attractive, flirty men before now.

It never affected me like this before, though, turning me into a frazzled mess of hormones.

I was deep in thought about whatever mysterious chemistry seemed to exist between me and Henry when a light knock sounded at the door. Steeling myself, I opened it wide and watched a slow smile spread across his face.

"Hey, Red," he said. "That's a good color on you."

Though the telltale flush crept along under my skin, I responded with an arched brow and demanded, "Do you compliment everyone in town like this?"

Henry sidled by me to set the bags of Chinese takeout on the kitchen counter, then he turned to let his gaze wander more slowly over me, from head to toe and back up again. There was no mistaking his interest this time—and my rebellious body was responding to it.

"Nope," he said once he'd finished his perusal, turning to unpack the bags.

I pulled plates from the cupboard, flustered into silence. A smile lingered on his lips when I finally turned back to him, but I scowled.

"What are you grinning about?"

"You look good. Sunburn from yesterday has faded, your forehead is healing right up, no wrap on your wrist, no limp." I rolled my eyes, but he only winked as he added, "And now I can't decide what hairstyle I like better, because that ponytail shows off your neck perfectly."

Before I could react, he reached out and stroked his knuckles along the side of my throat. My mouth dropped open, but then my phone vibrated on the countertop between us, shattering our connection. We both glanced down out of reflex, and Henry let out an amused snort when he read the text from Sarah.

Off to Amsterdam tomorrow. Any new run-ins with that dickhead from the inn?

I slapped one palm over the phone and the other over my eyes. Henry grinned at my pained expression when I peeked between my fingers. Crossing his arms over his chest, he leaned one hip against the counter.

"So I take it you haven't told your friend how I swooped in to rescue you yet? You wound me, Juliet."

"No, I have not. I didn't want her to worry and end up rushing out here or something. I'm sorry, I won't let her keep thinking you're an asshole, I promise. Not for much longer, anyway."

His smile had my stomach flip-flopping madly, then he nodded, tapping a finger against his chin as a glimmer of mischief crept into his expression.

"I've never played the villain before, but if you're into roleplay, I suppose it could be fun," he replied, offering a teasing smile that made my breath stutter for a moment.

I groaned as I dumped a container of noodles onto my plate. "Fess up, Walker. Do you intentionally say things like that just to make me blush? It goes with the pasty complexion, all right? I can't help it and it is definitely *not* amusing. It's physiological."

He reached over and brushed his thumb over the hot splotch of color along one cheekbone, causing my eyes to widen even more. When my lips parted in surprise, his gaze landed on my mouth and, for one breathless moment, I thought he was going to lean in and kiss me.

"Yes, I do it on purpose. I admit it freely," he said softly. "You're gorgeous anyway, but damned if blushing doesn't make you ten times more tempting. I wouldn't call you pasty, though. Just fair, like fresh cream."

"Henry," I began, but his fingers dropped and he shook his head with a rueful smile.

"I'm not pushing for anything you're not interested in, Juliet. If you want to just be friends or work colleagues or polite strangers, I'll abide by whatever boundaries you set. If you don't want me touching you, you only need to say the word and it won't happen again."

His hazel eyes glinted gold when they dropped briefly to my lips once more, but everything about his bearing in that moment indicated utter sincerity. I stared at him until he spoke again.

"Whatever's between us, this spark, it feels right. I'm sorry if I crossed a line."

"No, you didn't cross anything."

A relieved breath whispered past his lips and he nodded. "Good."

"Spark seems like a good word for it. I was thinking chemistry. It's not—I'm not opposed to you touching me," I said, cheeks heating further even as I held his gaze. "I just want to be sure I'm not misinterpreting it."

One corner of his mouth curved upward. "Believe me, you're not."

I held up a hand and added, "But before anything else happens, I also want to know that this *spark* isn't going to screw things up between us, in terms of the inn. Maybe this is me being overly cautious, or maybe it's feeling off-kilter being new in town, I don't know. I don't want anything to turn weird."

Henry reached out to cup my chin in his hand. "You're talking to the guy whose ex-wife is still one of his best friends," he reminded me with a grin.

That statement was absurdly comforting as I considered it. I had no intention of ever actually working at the inn, and I'd already been through the strain of avoiding the place because of him. The realization that maybe this, the two of us, might be possible brought a smile to my face. Henry lifted a brow in question.

"Okay," I said simply.

"Okay," Henry repeated, running his thumb lightly along my jaw.

His focus dropped to my lips again. I tensed, wondering again if he would kiss me. Instead, he let his hand fall—though he didn't look away from my mouth for several seconds—and he stepped back.

"We've got plenty of time, Red, and your noodles are getting cold."

We ate side-by-side at the counter. Henry asked about Sarah and Andre, teased me for keeping secrets from my best friend, and miraculously took my mind off the thought of kissing him.

At least, my mind *was* off of it until he casually reached over to tuck a stray curl behind my ear. Then my lungs forgot how to function.

"You were saying?" he prompted, clearly enjoying the effect his touch had on me.

"You, sir, are a tease," I threw back. When I narrowed my eyes at him, he only grinned at the accusation.

"A tease, huh? Does that mean you want me to kiss you, Juliet? I'd be more than happy to oblige."

A lock of dark hair fell across his forehead and I seized the impulse to reach out and smooth it back into place. His eyes darkened in response, so I let my fingers drift along the sharp line of his jaw. When my thumb brushed over his lower lip, he caught my hand in his and watched me in silent challenge.

"Yes," I said simply.

He blinked, clearly trying to remember what he'd even asked before I touched him, but I slipped off the stool before he could respond. Holding his gaze with my own, I laid my hands firmly against his chest, enjoying the feel of warm, hard muscle beneath his shirt. He shifted so I could stand between his knees as he set his own hands at my waist. My palms roamed from his chest to his shoulders before slipping around to cradle the back of his neck.

"Yes, I want you to kiss me."

"Thought you'd never ask," he murmured, shifting his thumbs under the hem of my shirt to brush across my skin.

I shivered at the caress. "And I think I underestimated."

"Oh?"

"When I said I'm not opposed to you touching me, I mean."

It was laughable just how big an understatement that was. At the moment, I was sure I'd combust if he stopped touching me.

"I'll take that as a good sign."

The words teased over my skin. Henry laughed softly at my dazed expression and tugged me closer. When he nuzzled the edge of my jaw, I shivered in his arms and did the only thing left to do.

I kissed him.

Seventeen

HENRY

WHEN JULIET FEATHERED HER lips across mine, my ability to formulate a coherent thought about anything other than her evaporated. She fit so well in my arms—so soft, so right.

I was determined to let her set the pace, even when the gentle insistence of her mouth made me want to groan. Instead, I let one hand slide to the small of her back, then grinned against her mouth when her fingers curled into my hair to angle my lips for better access.

She wasn't shy or tentative in any way, merely painstakingly thorough. I'd always considered myself a patient man, but this slow progression sent tempting streaks of liquid fire through my veins. While she directed the kiss, I focused on learning her: the flare of her hip, the sweetness of her mouth, the soft hum of pleasure in her throat when my fingers stroked along her spine.

I couldn't remember ever being so completely enthralled by another person before.

When she finally drew back, I swallowed a sound of protest. My hands stayed right where they were as I studied her expression. If her inadvertent blushes were appealing, the flush of passion under her fair skin was absolutely intoxicating.

"Wow," she breathed. "Even the unflappable Henry Walker finally looks a bit ruffled. Definitely a spark."

"More like an inferno," I said as I drew her mouth to mine once more.

This time, she sighed against me, ceding control in the sweetest possible way. We went no further than kissing, but that invisible thread between us wound tight, tugging until her body melted into mine.

After several more long, thorough kisses, we managed to safely bank that fire, though heat still smoldered in her eyes. I touched my lips lightly to hers one last time before she served up bowls of ice cream from the freezer and we moved to the living room with our dessert. When she settled herself a polite distance away, I set my bowl down on the arm of the couch to tug her close to my side.

"I think we're a bit past the 'leave room for the Holy Ghost' stage," I teased.

Once she was snuggled up against me, I noticed a sketchbook lying on the side table. Curiosity got the better of me.

"Can I look at this, or is that too personal?"

"Be my guest."

Juliet gestured regally with her spoon, though her smile looked a little self-conscious. I ignored my ice cream to flip slowly through the sketches. Most were landscapes, but there was one of Gramps working in the gardens at the inn. Even though he was turned away, I recognized him immediately and grinned.

"These are fantastic. You're incredibly talented," I said, lingering on the drawing of my favorite spot on the lake. She'd captured it perfectly, right down to the soaring eagle overhead and Blue pouncing in the waves.

When she scoffed around a mouthful of ice cream, I turned and took her chin in my hand, ignoring a tiny dot of mint chip at the corner of her lip.

"I mean it. Nan was probably the most amazing artist I've ever known, and you blow her out of the water. You better learn how to take a compliment, because there are going to be a whole lot of them coming your way."

She shrugged it off despite my admonition. "If you're lucky, maybe I'll show you my paintings someday."

Setting aside the sketchbook, I leaned over to kiss her, enjoying the taste of mint against her lips.

"I'm feeling pretty lucky already."

Juliet hummed contentedly and we finished our dessert in silence. I returned the bowls to the kitchen, noticing when I came back that she was absentmindedly rubbing her injured knee. I sat back down at the end of the couch, grabbed the pillow I'd slept on the other night, and settled it on my lap.

"C'mon, lie down."

Her eyebrows lifted. "I beg your pardon?"

"If your knee is getting stiff," I said patiently, "the best thing to do is stretch out and relax. I won't bite. Not unless you ask me to."

She looked skeptical, but I bounced my eyebrows to make her laugh. Grudgingly, she did as I suggested. I realized this might have been a bad idea as soon as she lowered herself to my lap, but as I stroked my fingertips through her hair, I couldn't regret the feeling of her soft, warm body against me.

"What is this cologne you wear?" she asked, closing her eyes.

I scoffed. "I don't wear cologne. Always seemed too fussy, which isn't really my style. I *might* have gone through an Axe Body Spray phase in high school, but we don't have to talk about that. Ever."

Rolling carefully, she opened her eyes to glare up at me for a beat before pressing her face to my chest. She drew a deep breath, settled back down, and shook her head.

"There is no way in hell you just *naturally* smell this good. Like ocean waves and sunshine."

Laughter rumbled through my chest when I realized what she meant and I returned to sifting my fingers gently through her hair.

"Oh, that must be the soap. Libby's husband, Mark, makes organic bath and body products. He runs a gift shop in town.

This one is my favorite, I think he calls it 'sea salt and drift-wood' or something along those lines. I try to keep it stocked up at home, since he sells out regularly."

She hummed in approval. "Well, it's my favorite too," she assured me, then peeked up at my face. "Your doctor ex-wife is married to a man who makes soap for a living? That's an interesting pairing."

"They're happy," I said simply.

Damned if I wasn't happy, too, sitting right here with Juliet curled up on my lap. While one hand toyed with her hair, the other stroked lightly along the delicate skin of her forearm, swirling between a constellation of freckles. I watched, fascinated, as her eyelids fluttered closed again, but my entire body tightened when a soft sigh drifted past her lips. It was like every move she made was an aphrodisiac designed just for me.

"You have such sensitive skin. You respond to the barest touch, even in the most innocent of places," I mused.

The dark teal shirt she wore pulled taut over the curve of her breast as she twisted to shoot me another glare. It wasn't nearly enough to stop me from wanting to touch far more than her arm.

In fact, it only spurred my imagination onward.

So responsive, indeed. Now I was responding to her in return. I was grateful for the pillow under her head.

With a broad smile, I shrugged off her scowl. "Just an observation."

Juliet let out an indignant sound, but she snuggled back down onto the pillow and closed her eyes again. It seemed she enjoyed these soft caresses enough to let go of a brewing argument. I noted that little fact for the future, since I was sure her temper would make a regular appearance when we spent more time together.

"What was it like, growing up here?" she asked softly.

A sharp pang of sympathy for her stabbed at my chest. Not only had she lost her mother, she'd also lost the chance to meet a grandmother everyone in this town had loved dearly. The only friend she'd ever mentioned was on the other side of the world while Juliet packed up her old life and moved halfway across the country on her own. It was no wonder she was lonely.

While I stroked her hair, I told her about things I rarely spoke of because everyone in our small town knew it all already—my enduring friendship with Libby and Mark, my close relationship with my family, the homesickness that hit when I went away to college, my joyous return to Spruce Hill after graduation.

"I worked a boring, soul-sucking job for a long time after college. A few years ago, Nan went through a bout of illness that made it difficult for her to handle everything she'd been doing at the inn by herself, so she offered me a job one day when I stopped by to visit Gramps. I almost turned it down, mostly because it was a pay cut, but I've been grateful every day since I started working there."

"I'm glad you got that time with her," she whispered.

"I'm glad, too. Working at the inn taught me that there's more to life than a paycheck. We never know how much time we have left with the people we love, so we should do everything we can to take advantage of each day with them."

When she drew a shaky breath, I cupped her face in my hand and smiled down at her.

"I was there the day she saw your picture from that art gallery, you know," I said, running my thumb across her cheek. "I don't remember ever seeing her so happy. I don't cry very easily, but...when she ended up in the hospital right after that, I wept like a baby. It just wasn't fair."

Tears slipped past her long lashes, rolling silently down her cheeks, so I shifted us both in order to cradle her against my chest. Her fingers tightened into the fabric of my tee. I held her like that for a few minutes, then pressed my lips to the top of her head.

"None of it makes any sense," she said, her voice muffled against my sternum. "Why would my mother leave here? Why would she lie to me? All that time, all those years I could have known Nan. Why would she take that from me?"

"I don't know," I said softly, "but I'll help you figure it out."

When she looked up at me, her eyes shining under a veil of tears, I kissed her with a tenderness that soothed the pain rising in my own chest at her grief. I hoped it would help to soothe her, as well.

"Thank you," she murmured, lifting her hand to my cheek.

"Anything for you, Red."

She bit her lip for a heartbeat, then tilted her face up for another kiss. I grinned as her expression shifted from sadness to something entirely different, something I recognized all too clearly as a reflection of my own desire every time her lips touched mine.

Juliet might not have a wealth of happy memories in this town, but as my fingers tangled in her hair to draw her closer, I was determined to create a few for her.

Eighteen

JULIET

OVER THE NEXT WEEK, I focused on my artwork with an intensity I simply hadn't had time for in years, then started researching local art galleries. After I finished a few more pieces, I might be able to pitch a Spruce Hill installment somewhere nearby—but the closest gallery was almost to Rochester. I'd finally started painting the image of the lighthouse and Blue on a canvas, but I earmarked that one as a gift for Henry when it was done.

Each day ended with Henry coming by after work to have dinner, help me sort through the boxes in the living room, and generally kiss me senseless.

It was a bit like being a teenager again, without the disapproving parent in the next room.

All in all, it was a routine that made me inordinately happy, though my patience with our slow pace was wearing thin. I had only myself to blame, since Henry was clearly letting me set our trajectory, but that didn't lessen my frustration.

In direct contrast to that, I was enjoying my time with him so much that I was afraid to rush ahead and ruin it.

When the weather cooperated, he brought Blue with him, but Henry teased that unless I was going to let him scrub the wet dog smell from us both in Nan's fancy bathtub, he wasn't willing to bring her over in the rain.

Though I wouldn't admit it to him just yet, I *might* have entertained a dozen or so fantasies about taking him up on the offer to lather up my skin with those strong hands of his.

We made progress working through the boxes, enough to let Henry cart some back up to the second floor to get them out of the way when we deemed the contents not worth deeper investigation, but I'd still found very few answers. Even if it was a study in disappointment, it helped to have Henry at my side through it all. He had an innate ability to tease a smile out of me, to distract and reassure me when I was ready to admit defeat.

"I wish I'd had you around while I was going through my mom's attic," I muttered one evening.

When I heaved a sigh and rubbed at eyes gone blurry from paging through decades of old ledgers, Henry's strong fingers cupped the back of my neck, pressing into the knotted muscles until a soft sigh whispered past my lips.

"I wish I could have been there for you, Red. No one should have to do that kind of thing on their own. It makes me grateful for my brother, even if he annoys me at times."

I stayed silent while he rubbed the tension from my neck. It was so easy, so natural being here with him. There was no pressure from him to move faster, give more, skip ahead—he seemed happy to let me set the pace, though I would swear there was a growing heat in his eyes every time we pushed the boundaries of our interactions.

Even if there were frequent moments when I was tempted to set aside all of my reservations, strip him naked, and while away the hours in bed together, for the time being, things stayed impressively chaste.

Of course, keeping it that way would be another matter entirely.

LATE FRIDAY AFTERNOON, AS I stood at the stove stirring a pot of sauce, Blue's joyous bark sounded from the front yard. I set a timer and gladly abandoned my task to open the door and admire the smooth ripple of muscle beneath Henry's t-shirt as he pulled a heavy box from the back of his truck.

Blue galloped straight toward me, accepted a quick head rub, then traipsed off to sniff at the wildflowers lining the walk.

"I come bearing gifts," Henry called.

He paused at the doorway, shifting the box to one hip so he could kiss me in that slow, languid way that set my nerves aflame, while Blue trotted past us and settled into her favorite spot in front of the couch.

"I see that," I said when he drew back to wink and lug the box into the living room. "Dinner's almost ready. I'm no master chef, but it should be edible."

Henry set the box on the floor and returned to my side to kiss me again now that his hands were free. The man could work wonders with his mouth alone, but when his hands joined the action, I was a goner. He'd spent the previous evenings learning my responses until he knew exactly where to trace his fingers along my spine to draw that purr from my throat, where to cup his hands without tickling me, just how I liked to be kissed and held and cherished.

When he reluctantly released me, I gazed up at him in that dazed way that always drew a smile from his lips.

"What's in the box?" I asked once I'd recovered my senses.

Henry grinned, looking excited enough that I didn't think it was full of tax documents or elementary school report cards.

Thank heavens for that.

"Gramps found some stuff in the basement of the inn, he thought it might help in our quest for information," he said, gesturing to the other boxes still lining the floor. "They're not diaries, but there are some sketchbooks and notebooks in there, along with a bunch of file folders. He didn't want to pry and neither did I, so they're yours to discover."

As much as I wanted to dive immediately in, the timer I set for the pasta went off with a loud ding. I sighed as I returned to the stove, waving off Henry's offer of assistance. When I laid our plates on the counter, his expression shifted from excitement to something darker, more troubled. He was almost always smiling these days—either that or giving me the intense, heated look I was coming to know so well, the one that made my breath catch in my throat with anticipation.

After I sat beside him, he tucked my hair behind my ear, his fingertips lingering on the sensitive skin.

"What is it?" I asked.

"This smells delicious," he replied, but I narrowed my eyes at him. "Right, fine, I'll stop buttering you up. It's probably nothing, but I've been asking around about the sound you heard that day at the Point."

I had nearly forgotten he'd promised to do that, distracted as I'd been by this thing that was developing between us.

"So? Spill it, Walker."

Henry flashed a grin and leaned over to kiss me before he continued, but he knew better than to press his luck, so he kept it quick.

"The Partridges, who live along the road by Cooper's Point, thought they heard a gunshot that day, too. They were outside in the yard with their grandchildren that afternoon so everybody heard it. Mr. Partridge assumed it was either a hunter or some kids messing around out in the woods."

"But you don't think so?"

"I don't know what to think, to be perfectly honest. Folks in Spruce Hill are pretty careful. I've talked to enough people that word will get around, so maybe we'll find out more. Either that or whoever was responsible will realize they're about to get busted, and it won't ever happen again."

Something in his expression said he didn't agree, but he reached over to touch my cheek, his gaze softening. A faint streak of heat blossomed under his fingertips.

"It pisses me off that you were hurt because someone was out there dicking around. I'm still amazed your injuries weren't worse."

"Well, thank you for asking about it," I said softly. "My knee is feeling better, and I don't look like something from a horror movie anymore, so that's definite improvement."

"Oh, I don't know, sometimes there's a hot redhead at the beginning of the movie, right before everyone starts getting murdered. You might still have a backup career in film, you know," he replied, his eyes twinkling with mischief now.

I snorted and whacked his arm. "Eat your dinner, you scoundrel."

He did, with such gusto that it made me feel marginally better about my subpar cooking skills. I'd managed to feed myself for years, but between popping over to the inn for breakfast, exploring the town's takeout options, and letting Henry cook for me, I was spoiled now.

And enjoying the hell out of it, to be perfectly honest.

After dinner, he insisted on taking care of the dishes. I propped my chin in my hand and basked in contentment as I watched him bend over to load the dishwasher, giving me a pristine view of his ass in those faded jeans. There was something so captivating about him, all lean grace and understated strength.

After a few minutes, he threw a glance rife with promise over his shoulder and smirked ever so slightly.

"I can take off my shirt, if you'd like a better view," he offered.

I learned very early in this budding relationship that he enjoyed throwing me off balance with such comments, but I'd also come to understand that he didn't generally expect me to call his bluff.

Lest he start to think I wasn't up to the challenge, I decided it was time to change that.

"Yes, please," I answered, delighted by the flash of surprise that crossed his face.

It was followed by a slow, devastating smile as he drew the shirt over his head and tossed it onto the counter next to me. My breath caught in my throat as I studied him.

He really was beautiful. Sleek curves of muscle bunched and shifted beneath olive skin that was dusted with dark hair, trailing down toward the sharp vee of his hip bones before dipping below the waistband of his jeans. His muscles were smooth, defined but not bulky. I knew firsthand just how strong they were—strong enough to sweep me off my feet. Literally.

The late afternoon sunlight streaming through the window flowed lovingly over his chest. My fingers itched to do the same.

He seemed neither bashful nor impatient, so I contented myself with absorbing every detail of his bare torso.

There'd be time enough for touching.

"You know," I said lightly, trying to ignore the low simmer of blood in my veins, "art schools always need nude models. You really should do your civic duty and volunteer. An entire generation of artistic talent is missing out on all this beauty."

Henry dried his hands and set aside the dish towel before leaning toward me across the counter. I dragged my gaze from his chest to his face, meeting his amused smirk.

"Beauty, huh? You should know by now that the only artist I'd ever pose nude for is you, Red."

"Hmm," I replied. "There's a thought."

It wasn't the first time I'd thought about drawing him, but the image of him lounging naked before me inspired a variety of desires that had nothing to do with art. Especially now that I could see what I'd been missing.

When he raised a questioning brow, waiting for me to speak, I cocked my head and said, "I think you should come over here."

Nineteen

HENRY

WITH A SMILE, I rounded the counter, watching her eyes darken as I closed the distance between our bodies. An involuntary shiver ran through her and I recognized it immediately, knew it for the aching need it represented.

I felt it just as keenly myself.

As I moved to stand between her knees, she shifted on the chair, spreading her legs to make room for me, and I had to remind myself to go slow.

Even if every inch of my body wanted to capture that sweet mouth and ravish her until morning.

"And now?" I asked, my voice low and husky.

"I'd like to touch you," she said simply.

I spread my arms wide in invitation. Without hesitation, she reached out to smooth her palms over my shoulders, down my biceps, and back up again, the hunger in her beautiful eyes intensifying throughout the exploration. I stood perfectly still, watching her face and realizing she wore the same look of wonder I'd noticed that day at the beach.

A guy could get used to dating an artist.

Her expression alone was thoroughly arousing, nevermind the trail of heat left by her fingers. It might kill me to keep still, to be patient, but it was worth the effort just to watch her watching me.

"You're beautiful," Juliet told me as her hands splayed over my chest.

A groan dragged from my throat when those soft fingers moved through the rough hair there. Even with my gaze focused on her expression, I could feel the weight of her regard on my skin. This bold intensity from her was electrifying.

When I couldn't bear to stand still for another moment, I set my hands on her knees. I hadn't seen her bare legs since that day in the forest and wasn't sure if the tenderness of the bruise was completely gone, so I kept my touch light as my hands slid slowly upward from her kneecaps, coasting along the outside of her thighs.

Once they reached her hips and cupped those perfect curves, Juliet finally lifted her eyes to meet mine. I held her gaze for a moment, then lowered my lips to graze her jawline, nuzzling the soft skin.

"So are you," I whispered against her ear.

This time I felt the tremor go through her, and a swift rush of satisfaction coursed through my veins. Her hands left my chest to twine around my neck.

"I can take my shirt off, if you'd like a better view," she breathed, echoing my offer.

"Yes, please."

A laugh escaped her lips, a hint of sound that was breathless and so erotic I wasn't sure I could wait to get my hands on her bare skin. It took all of my strength to straighten up and let her lift the shirt over her head, revealing the turquoise bra I'd caught sight of in her bathroom that first night when I brought her home—and the creamy, freckled skin I knew would feel like silk under my fingers.

I growled as a bolt of raw desire shot straight through me.

My eyes feasted on her, stroking over her skin in a way that made her breath come a little faster, a visible sign of my effect on her. When my gaze landed on the dainty silver ring hanging on a chain, nestled in her cleavage, I had to bite back a groan. Instead of burying my face there as well, I touched the ring with a careful fingertip, fully conscious of her sharp intake of breath when my knuckle brushed the swell of her breast.

"What's this?"

"It was my mother's."

When I traced the edge of her bra with my fingertip, she broke off, apparently having no desire to talk about her mother at that moment. I read the sentiment in the way her head fell back slightly as I retraced the path again, and I didn't comment on the ring any further.

"This color brings out your eyes," I murmured as I swept my thumbs lightly over her satin-covered nipples, watching her eyelids flutter.

"Does it?"

"Damned if I know," I groaned, finally setting my mouth to hers.

As I kissed her, I lifted my hands from her breasts to follow the same path along her shoulders and biceps that she had explored on me, equally intent, equally hungry. When her arms tightened around me, the brush of that turquoise satin against my chest was torturous. My palms coasted up her spine, spreading across the bare skin that had haunted my dreams since that night I spent on the couch, then back down, leaving a trail of heat in their wake.

We'd been moving slowly these past weeks, cautiously, as though one of us might spook. It had seemed important to learn more about one another before rushing ahead, but now I could think of nothing more vital than learning her body.

"I want to touch you," I whispered, letting my lips drift over her cheekbone.

A quick nod from her was permission enough—I unclasped the bra and she shrugged it off, letting it fall to the floor. My exploration grew ravenous as I drew back to look at her, admiring the way her skin flushed under my gaze.

"So, so lovely," I said hoarsely as my hands slid upward to cup her breasts again.

I was no artist, but I couldn't imagine anything more beautiful than those rosy nipples growing taut as my thumbs swept lightly over them, back and forth. Her head fell back on a sigh and I kissed her again, sinking deep into the lush heat of her mouth.

She barely noticed when I leaned her back more, supporting her with one arm wrapped around her waist, until I kissed a path down her neck and took her nipple into my mouth.

Juliet gasped, then tangled one hand in my hair, clutching me there against her racing heartbeat.

I gloried in the soft whimpers that burst from her lips as my tongue worked over her skin, teasing and then sucking deep, circling and soothing, spiking the pleasure higher with each pass.

"I can't get enough of you," I whispered, desperate to fill my hands and mouth with every inch of her soft skin.

"I was thinking the same," she replied with a strangled laugh, then my teeth grazed her nipple and she arched over my arm.

I drank in every response, delighting in each sweet sound I drew from her. Just as I suspected, her skin here was even more exquisitely sensitive than the rest of her. I'd just shifted to her other breast, swirling my tongue over its peak, when a cold, wet nose pushed between our bare stomachs.

"Oh!" Juliet yelped, jerking back just in time to avoid a collision with the top of my head as I stood upright.

Blue's tail wagged and she offered a canine smile that normally would have charmed us both. At that precise moment, though, we were not amused.

I rubbed my hands over my face to clear my head. Juliet's cheeks were flushed, her lips rosy from my kisses. Though I tried to keep my gaze from dropping to her breasts, heaving as she struggled to catch her breath, I gave up, taking in the perfection of her bare skin before me.

Blue woofed impatiently. Juliet stifled a laugh while I cursed beneath my breath and strode to the door to let the dog out into the yard.

Once I returned to stand before her, she laid a hand on my chest. I sighed as I sank down onto my stool. Her curls tumbled wildly about her bare shoulders, but I knew the look on her face meant we wouldn't be picking up right where we'd left off. I took her hands in mine, running my thumbs over the back of her knuckles.

"I'm sorry," I said, feeling a rush of guilt that threatened to kill the mood. "I didn't mean to push you."

Juliet arched a brow, still looking a little dazed and distracted. "I'm not stopping you because I don't want to . . ." She lifted one hand from mine in a vague gesture and I bit back a smile. "But I feel like there are some awkward conversations we should have first."

"Okay. Let's move this somewhere more comfortable, then," I said, lifting her down from the stool.

She grabbed her shirt off the floor, clasping it to her chest as we transferred to the couch. This spot was probably even less conducive to conversation than the stools, but at least I wouldn't be staring straight at her bare skin. The shirt barrier was reminiscent enough of that night in the bathroom to make me laugh softly as I sat beside her.

"Probably for the best you have a shield, if you expect my brain to function," I said, stretching one arm along the back of the couch so my fingers were close but not quite touching her.

As tempted as I'd been to tug her back into my arms after letting Blue outside, it was clear that she wanted to get solid ground back under her feet.

"What's on your mind?"

"I don't really know how this kind of thing goes," she said, waving her hand between us.

My brows lifted as I waited for her to continue. When she stayed silent, I murmured, "What kind of thing?"

"This. Us. I've never had a...casual relationship."

I drew a sharp breath as her words struck home. Did she think I was just sticking around for a roll in the hay?

"Oh, Juliet," I said gently, reaching over to cup her face in my hand. "My feelings for you are anything but casual. If I've given you the impression that they were, I really, truly apologize."

"Oh," she said in a small voice, then a little louder, "Oh."

She jerked slightly then, as though startled, and her cornflower eyes searched my expression for a moment. A flash of something that might have been panic crossed her face.

"Easy," I said, keeping my tone light even as I wondered why that would frighten her. "I'm not pushing anything, I hope you know that. We don't have to do anything you don't want to do."

Juliet sucked in a deep breath, but she nodded while she let it out. "I didn't think you were pushing, I just...I don't have a great track record with relationships of any kind, period. You know about my ex, and the ones before that weren't much better."

I stroked her cheek gently, a soft movement meant to soothe. Maybe her admission shouldn't have made me want to sucker-punch the past partners who'd hurt her, but it did. Especially the one who'd proposed on her mother's deathbed.

On the other hand, I couldn't ignore my relief at the fact that things hadn't worked out between them.

I was dedicated to making sure we were both clear about exactly what she deserved, and I was more than willing to let her determine how she wanted this to play out, even if she worried it was my heart at risk rather than her own.

"If you're not sure about anything, you say the word and it stops. Physical or emotional. What you want is important to me. I'm not asking you to profess your undying love, I just need us to be clear on what you want."

The smile she gave me was heartbreakingly vulnerable, so I rubbed my nose against hers until a soft laugh escaped her lips.

"So, are we getting dressed, or do you want me to kiss you some more?"

"Oh, I want you to kiss me some more," she said, tossing the shirt aside and rising to her knees so she could throw one leg over and straddle my lap.

"Excellent choice."

She draped her arms around my neck, her nipples brushing my chest as that smile blossomed into an expression of exquisite promise. "Then I guess we'll see where things end up."

"I like the sound of that."

In fact, as my hands explored the softness of her skin, I could think of nothing better than following her lead.

Twenty

JULIET

S OME TIME LATER, WE moved to the bedroom, parting only long enough for Henry to let Blue back inside.

We paused just inside the door, still wrapped around one another. When a few minutes of pathetic whining at the bedroom door still didn't gain her an invitation to join us, the dog's footsteps padded back to the living room for the night.

I discovered soon enough that Henry had very much meant it when he said he wouldn't rush or pressure me, even now that things had progressed—the man had the patience of a saint. That wasn't to say he wasn't an active and enthusiastic participant, but something about knowing he wanted me to set the pace gave me a heady sense of power.

As a result, I grew bolder with each passing minute, with each kiss and caress that spurred that raging fire into a million individual flames burning so hot I thought I might melt.

And, when I did, Henry was right there to catch me.

He swept me into his arms as he had in the forest and laid me on the bed, stretching out alongside me.

"You're the boss," he murmured, trailing his lips across my collarbone. "Tell me what you want."

In reply, I reached for the zipper of his jeans, though my fingers grew clumsy when his teeth grazed the base of my throat. A fierce grin split his face when I fumbled and tilted my head to give him better access.

"If you don't stop distracting me, I'm not going to be able to tell you a damn thing," I gasped.

"My goodness, Juliet Morrison speechless? Now that *is* a surprise."

Henry drew back, giving me a lazy smile. Even with his head raised, his fingers stroked over my breast in a way that had my back bowing right off the bed.

"Henry!" The breathless exclamation tore past my lips as he rolled my nipple between his thumb and index finger.

"Yes, Juliet?"

When I pried my eyes open, he was looking down at me with a polite expression on his face, as though we'd been discussing the weather. Only the molten heat in his eyes betrayed how much he was enjoying this. That in itself was as arousing as the things he did with his hands.

I dropped my head back onto the pillow, mumbling, "I need you to get these jeans off. Right now."

He grinned. "Mine or yours?"

"Yes!"

Even as I blurted out the word, Henry's fingers danced down along my rib cage to the waistband of my jeans. He flicked the button open with annoying ease, given my inability to manage that move with his, then he let one fingertip hook under the edge of the denim to tease a fiery arc from one hipbone to the other.

I made a sound, something between bliss and frustration, but in the next second, he tugged my jeans and underwear down my legs. My eyes flew open again in order to watch him discard his own before he returned to my side.

"Is that better?" he asked, cocking a brow as he smiled down at me.

One of his palms slid upward from my knee to the flare of my hip so slowly that I thought I might ignite right then and there.

"Much better," I breathed when his hand reached its destination, cupping the curls between my legs.

He watched my face while he stroked and teased, looking just as entranced by my response to these intimate caresses as he had been by my reaction to the more innocent ones.

My skin became exquisitely sensitive under his fingers as I arched and shifted, making little sounds of need that I couldn't have held back if I tried—especially when he slid one finger inside me and curled it until my back bowed nearly enough to dislodge him. He only adjusted his position as he put this new discovery to good use.

Distracted as I was, I still couldn't help but appreciate how his eternal patience translated into a level of concentration I'd never been the focus of before. It was like he was cataloging the results of each stroke of his fingers, each touch of his lips.

Eventually, he leaned down and nipped the edge of my jaw. My fingers tangled in his hair, clenching against his scalp. Before long, I was panting his name as the tension built, writhing helplessly while his hands and mouth moved over my skin.

When an explosive release finally shuddered through my limbs, I collapsed in a boneless heap and his touch turned soothing. Though I caught him staring at me when I managed to focus my eyes again, I was too blessedly limp to blush. His eyes were filled with something hot and hungry, something that obliterated any remaining trace of self-consciousness that might have lingered.

After catching my breath, I summoned enough strength to roll over and shove him onto his back, my hair falling like a curtain around us as I dropped my head to kiss him. When I wrapped a hand around his hard length, he groaned into my mouth.

"You're killing me, Red," he whispered.

I drew back with a jerk, my brows drawn together in concern that my plans might be foiled. "Do you have condoms on you? I should have thought of that earlier."

He laughed as he smoothed one finger over the furrow between my eyebrows. I shifted slightly over him and he growled low in his throat before replying.

"Yes. Back pocket of my jeans."

I released him to roll off the bed. When I glanced over my shoulder, he was studying my ass intently as I bent down to locate the condoms.

"Do you have any idea how gorgeous you are?" he asked, his voice husky with desire.

My brows lifted as I returned to the bed. "Not really, no, but if you're carrying these around, I'm going to guess you find me at least passably attractive."

Though I was joking, Henry caught my wrist in a gentle but firm grasp as I knelt beside him.

"I only started carrying them when things were getting a little more heated between us," he said softly. "I don't want you to think I'm a complete cad. I promise I wasn't making any assumptions."

I gave a breathless laugh as I leaned down to kiss him. "A cad, hmm? I think you've spent too much time reading an old lady's journals, Mr. Walker."

He grinned. "I think 'cad' was one of Nan's favorite words."

"That doesn't shock me. In any case, I'm glad you thought to stock up, or this might have been an exercise in frustration."

"We can stop any time you want."

He threaded his fingers through my hair and drew me back down, placing tiny, playful kisses along my lips.

"What I want," I murmured against his mouth, "is you inside me."

I handed him one of the condoms and tossed the others aside as he rolled it on. Henry gazed up at me like he wanted to devour me as I straddled his body. When I guided him into place and sank slowly downward, his eyes fell shut on a strangled groan.

Every sense sharpened, heightened at the feel of him buried so deep, like puzzle pieces slotting into place.

His words echoed in my head—*anything but casual.* I hadn't planned to add a new relationship to the mix when I showed up here, but he was right. Whatever was growing between us felt serious. Meaningful. Utterly beautiful.

As I lifted away again, his fingers gripped my hips, dragging me slowly back down. My hands caught his shoulders for balance when he shifted so he was only half-reclined, angling us until he was so impossibly deep that I gasped. One of his arms banded around my lower back and the other tangled in my hair again, drawing my lips down for another kiss—this one scalding hot, the teasing playfulness long gone.

I felt the soft moan that escaped his lips reverberating inside my own chest, a siren song that I happily surrendered to.

Breaking the kiss, I sat up and rode him, arching until the tips of my hair cascaded across the arm at my back and over his thighs. His teeth caught one puckered nipple and the air left my lungs in a swift woosh.

Before I could draw another breath, he rolled us over so I was blinking up at him from my back.

"Juliet," he whispered.

My name sounded like a prayer on his lips, then his mouth was everywhere all at once. My cheeks, my jaw, my throat. I locked my legs around his waist, drawing him deeper as he rocked his hips against mine.

When his hand snuck between us, stroked and circled, then pressed against my clit, I whimpered his name. He thrust harder, faster, keeping time with the frantic sounds coming from the back of my throat.

I clenched around him, my muscles quivering. His teeth nipped at my earlobe and I arched beneath him, giving a sharp cry as I shattered once more. A bare second later, he followed me over the edge, burying himself deep as the release swept through him.

For a few minutes, he stayed there, letting the last of the waves lap at us both. Once I was sure my heart wasn't going to beat right out of my chest, I unhooked my legs from around his hips and he carefully withdrew. He pressed a kiss just over my racing heart before he rolled off the bed to throw away the condom.

The room was already dark when he slipped back into bed and tugged me against his side. I settled in, draped across his chest.

"I'm never moving from this spot again," I declared, sounding as drowsy as I felt.

Henry chuckled against my hair as he drew the blanket up and over us both. "Sounds good to me."

"That was—I mean—wow," I murmured into his chest.

"An inferno?"

With a low hum, I nodded. "An inferno."

There in his arms, I'd finally found something to hold onto. As my eyes drifted shut, I let the colors of flame swirl behind my eyelids, painting a landscape of heat, pleasure, and comfort.

Twenty-One

HENRY

THE NEXT MORNING, I awoke in confusion, tangled up in Juliet's sweet limbs. I squinted against the bright morning light as memories rushed back in a flood of sensation and satisfaction.

One of my hands rested possessively along the curve of her ass, the other atop her arm, which was flung across my chest. Her left leg draped over one of mine like a soft, seductive anchor. When she shifted, her thigh brushed across my groin, drawing a strangled groan from my throat.

"Again? You are a demanding wench," I grumbled playfully against the top of her head.

She laughed, her voice still husky with sleep. "I didn't mean to wake you. I don't even know what time it is. Do you need to be at work? I don't think I can move, so if you need to call in sick, just tell them you have a parasitic infestation or something."

I laughed and rolled toward her, sliding my hand along her leg to draw her knee up over my hip as I said, "No, today is my day off. Good morning, beautiful."

"Good morning."

At the shy, slightly hazy look in her eyes, I grinned. Tousled, gorgeous, and utterly kissable—waking up beside her was something I could get used to *very* quickly. I trailed my lips along her hairline and she burrowed closer just as a loud bark sounded from the other side of the door.

"I'm never bringing her here again," I muttered, then gave Juliet's ass a gentle squeeze, followed by a more lingering caress. "Don't you dare move."

She threw her arms wide once she had the bed to herself, mumbling, "Yes, sir."

I paused to pull on jeans and stifled another groan when I glanced back at her sleepy sprawl. Morning sunlight danced across her skin through the lacy curtains. My gaze roamed hungrily over her, though I grimaced at the faint shadow of bruising on her knee. The rest of her scratches and scrapes had healed well, even the deeper cut on her forehead.

Despite the line of conversation she'd broached the night before, there had been nothing awkward about our coming together. I soaked in the sight of her for another moment, then forced myself to leave the room so I could take the dog outside.

Blue didn't look nearly as reproachful as I'd expected, simply happy to see me. I let her out into the yard and squinted into the brightness of the morning. Leaving the dog outside unsupervised was a surefire way to invite another interruption far sooner than I wanted, usually in the form of her barking her head off after chasing a squirrel up a tree, so I waited in the doorway while she relieved herself.

The lake glittered almost painfully bright in the morning sun, but as I turned to follow Blue back into the cottage, a flash of movement near the edge of the forest caught my eye.

Before I could blink, it was gone, but I was sure it had been there.

"What the hell?" I muttered, cupping a hand over my eyes.

Whatever the source of movement had been, I saw nothing unusual as I studied the stretch of yard between the cottage and the treeline. I chalked it up to some animal heading back into the trees, but I cocked my head when I looked down at the dog, who loved nothing more than bolting after a deer in the woods.

Then again, this wasn't her usual stomping grounds; maybe she'd been too distracted by new yard smells to notice the creature.

Though Juliet had been a phenomenal distraction these past days, I was unsettled by the increasing probability that it had been an actual gunshot she heard that day in the forest. Whether it was a clueless hunter or something more sinister, it was a danger that didn't belong in Spruce Hill, certainly one I didn't want anywhere near Juliet.

With nothing more to go on, though, I pushed down my concern, determined to enjoy my day with her to the fullest.

I closed the door behind us and threw the bolt before returning to the bedroom. Juliet was much as I'd left her, except with one arm now thrown across her eyes. She lifted it to peek at me when I stopped at the foot of the bed, gazing down at her with raw appreciation.

"Remind me to get some blackout curtains soon," she grumbled as I tossed my jeans aside and crawled toward her.

I paused at her knee, laying a lingering kiss against the pale purple bruise. The sharp intake of breath that passed her rosy lips inspired me to continue a trail of feather-light kisses up the impossibly soft skin of her thigh. With my shoulders, I nudged her legs wider and settled myself between them.

"Henry," she gasped when I reached the soft copper curls that had captivated me for the better part of the night.

I rubbed my cheek against the inside of her thigh, the faint shadow of stubble along my jaw teasing the sensitive area. Her legs shifted restlessly on either side of my body.

"Yes, Juliet?" I replied, then swirled my tongue over her skin, dewy and pink under a beam of daylight from the window.

When her only reply was a soft moan, accompanied by the faint quiver of her limbs that had become familiar to me already, I grinned and focused on my task. Though we'd made love twice more during the night, I hadn't had the chance to taste her, and I savored the experience.

Everything about her—the little whimpers, each helpless roll of her hips, her wetness against my tongue—tempted me to linger here for the rest of my days. It didn't take long before she came apart with my name on her lips, her body trembling under my hands and mouth.

I found her swift and intense release incredibly gratifying.

When I crawled back up to the pillows and gathered her boneless form into my arms, she sighed contentedly, nuzzling her face against my neck as she murmured, "You're too good at this."

"We're good together."

"Very, very good."

I hummed in agreement, my fingers stroking lightly over her hair, soothing her as her pulse slowly returned to normal. After a moment, I drew back just far enough to see a tiny crease between her brows.

"I can see the wheels turning in that pretty head of yours. What are you thinking about?"

"Just this." She waved a hand over us.

"What? Incredible, heart-stopping sex?" I asked, running my palm over her hip to cup her ass. Every inch of her anatomy delighted me, but this exquisite curve practically inspired me to write poetry in its honor. "The way I fit so perfectly inside of you? That little sound you make when my fingers—"

She laid a hand over my mouth and I chuckled against it. Now I was thinking about all of those things, but she looked so serious that I dipped my head to kiss her one more time before she replied.

"This, us, everything," she said vaguely.

I got the picture as I noted the deep blush spreading across her cheeks. Juliet was gloriously expressive, physically and emotionally, but it wasn't until her revelation about the ex-boyfriend's proposal that I realized she was also wary. I slid my hand to her back, rubbing soothing circles across her shoulder blades until she sighed and dropped her head to my chest, burying her face against my throat.

Though it was clear she was still sorting through what had happened between us, I could think of little aside from how stunning she looked when she'd been thoroughly and repeatedly satisfied. Despite a week of kissing, cuddling, and talking late into the evening on her couch, it took a night of passion to reveal just how affectionate she really was.

It was a beautiful discovery.

"Definitely worth thinking about," I murmured against her hand. I felt her lips curve against my neck and my arms tightened reflexively around her. "We have the whole day together, if you don't mind me hanging around. What should we do with it?"

Juliet gasped. "Oh, the box. I totally forgot."

"You were a tad distracted."

"Maybe a little."

"I'm happy to make us some breakfast, but we can save time by showering together." I waggled my eyebrows and she laughed.

Rising up on one elbow, Juliet leaned over and kissed me, flashing a challenging grin when she drew back.

"Last one to the bathroom has to do the soaping," she said, then she bounded off the bed before I could react.

A broad smile spread across my face as I rolled out of bed to follow her. This was one race I didn't mind losing.

Twenty-Two

JULIET

I N THE END, WE both triumphed in the shower contest, then ate breakfast together at the counter. What Henry had said about us being good together was absolutely true. Every time he came near me, I was struck by the overwhelming sensation of being *whole*. Even the cavernous emptiness that had inhabited my chest since my mother's death evaporated, replaced with something warm and fulfilling.

It was beautiful and terrifying all at once. I wasn't sure how to articulate those thoughts to him without it sounding like some kind of declaration I was in no way ready to make, but from the expression on his face when I caught him looking at me, I suspected he felt it, too.

While Henry finished taking care of the dishes, I sank down to the floor in the living room beside Blue and opened the box.

I drew a deep breath, letting it out slowly as Henry came to sit beside me. There was a faint tremor in my hands, but I wasn't sure if it was from anticipation over the box or a result of his dedicated morning attentions. All of my nerve endings were still singing, so I decided to blame the latter.

"Ready?" he asked.

"Ready as I'll ever be."

A leatherbound book lay atop the rest of the contents. I leaned against Henry's shoulder, appreciating his support, and flipped the book open. When a brittle pressed violet fell from inside the cover, I lifted it gently between my thumb and forefinger.

"Nan made me one of these," I said quietly. "I found some letters and cards she'd written to me, stashed away in the box of journals from the attic. She wrote to me for years, even though she didn't know my name. Like she knew I'd find them one day."

Henry put his arm around my shoulders. "Nan loved you, Red, even without ever meeting you."

The assurance strengthened my resolve. I flipped through the book, running my fingers reverently over pencil and charcoal drawings of the inn, the cottage, even some of the landmarks from my list. There were two more sketchbooks in the box, very much like the first, but I paged through each of them with intense concentration.

Henry seemed less interested in the artwork they contained than in my expression as I studied every sketch. I felt his gaze, warm and soft on my face, and when I glanced up at him, his smile was sweet enough to momentarily distract me.

When I managed to refocus on the last sketchbook in my lap and turned the final pages, my eyes shot wide. Instead of landscapes, these last few drawings were portraits done in bold, dark strokes of charcoal.

At my gasp, Henry's gaze dropped to the artwork.

"That's your grandfather," he said, pointing to the first. "There are some other old photos of him around the inn. I'll show you, if you haven't seen them yet."

Nan's husband was a handsome, distinguished man with soft eyes and a gentle smile. I recognized him from one of the pictures on the mantle, but seeing him through Nan's eyes was different. After studying his features for a moment, I turned the page, revealing an achingly beautiful image of my mother's face.

"That's my mom," I told him. Carefully, so as not to smudge the charcoal, I laid my fingertips over my mother's cheek. "She looks so sad here, so young."

Henry squeezed my shoulder gently and pointed to the date at the bottom of the page. "This must have been around the time she left town, right?"

I nodded. "She was just a kid. I never really thought about what it must have been like for her. She left everything she'd ever known to make a new life, not just for herself but for me, too. I always knew being a single mom was difficult at times, but she was barely eighteen when she left Spruce Hill, pregnant and on her own. It must have been so hard."

My words faded into silence as I flipped to the final page. This picture was of a young man, older than my mother's portrait but not by much, with a cruel mouth and cold, dark eyes. Something about him seemed almost familiar at first, but at second glance, the sensation was lost. The date was the same as the previous page.

I stared down at it, studying each harsh line, before saying, "She left a note for me to contact the inn. I found it right before the house was sold."

"Your mom?"

"Yes. She said lives were at stake and I needed to protect myself."

Henry tensed at my side. "Protect yourself from what?"

"I don't know. I thought she was just being dramatic. She told me to call the owner of the inn, who would explain things to me."

"Shit," he whispered.

"Yeah, that about sums it up." I tapped the sketch in front of us. "Could this have been her boyfriend? His name was Lewis, I found it in one of the journals."

"No," Henry said slowly. "I'm pretty sure that was Lewis Zoratti. There was a framed photo of him and your mom from a school dance in the office at the inn. This is definitely not him."

An unreasonable twinge of jealousy struck me, then flitted away. It wasn't Henry's fault he'd grown up so close to my family history while I'd been a thousand miles away. He must have seen the disquiet written on my face, because he pressed a kiss to my temple.

"It's all yours, Red. I'll help you track down every piece of history in every hidden corner of the inn, if that's what you want. We can even visit Lewis this weekend, if you'd like to talk to him. I'm sure he'd be willing."

I tore my eyes from the sketchbook and looked at his handsome face, shadowed now by morning stubble. Somehow, the scruff made him even more alluring.

"Thank you," I said softly, then dropped my eyes back to the page, frowning down at the drawing. "Nan's journals mentioned another guy, one who fought with my mom and showed up drunk, but she only used the initial T. This could be him. This...this could be my father."

"Then we'll find out who he is."

My heart leapt into my throat at the prospect of learning more. I knew well enough that Nan's view of this man had very likely influenced her portrayal of him, especially if she blamed him for my mother's abrupt departure from town, but the sketch left me uneasy.

Henry's strong fingers massaged the back of my neck as another rush of affection swept through me. I'd come to Spruce Hill looking for answers and instead I kept finding so many more questions. Anything he could do to help me in that quest, Henry seemed ready and willing to do it.

I appreciated it more than I could say.

And yet...I had a bad feeling, deep in my gut, as I studied the image.

"Maybe he was the reason my mom left town," I said. "Maybe he was as malicious as he looks here. Maybe that's the danger she was warning me about."

The possibility had clearly crossed Henry's mind as well—I could see it in his eyes, now solemn and worried. Spruce Hill was known for its low crime rates, but I couldn't quell the thrum of anxiety that took root inside me.

"Maybe," he agreed, his tone so serious that a chill ran down my spine.

"But you'll help me find out who he was anyway?" I asked, studying him closely.

He nodded. "Of course I will. You should know by now that I'd do anything you asked."

I got the feeling there was something he wasn't saying. Even after the turn our relationship had taken, I was still a little flustered by that willingness to help, but then he cupped my cheek in his hand. His cautious expression was making me nervous.

"Will you do something for me?"

"What is it?" I asked, laying my hand over his.

"You're a grown woman and I would never imply that you need a chaperone or a babysitter," he began, "but I'd feel a lot better if you'd hold off on any more outdoor adventures by yourself. I'll come with you anytime you want, but I don't like the idea of you out in the woods or trekking the countryside alone until we get to the bottom of this."

"You think there's actually danger?" I drew back a little, searching his hazel eyes.

Before seeing the charcoal portrait on my lap, I might've laughed at his concern, brushed it off as an overreaction, but now, with those bold black strokes in my mind, I felt as unsettled as he looked. It seemed like he was torn between not wanting to scare me and not wanting to keep something from me.

"Probably not," he admitted. "But I thought I saw something out back this morning, by the treeline."

I jerked in surprise. "What?"

"It could have been a deer, a raccoon—anything, really. I just got a weird feeling from it and I'd rather be safe than sorry, especially when it comes to you."

The simple words caused a flutter inside my chest, followed by a strange warmth that radiated throughout my body. I'd explore that at a later time.

"Okay."

"Okay?" He cocked a dark brow, clearly surprised by my swift agreement.

My responding smile was equal parts rueful and amused. "Yes, I promise I won't go traipsing around by myself. You might eventually regret your offer to come with me, though. I still have a lot of ground to cover and it gets pretty boring for onlookers when I go into artist mode. Sarah once said it's like watching paint dry. Probably because it literally is that, sometimes."

Henry dropped his lips to mine in response, kissing me until I set aside the sketchbook and nearly climbed onto his lap.

"I won't regret it, Red," he whispered against my mouth. "Not a single moment."

When I drew back, breathless and flushed, Henry couldn't hold back a grin.

"What are you smirking at, Mr. Walker?" I asked.

"You taste like maple syrup," he said in a low voice that sent goosebumps dancing over my skin.

"Hmm," I murmured, running my tongue across my lower lip in a way that caused his pupils to blow wide. "What a fascinating idea."

Henry's gaze sharpened on my face. I wanted to kiss him, wanted him to sink into me again, right here on the floor. Even with the damn dog looking on, I suspected he would be willing to oblige, if I asked.

Instead, he kissed me again, hard and swift.

"I'm more than happy to participate in whatever dirty thoughts are going through that beautiful head of yours," he said, "but I don't want you to get upset with me for distracting you from the box."

"Right. Let's finish this." I leaned my forehead against his while I caught my breath, then I wrinkled my nose. "Man, am I a terrible person to be thinking about sex while we're sorting through my dead grandmother's belongings?"

Henry's laughter reassured me. "Juliet, I will *never* fault you for thinking about sex around me, no matter what we're doing."

He brushed his lips over mine one last time before I shifted back to my spot beside him and reached into the box. The notebooks were much less interesting—and far less revealing—than the sketches, but we scanned each page for anything pertinent. Mostly they held lists of supply orders, cost comparisons between local stores, and records of repairs to the building and grounds.

With a sigh, I tossed aside the final notebook and stretched my arms over my head. Henry didn't even try to hide his appreciation for the way my breasts strained against the fabric of my shirt as I arched.

"Last stop, file folders." I shot him a warning glance when I noticed where his gaze lingered.

"Yes ma'am," Henry replied, pulling out the small stack of folders.

We each opened one, reading off headings to one another as we sorted through them. I sucked in a sharp breath as I pulled out a document.

"This must be a copy of my grandfather's will."

Henry leaned over to look, then let out a low whistle. "He left Nan a small fortune. I knew she owned the property outright, but I figured she'd just owned it for so long, she'd probably paid off the mortgage over the years. I think his family was pretty well-off, but he had no siblings and his parents died before your mother left town."

I looked at Henry curiously. "The inn makes enough of a profit to stay in operation, though?"

"Oh, yeah," he said, nodding enthusiastically. A glint of pride crept into his eyes. "I only took over full time with the bookkeeping about three years ago, though now I have Nan's remaining responsibilities rolled into my job. She was a damn fine businesswoman. The inn became a popular getaway spot back in the early seventies."

"I should have asked you for a history lesson that first day instead of fighting with you. People still visit in the off-season? I've heard winters can be brutal out here."

Henry grinned. "Oh, they can be, but yes. We're almost always at half-capacity, at least, even during slower times. We host a few small weddings each year, and Nan created different seasonal packages that still sell out every time."

"That seems like a good way to keep people interested. Nan had some entries about weddings in the journals—those must be beautiful, especially with the gardens in bloom."

"Definitely. She never wanted to update the damn website, though. I guess she thought calling for reservations was a nice personal touch, but I've been working on upgrading the site recently. Talking to someone on the phone might be more personal, but for the younger generations, it's just an added aggravation. I want to allow for online booking, even if we hold back some availability for phone reservations."

"That sounds perfect," I agreed, smiling at him.

His enthusiasm charmed me. Then something occurred to me and my smile faded—I watched Henry's expression fall right along with it.

"What would have happened to the inn if Nan hadn't left it to me?" I asked quietly.

"I don't know, actually," he said, frowning a little. "We all assumed it would have been left to your mother, as next of kin—I figure it would have fallen on the lawyers to track her down. Nan changed her will after learning your mother had passed," he added gently, "but I don't know what exactly she changed, apart from naming you as her heir instead of your mother."

I dropped my gaze back to the paper in my lap, nodding silently.

"No one at the inn has any hard feelings toward you, Juliet. They were as delighted to know you were coming out as Nan was when she found your picture. Believe me, I had to sit through a staff meeting about how amazing you would be right before you got here."

I laughed at that. "Then I guess I can't blame you for thinking I was a spoiled little heiress when I came into the office."

"Well, I might have jumped to conclusions."

"Only a few."

He grinned. "I learned my lesson, though."

"Good. This is the last one," I said as I set aside the folder containing Philip Montgomery's will and reached into the box.

Under this file folder was a small metal box fitted with a tiny lock. My eyes flew wide.

"I can go get some tools to break into it," Henry offered.

"No," I said slowly, "I think I have the key."

I reached across him to grab the set Gerard had given me from the side table, then held up the tiny third key to show him. We were both silent as he watched me insert it into the lock. It popped open and I set the lock aside to open the lid.

Henry wrapped his arm around me as we leaned forward to look at its contents together. The box held a number of yellowed local newspaper clippings spanning nearly a decade, from years before and after my mother left town to create a new life a thousand miles away.

I gingerly lifted them one at a time, scanning the front and back of each brittle page. None of the articles were about the inn, my grandmother, or my mom.

"I don't understand," I said finally. "Maybe Nan was running the local conspiracy site I found before I moved here."

Henry huffed a laugh. "Nan is the one who refused to let me update the website. I can't imagine her figuring out how to run one herself."

I opened my mouth to respond, but his finger landed on a headline and he froze.

"Look at this," he whispered, pointing to the tiny print.

Body found during construction on Lakeview Drive.

We read the article in silence. A young woman's body had been unearthed during foundation work in a new subdivision in the early nineties. It was eventually ruled a homicide. Her identity was listed as Lynette Jenkins of Oakville, which I remembered Henry said was the next town over. There were no suspects at the time.

"Lakeview Drive isn't too far from Cooper's Point," he told me.

"Oh my god," I whispered. "That conspiracy site, it had a page about unsolved murders. This must be them."

A chill slithered down my spine at his words. With fresh insight, we flipped back through the other pages and found a number of similar articles—nearly a dozen bodies had been found, all told. A shudder rocketed through me and Henry pulled me onto his lap, wrapping his arms securely around my body.

A matter of life and death. Was this what my mother was referring to in her note?

"What do you think it means?" I asked, my voice muffled against his shoulder. "Why would Nan have kept these—and why would she lock them up?"

Henry only shook his head and held me tight to his chest. Neither of us knew the answer to that, and I wasn't convinced we'd ever find out without Nan there to ask.

Just as I'd assumed my mother's warning was a dramatic exaggeration, I had been damn near certain Henry was overreacting by asking me not to trek through the woods alone, but now? I was no longer sure what to think. Blue must have sensed our discomfort, because she immediately relocated to press her furry body against us both.

A sudden vibration from one of our phones made us both jump. Henry kept one arm around me while he grabbed his from the floor behind him, then he gave a short laugh.

"Libby's inviting us over for dinner tonight," he said. "We don't have to go if you don't want to."

I peered up at him while I considered the offer. Though I was a little shell-shocked in light of our discovery, I felt strangely calm about Libby's invitation. Being nestled in his arms slowed my heart rate for once instead of speeding it up.

We were safe. These crimes were decades old and we had no reason to truly believe anyone was at any real risk. Even if my mother was right about it being dangerous at the time, that was three decades ago.

"I don't think this day could possibly get any weirder than it already is, so yes, let's do it."

Henry kissed the tip of my nose and cocked an eyebrow. "By 'do it,' you mean go to dinner, not get naked," he clarified.

The words sent twin streaks of heat through my body, one straight to my heart and the other between my legs. I poked him in the chest.

"Cad," I teased, remembering his comment about Nan loving that word, but his fingers were running lightly over my arm in a way that promised he'd be happy to deliver. The temptation of forgetting about these stupid articles proved irresistible, so I caught his earlobe between my teeth. "But why not both?"

His eyes went dark with desire and he fired off a response to Libby as succinctly as possible before tossing the phone aside.

"Your wish is my command," he said with a smirk.

The sketch, the headlines, every real or imagined threat—it all fell away as Henry set about distracting me as thoroughly as he could manage.

Twenty-Three

HENRY

WHEN JULIET FINALLY INSISTED she needed to shower and get ready for dinner with Libby and Mark instead of lounging naked in bed, I groaned with genuine reluctance. Watching her stroll through the room, glorious in her nudity, as she gathered an armful of clothes from the closet and headed toward the bathroom was only a small consolation.

Once she was out of sight, I leaned back on the pillows and closed my eyes. All I wanted to do was spend my days with her: next to her, over and under her, inside of her. Any of those would satisfy me, but I wanted it all.

It was intensely rewarding and more than a little amusing that I was able to distract her so easily, take her mind off things with just a touch of my mouth or a sweep of my hand. I wasn't usually the jealous type, as evidenced by my heartfelt support of Libby and Mark's relationship, but I imagined that her idiot ex hadn't possessed this particular ability when it came to Juliet Morrison.

My smugness was immediately dampened by the reminder that she'd not only had to deal with her own grief at the time, but also a selfish, oblivious boyfriend.

I shoved the thought aside and wondered why the hell I'd agreed to this dinner instead of spending the rest of the day and night in bed with Juliet, but I finally rolled to my feet so I could pull on my jeans. My shirt was nowhere in sight, so I strolled out of the bedroom to check the couch.

Along the way, I popped my head in through the open bathroom door and found Juliet applying mascara. She wore black leggings and a silky blue blouse that made my fingers itch to touch her, to see if the fabric was as soft as the skin underneath.

Pausing with the mascara wand aloft in front of her face, she gave a slow perusal of my bare torso in the mirror.

"I didn't realize dinner was clothing optional," she teased, but there was no mistaking the appreciation shining in those brilliant blue eyes.

I moved to stand behind her, setting my hands on her hips. My thumbs slipped under the hem of her blouse and I gave a slow smile when she shivered at the brush of my fingers.

"You look incredible," I murmured against her ear. "Good enough to eat."

Her cheeks colored, but instead of shooing me away, she closed the tube of makeup, turned, and ran her hands over my chest.

"As much as I like this look, I'm not sure your ex-wife's current husband will appreciate you flaunting all that muscle. If he cuts off your soap supply, you'll need to find a new reason for me to nuzzle you all the time."

"Party-pooper."

I kissed her freshly-glossed lips before trudging to the living room to locate my shirt. Somehow, it had ended up wedged between the couch cushions. I pulled it on and gave Blue a quick belly rub.

"C'mon, I'll take you out while the lady does her thing."

Before opening the back door, I peeked out through the sheer curtains, but the yard lay still and silent. For the briefest moment, I wondered if I'd only imagined that flash of movement earlier, but I would take no chances when it came to Juliet.

I stepped out into the afternoon sun, watching Blue as she pranced across the lawn to explore new scents. Casually slipping my hands into my pockets, I wandered up the side of the yard nearest the woods. The only sounds were birdsong and some occasional snuffling from Blue as she joined me to investigate.

Though I wasn't completely sure what I'd hoped to find, I saw nothing that screamed lurker to me, no footprints or cigarette butts or anything the movies suggested might signify a threatening presence.

Once Blue and I had scoured the area where I thought I saw movement, I turned back to the house to judge the distance.

"Smell anything, girl?" Blue sniffed at a few trees but trotted calmly back to my side after another minute, prompting me to mutter, "Should've gotten a bloodhound."

Just as I turned back to the cottage, though, my gaze caught on a tree trunk sporting deep gouges in the bark. I moved closer, running my fingers over the lines. It was the letter M, but it looked like an old mark, worn into the rough surface.

"What the hell?"

Standing by the marked tree, I looked back across the lawn and watched as the lacy curtains in Juliet's bedroom shifted in the breeze. The thought of someone standing here while we were inside the cottage—while we were in her bed—filled me with twin bursts of nausea and fury. We'd kept the lights off, as far as I could recall, so there was only a slim chance of seeing much from here.

Shit, I didn't want to scare her, not when I couldn't be sure the marks weren't from as far back as her mother's childhood. Maybe I'd just make sure we replaced those curtains sooner instead of later.

"Weird," I muttered.

Blue cocked her head at me, then she nosed at the base of the tree and I spotted a piece of paper half-buried under the weeds.

I picked it up by the corner, shaking off bits of leaf and dirt to reveal thick, fancy paper with swirling cursive across it.

My dearest Juliet.

It was the note from her mother, the one she thought she'd lost. I glanced back toward the cottage, its tidy garbage cans outside the back door. Their covers fit snugly to deter animals from rifling through them, but it was possible the note had blown across the yard when she took out the trash.

Blue and I returned to the house to find Juliet waiting in the doorway, looking impossibly beautiful. The blouse flattered every lush curve and its pale blue shade turned her eyes the same vibrant cerulean as the afternoon sky. Her hair was drawn up and back, with curling wisps around her face.

"Find anything?" she asked.

"Looks like maybe your mom scratched her initials on a tree when she was a kid," I replied. "Oh, and this."

I handed her the note and watched those blue eyes immediately fill with tears. She smoothed it out, brushing a smudge of dirt from the paper, then clasped it to her chest.

"I can't believe it was out there all this time. Thank you."

"Of course," I said gently. "I didn't spot anything else outside, but I'm definitely glad you're so obsessed with locking the doors."

Juliet gasped in mock outrage, but when she jokingly moved to flounce away, I caught her around the waist, swung her into my arms, and kissed her, a light, teasing graze of my lips across hers. As I'd hoped, her hand immediately slipped around the back of my neck to draw me down for more.

When we finally parted, I took great pleasure in studying that sweet, dazed look in her eyes. Juliet blinked it slowly away, like she was waking from a particularly pleasant dream. I kissed the tip of her nose and set the letter on the counter, then bolted the back door and took her hand as we headed to the front of the house.

"We can park at my place," I said, watching as she locked it with her key. "I'll get changed and we can walk over."

"You live that close to them?" Her eyebrows arched upward, then her mouth dropped open in horror. "I didn't mean for that to sound so clingy. I'm just curious, I swear."

I grinned at the way the words tumbled from her lips, enjoying the tiny hint of jealousy that colored the question. "Relax, Red. Yes, they live across the street."

"Not a single one of my past relationships ended well enough to stay friends. Then again, I guess none of them started with friendship, either. It's probably a good thing none of them live nearby."

"I had an apartment in town for a while, but my parents sold me their house when they got the RV. When they're done traveling, they're planning to downsize. Libby and Mark bought a house across the street when they got married, maybe four, five years ago now? I was their best man. I look pretty damn good in a tux, in case you wondered."

"I did wonder, actually. It was an important consideration before I allowed you to rescue me in the woods," she replied.

I laughed as I opened the door of the truck for Blue to jump in, but I caught Juliet around the waist before she followed. She smirked at me for a second, then rose on her tiptoes to kiss me.

From up close, I watched her eyelids float down just before her mouth opened under mine and her body softened against my chest.

When we finally drew apart, I brushed the tip of my nose against hers and winked, then gave her a hand to help her climb up into the truck. Once I was in the driver's seat with Blue wedged between us, Juliet grinned over at me.

"I do truly look forward to seeing firsthand this fascinating triangle you guys have going," she said earnestly. "The evening promises to be quite illuminating."

I shook my head. "I guarantee you it isn't as interesting as it sounds. We're all just friends."

"Friends who used to be married but aren't anymore, plus friends who used to not be married but now are, plus friends who just spent a night and the better part of the day in bed together?"

"That sounds about right."

Her laughter filled the cab and I stopped wondering why I'd agreed to dinner at Libby's. Juliet had been alone for too long. She needed to feel like she belonged in Spruce Hill, because she *did* belong here.

When we reached my house, her eyebrows rose once more. It was a quiet neighborhood close to the center of town, and the house was much like the other old Victorian homes found nearby. The siding was a soothing sage, with darker green shutters and tiny rose-pink accents along the scrolling woodwork.

"Oh my god," she whispered.

I parked the truck and cocked my head at the house. It had been a long time since I'd tried to look at it objectively. Even when I moved back in, the lingering traces of my childhood had kept me from noticing much beyond glaring spots that needed repair.

"The pink's a little girly, I guess, but it didn't seem worth changing. I'm comfortable in my masculinity."

"Henry," she breathed, "it's not girly. It's amazing. Would you mind...can I take some pictures? I already sketched both the cottage and the inn, but this house, this is the embodiment of Spruce Hill in my mind. I want to turn it into art."

I smiled indulgently at her excited tone. "Well then, be my guest. Do you want to come in while I get changed or are you too enamored with the exterior for that?"

"If you think I'd miss out on the opportunity to see inside, you're sadly mistaken," she informed me, but she snapped more than a few pictures with her phone before we entered the house.

The interior was apparently just as captivating as the outside, if Juliet's crooning appreciation for the dark woodwork, so carefully maintained over the years, was anything to go by. I left her to investigate the array of family photos decorating the mantle and hanging by the stairs while I gave Blue dinner.

Juliet was still admiring the pictures after I ran upstairs to grab a quick shower and change into a crisp gray button-down shirt with a clean pair of jeans. I came up behind her, fastening buttons as I peered over her shoulder.

"Is this you and your brother?" she asked, trailing her fingertips across a pewter frame.

"Yeah, that's Aaron," I said fondly. "He works with Libby and I'm sure she'll tell him all about dinner tonight, so expect another invitation to be coming our way. He and his husband don't like to be outdone when it comes to social gatherings."

Juliet's gaze lingered on the picture for another moment, then she turned and gave a low whistle, sweeping her gaze over me from head to toe.

"You were right. You do clean up well, Mr. Walker."

I winked at her, then offered my arm. "Ready?"

"Let's hope so," she replied, slipping her arm through mine.

Leaving Blue with her favorite stuffed octopus for company, we crossed the street and made our way to Libby and Mark's place. It wasn't quite as elegant as my parents' Victorian, but the house was well-kept, cozy and loved. Flower boxes in the front windows overflowed with blossoms, adding a splash of bold color against the pale yellow siding.

Juliet slipped her phone from her pocket and snapped a few photos before grinning sheepishly up at me. I only smiled, enjoying the opportunity to witness her excitement. Somehow, I'd known she wouldn't be swayed by elegance, focusing instead on the loving little touches, the evidence of warmth.

I led the way to a side door instead of the front and let us in without bothering to ring the bell or knock.

"Anybody home?" I called as I kicked off my shoes in the mudroom.

Juliet slipped hers off as well, then scowled at me when I laughed at her rainbow striped socks.

"I was distracted," she hissed under her breath.

"Yes, come on in," Libby called from the next room. "Mark's out back grilling some sides, I'm just getting dinner out of the oven."

The mudroom led to a beautiful kitchen, well-lit and perfectly appointed. Juliet's gaze went straight to the high-end appliance in question.

"I never knew stove-envy was a thing, but apparently I have it."

Libby laughed and set a casserole on the kitchen island, then wrapped Juliet in a warm hug. I snickered when her eyes widened in shock.

"I forgot to tell you, she's a hugger," I whispered loudly.

Juliet glared at me, but she awkwardly patted Libby's back. "Thank you for having us."

When Libby drew away, she held onto Juliet's shoulders and studied her forehead closely. "That's healed up nicely. I hope you've been resting that knee?"

Juliet flushed scarlet under the fluorescent kitchen lights, clearly thinking about all the things she'd done on her knees in the past twenty-four hours. I burst out laughing, so Libby turned and whacked me with an oven mitt.

"Nevermind, I don't need the details," she sang out. "Henry, why don't you go help Mark outside?"

Juliet turned her face to me in a silent plea not to leave her alone while Libby's back was turned, but I winked at her, pulled my shoes back on, and headed toward the yard. Mark stood at the grill, wearing sunglasses and humming along to the music streaming from his phone. He turned when the screen door closed behind me.

"Hey, man." He reached over to grab me around the neck and dragged me in for a hug. "It's about time I finally get to meet your lady, you jerk. What's taken so long?"

I scrubbed a hand over my face, realizing I still hadn't shaved. Juliet seemed to like the scruff, so maybe I'd leave it—she certainly liked it when I ran that roughness along the inside of her lovely thighs. With Mark still studying me, I forced the image from my mind and gave a shrug.

"I've been helping her sort through Nan's boxes after work," I said simply.

Mark slid his glasses down his nose to look at me. "I have to call bullshit on that one, buddy. I know what happiness looks like on you. It's been too long since I've seen it."

It was true; I *was* happy, and I couldn't remember when I'd last felt like this. Not for the first time, a knot of emotion lodged in my throat when I thought about how lucky I was to still have such good friends in Mark and Libby. I didn't regret much in my life, but if my failed marriage had led to losing the two of them, I wasn't sure I could have handled that.

"She's...special. And I almost ruined my chance with her before we even knew each other."

"Almost doesn't matter, man. You're with her now. Don't blow it, yeah?"

"I'll do my damnedest," I replied.

He studied my face for another moment, then said, "What else is up?"

In a quiet tone, I gave him a rundown about the news articles Nan had hidden away, the incident at Cooper's Point, my odd experience that morning at the cottage, and the gouges I'd found in that tree. Mark was an avid historian and eager to help dig into the events surrounding Melissa's departure from Spruce Hill—and he was more than willing to recruit others from our small circle of friends to keep an eye out for any strange happenings around town.

I felt a hundred pounds lighter knowing that Juliet would have other people looking out for her, as well.

"Libby was pretty taken with her," Mark offered, "and, of course, with your knight in shining armor routine. You should have heard her gushing about it. Hell, man, if you were any other guy, I would've punched you right in the balls. Good thing I know I'm better in the sack."

I put my arm around Mark's shoulders, then wrangled him into a headlock. "Punched me, huh? You could have tried."

After a few minutes of tussling, I caught sight of Juliet through the big bay window of the dining room and lost my train of thought. Mark followed my gaze, chuckled, and shook his head in amusement. Of course, he then used my distraction to reverse our positions, dropping me to my knees with his forearm around my throat. As long as Juliet was in view, I was willing to cede the high ground.

"Damn, bro, you've got it bad," he muttered.

"I've never met anyone like her," I replied. It was both that simple and that complex.

Through the window, we watched as Juliet focused on placing the plates and napkins just so, then on repositioning the flowers in a vase at the center of the table.

My beautiful artist, I thought with a surge of affection.

Mark was absolutely right. I had it bad.

Twenty-Four

JULIET

As soon as Henry left the kitchen, Libby turned to give me an apologetic smile.

"Oh honey, I'm so sorry," she whispered, taking my hands in hers. "I swear I didn't mean to embarrass you. Henry's sense of humor hasn't changed since he was twelve years old. I should've waited for him to leave the room before I said anything that could be twisted into a dirty joke."

In my wildest dreams, I would never have imagined I'd be standing in a kitchen while my lover's ex-wife apologized for an unintended innuendo.

"Please, it's fine," I insisted, hoping the color in my cheeks was fading.

"I don't want things to be awkward between us. I haven't seen Henry this happy in a long, long time," Libby confessed.

She squeezed my hands once more before she moved to fuss over dinner. As I stood there, I chewed on that statement, realizing I hadn't been this happy in a long time either. I hovered awkwardly as I watched her slice into a loaf of fresh bread that smelled divine.

"Can I help with anything?"

Libby's smile hit me like a beam of sunlight. "The plates are on the counter, if you wouldn't mind bringing them to the dining room? It's just through there."

With a task to occupy my hands and take my mind off my nerves, I set the table. Though I tried not to think about the fact that Henry and Libby had once been married, I was buzzing with curiosity about their history.

When I glanced out the big window at the back of the house, Henry and Mark were wrestling in the grass behind the grill and I abandoned my task to watch them.

I recognized Mark as one of the men who'd been talking to Henry outside The Mermaid that night and wondered if Henry told him how I threatened to break his hand. With sun-streaked blonde hair and a physique to rival Henry's, Mark looked more like a surfer than someone who made bath and body products.

From all I'd heard from Henry, the two of them were as close as Henry was to his brother. Seeing them together, laughing in the midst of their roughhousing, I could almost feel it.

I'd always wondered what it would be like to have a sibling. For years, I begged my mother for a baby brother or sister, well before I understood the particulars of such a request. My mother always replied that we were a team, a dynamic duo, and vowed we would take on the world together.

Absently, I rubbed at the twinge under my breastbone as I continued to spy on Henry and Mark horsing around in the grass.

They grappled for several minutes, jostling to bring the other down like they were on an elementary school playground, until Libby poked her head in to fetch me. I followed her to the back hall, where she cleared her throat from the doorway. She stood there, arms crossed, watching them with amusement as both men shot upright and Mark saluted.

"Juliet, this is Mark Davies. Mark, Juliet," Henry said, elbowing his friend in the ribs when Libby wasn't looking.

"If you boys are finished wrestling, dinner is ready," she informed them. "Are those vegetables done or were you too busy for that?"

"Grilled vegetables, check," Mark said, then offered his hand to me with a broad, friendly smile. "It's a pleasure to meet you, Juliet."

Stepping forward, I shook it and couldn't help but smile back. I shot a curious glance at Henry, who now looked a tad ruffled and even sexier than usual. He winked at me.

"Thank you for having us. Sorry to interrupt your...uh, whatever this was," I said, gesturing between the two men.

Henry hopped up the stairs, slipping his arm around my waist as we moved to the dining room. When Mark pulled

Libby into his arms for a long, passionate kiss, Henry leaned in close to my cheek and whispered, "Show-offs."

Though I shivered as his breath tickled my ear, I rolled my eyes and shot him a smile.

The meal was delicious and so devoid of awkwardness that I was both amazed and humbled by the acceptance these people offered me. Since my mother's death, Sarah and Andre had forced me to go out with them more times than I could count, determined not to let me wallow in my grief, but it was never even close to as comfortable as this.

Bless her, Sarah had tried her hardest. I just always felt like someone on the outside looking in, a third wheel left out in the cold.

This evening was completely different. All three of them directed conversation toward me, making me feel totally included, fully immersed instead of lingering at the outer edges. It was enough to make my chest swell with emotion, so much so that I was afraid I might embarrass myself by bursting into tears.

As though he could see straight into my heart, Henry found regular excuses to touch my arm or my hair. The soft, comforting caresses settled me. When he set his hand on my knee under the tablecloth, though, he ignored the glare I shot in his direction. He smiled with wide-eyed innocence even as he stroked his fingers along the inside of my thigh.

"You know, we have a little hiking group that gets together on weekends. You're welcome to join us if you're interested in seeing more of the area," Mark said, distracting me from Henry's fingertips. "Henry and Blue come out sometimes."

"That's sweet of you, but I'll probably avoid forests for a while longer," I joked.

Henry grinned at me and said, "Well, if you change your mind, there'd be half a dozen people out there to keep you from falling down any hills. Safety in numbers, you know."

"Stop teasing her, boys," Libby ordered. "Juliet, I want to hear about your artwork. Nan showed everyone in town the article about your award. You're very talented."

Though I tried to demur, the three of them worked together to gently draw me out. Henry gushed about what he'd seen in my sketchbook, gazing over at me with an expression both sweet and soft.

Once I started sharing such a vital part of myself, I discovered how rewarding it could be to let them in. An unfamiliar feeling of contentment spread through my chest.

At the end of the meal, Mark and Henry rose to clear the table, leaving me and Libby sipping a local wine that I vowed to buy for myself as soon as possible. They returned from the kitchen with a beautiful fruit tart for dessert.

"Mark made it," Libby said with a conspiratorial wink. "I freely admit that I married him for his pastry skills, though Henry's a decent enough cook."

"This is true. She loves me for my desserts." With a laugh, Mark leaned down and kissed the side of his wife's neck before serving us each a slice.

"So you make pastries as well as soaps?" I ventured.

Mark's grin widened. "Yes, did Henry tell you about the shop? You should come in sometime."

"She's totally obsessed with how amazing I smell," Henry said as he slung his arm across the back of my chair. "I probably should have let her believe it was just my own manly essence."

Though I narrowed my eyes at him, I then smiled brightly at Mark. "Clearly, it's all thanks to you and has nothing to do with this oaf."

Mark and Libby burst out laughing. Henry grinned and tugged playfully on a lock of my hair.

"Oh," Mark said, waving his fork toward me, "I like you, Juliet. Stick around, would you? We need someone who can keep Henry in line, knock him down a peg when he gets too puffed up."

I let the sheer joy of companionship float over me. When I glanced over at Henry, I saw that soft look in his eyes and all of the broken pieces inside me finally slid into place.

This was home. This was *belonging*.

Now that I'd found it, I didn't think I'd ever be able to give it up.

Twenty-Five

HENRY

A T THE END OF the night, both Mark and Libby pulled Juliet into a tight embrace. I didn't miss the sheen of tears brightening her eyes, nor the way she clung to them both in return. What a contrast to her obvious uncertainty upon our arrival.

I could get used to this, this little circle of friendship.

They'd taken to Juliet as quickly as I had—or at least, after our first few meetings. Both of them hugged me as well before Libby released us with an invitation for a cookout the following weekend. With Juliet's hand tucked in the crook of my elbow, we strolled back toward my house just as twilight fell over the neighborhood.

"So," I prompted softly, "what did you think of them?"

"They're amazing. They both love you so much, I could feel it. You were right when you said you're all just friends. I don't know how you three pulled that off, but clearly, you did."

The soft, happy sigh that slipped from her lips filled me with joy. When she glanced up at me, I thought I caught the glimmer of tears in her eyes again, but a radiant smile lit her face. Something warm curled through my chest as I gently brushed a fingertip along her cheek.

"I love them, too," I said. "I know it might be weird, the three of us staying so close through all of this, but Libby and I realized pretty damn quickly that loving someone doesn't necessarily mean you're in love with them. They're part of my family, both of them. I just wish we'd realized sooner that Mark was the one destined to be with Libby. Maybe it would've saved us all some heartache."

Her hand squeezed my arm and she leaned her head against my shoulder as we headed up the path to my front porch.

"They're both lucky to have you."

I stopped, turned her to face me, and kissed her. It was a gentle meeting of lips, but imbued with all the emotion I could pour into it. It was clear Juliet felt it, drank it in, as she clung to me until we came up for breath.

"I feel like the lucky one," I whispered, pressing my lips to her forehead. "Will you stay here with me tonight?"

It was odd, the fact that this seemed like a precipice, a milestone. I'd already slept at the cottage, if one could call our night spent together *sleeping*. Having her beside me made everything better, brighter somehow.

She nodded, then a mischievous smile tugged at her lips and she said, "I didn't bring any pajamas, though."

I laughed, kissing her again before I unlocked the door. Blue greeted us joyously, practically dancing all the way to the back door so I could let her into the fenced yard. Though I was less unsettled after talking to Mark about the situation, I still flipped on the outside lights and lingered near the door where I could watch the dog as she inspected the yard. Even after a visit from Mark or Libby, Blue would trail intently through the area to sniff out their paths, but tonight she simply trotted to her favorite patch of grass.

I took that as a sign that no one had been poking around in my yard, at least. Juliet followed closely behind me, her attention on the kitchen I'd renovated the year before.

"I'm starting to feel a little slighted by all these amazing appliances," she grumbled.

"You're welcome to stay over whenever you want. I'm sure we can work out some kind of mutually beneficial...arrangement," I offered, then lifted a teasing brow.

Before she could respond, I twined my arm around her waist and buried my face in her neck. Juliet shrieked with laughter when I blew a raspberry against her skin as I tickled her ribs. Those blue eyes twinkled up at me when I finally lifted my head.

"Why, Ms. Morrison, I do believe you're ticklish," I said, grinning.

"Extremely," she agreed readily, "and prone toward violent responses, so you might want to watch it. The last guy who tickled me got kneed in the balls so hard he cried."

As she probably intended, the comment made me flinch. I nodded solemnly. "Right, no tickling. That's fine, there are plenty of better things I can do with my hands."

Juliet snorted, but before she could reply, Blue came bounding back across the deck to the door. Once she was inside, I turned off the lights, locked the door, and pulled Juliet into my arms. Though I didn't remember quite how it happened, we ended up in the hallway upstairs, flushed and breathless, fumbling with one another's buttons. I nudged open the door to my bedroom and Juliet peeked around me, taking in the decor.

"Was this your parents' room?" she asked.

I could tell she was trying not to sound weirded out by the idea, but she'd told me that part of the reason she decided to sell her childhood home instead of moving in permanently was the way she felt her mother's presence every time she passed through a room, suffocated by the memories of a lifetime spent there together.

It had been difficult to imagine being comfortable bringing a lover into the master bedroom here at first, but my parents weren't dead, just traveling. One of the first things I did upon taking ownership was to make this room my own.

"Yes, but I remodeled it completely so that I'd have no qualms about seducing the hot redheads I hoped to bring home," I informed her, finishing my own buttons so I could toss the shirt aside.

"Seducing, huh?"

Her expression turned sultry and I wanted to tear that damn silk blouse right off her body—except the color looked so good on her, I couldn't bear to ruin it. Her fingers toyed with the next button as I stalked toward her.

"Oh, yes," I breathed, pressing her back against the wall.

My mouth covered hers, savoring the taste of her, tinged with the sweetness of Mark's fruit tart. I finally managed to unbutton her blouse so I could peel the blue silk away, revealing even softer flesh beneath it.

When my hands began a slow, thorough exploration of her skin, Juliet sighed against my lips.

"You were right," she said huskily, dropping her head back against the wall.

"About what?"

I lifted my head and stared at her blankly. With a captivating twinkle in her eye, she tangled her fingers in my hair and kissed me, hard and deep. Once I lost track of whatever we'd been saying, she drew back, her words whispering across my lips.

"There are plenty of better things you can do with your hands."

Twenty-Six

JULIET

WAKING UP IN HENRY's bed filled my sleepy mind with images of the beach. I inhaled deeply, letting the scent of his skin—deliciously male, mixed with a lingering trace of that amazing soap—fill my lungs. When I finally dragged my eyes open, he was lying on his side, watching me with a half smile tugging at his lips.

"That's a little creepy," I informed him. Though I tried for a scowl, I failed miserably, too content to pull it off.

Henry just grinned. "It's only been a minute or two. I figured you must be waking up, since you started smiling like that."

"I like waking up with you, what can I say?" I rolled to face him and tucked my hands under my cheek.

"The feeling is mutual," he said, reaching over to brush a lock of hair off my face. "You are absolutely breathtaking."

His tone was low and sweet and it sent a wave of pleasure crashing over me. Then his fingers trailed down my bare shoulder, causing my breath to catch in my throat. Through the cotton sheet covering my breasts, he traced lazy circles around one nipple until my eyes fell shut again under the onslaught.

"So amazingly beautiful, not to mention courageous, talented, and passionate," he murmured, just as I pushed him onto his back to straddle his hips.

"You shouldn't start something if you don't intend to finish it," I warned, then covered his lips with my own.

Henry's hands gripped my hips as I rocked just enough to coax a groan from his throat. Once I released his mouth to raise a brow in challenge, he grinned and rolled us so his long body was stretched over me.

"Oh, I plan to finish it," he promised, reaching for a condom from the drawer in his nightstand before settling back beside me.

His lips trailed over my skin, gossamer light, finally closing over one peaked nipple as he sank two fingers inside me.

"Henry," I gasped, needing more.

Needing him.

"Juliet," he murmured into the crook of my neck, then his fingers moved away, circling my clit one final time before his hips took the place of his hand and he thrust home.

My head fell back on a sigh. Every movement was dreamlike, slow and drowsy in a way that made me feel like we were still only half-awake. The pace he set matched that sleepy haze around us, unhurried even when the depth and stretch of him filling me over and over again had me whimpering into his kiss, shifting my hips to spur him on.

He held out, resisting my attempts as amusement sparked in his eyes. Finally, when I was ready to beg, he nipped at my lower lip and lifted my knee higher, stroking deep inside.

I moaned, arching into every thrust. He rolled my nipple between his fingers until I clenched around his cock, then his hoarse groan melded with mine and he dropped his hand between us, circling his thumb at that same lazy pace.

God, those hands.

The orgasm crashed over me without warning, tightening every muscle in my body until Henry swore aloud and his thrusts grew frantic, each one prolonging the waves of my release. Then, with my name on his lips, he growled into my neck and shuddered through his own while I clung to him with all four of my limbs.

Time became irrelevant when I was with him. I had no idea how many meals we might've missed, whether days had passed or only hours. This boneless contentment was entirely foreign to me—and I was fairly certain I could get used to it without any trouble at all.

At some point later in the morning, I was vaguely aware that Henry had slipped out of bed to let Blue out and give the dog breakfast, but once he was back at my side, I was altogether happy to forget everything but him.

"I think you might be a bad influence," I said at one point.

He merely smirked in response and countered, "I think maybe you're the bad influence."

"Interesting theory."

It sent an odd thrill through me, realizing that I was having the same intoxicating effect on him that he had on me.

"Since you've clearly proven that your knee has recovered," Henry said with a grin, "I wondered if you wanted to go see my actual favorite place today?"

"Is it as interesting as this?" I asked, pretending to consider as I paused in my exploration of the planes of his chest to lift a brow.

When I remembered he'd mentioned bringing my camera and sketchbook, all pretense evaporated.

"Yes, I do want to see it," I said eagerly. "Can we stop at the cottage for my stuff?"

Henry grinned at my excitement and kissed me once more before answering.

"Of course. I'll drop Blue off with Mark while you get dressed." His eyes landed on where my blouse lay draped over a lampshade. "Assuming you can find all of your clothes."

While he threw on jeans and a fresh tee, I rose to the challenge, searching the room for undergarments that had been hastily discarded the night before. Henry was gone and back by the time I came downstairs, my clothes rumpled enough that his eyes heated. He handed me a sandwich, which I scarfed down in record time.

I lifted my chin when his broad, knowing smirk sent heat to my cheeks. "What? I worked up an appetite," I said primly.

He only shook his head and kept on grinning at me as we left the house.

When we reached the cottage, I changed into clean clothes, then shoved my camera and sketchbook into my backpack. After a bare second of hesitation, I discreetly added another change of clothes to the bag, just in case, while Henry checked the backyard again.

I tossed the backpack over my shoulder and returned to the kitchen, watching him through the window. The day was still and silent, without a trace of anything—or any-one—near the cottage.

He smiled at me when he came back in. "Ready to roll?"

"Yes. Where exactly are we going?" I asked as he looped the backpack over his shoulder and took my hand.

"Patience, Red. It's a surprise. Believe me, you're going to love it."

He kissed me quickly and led me out the back door instead of the front. My brows shot up in surprise. The fact that he paused to lock the door behind us managed to tarnish the haze of contentment around me, but only a little. Together, we cut across the yard, heading into the woods along a tiny trail close to the lake.

"You didn't bring your fanny pack," I teased. "What if I need first aid again?"

Henry snorted. "I'm hoping my presence is enough to keep you from falling down any hills today. If you stumble, though, feel free to grab onto me."

"My hero," I replied, leaning my head against his shoulder.

The trickle of sunlight through the branches overhead gave the world a glorious glow of green and gold, reminding me of his eyes. The trail here was easy to navigate and, fortunately for me, mostly flat.

After several quiet minutes, the path narrowed a bit as the forest grew more dense around us. Henry took advantage of the opportunity to tug me closer against his side, but he didn't speak. He'd watched me sketch enough times that he knew when my mind was tangled up in art. I was busy studying each color and texture as we picked our way between the trees.

The only sign that we were almost to our destination was his careful attention on my face when the path opened to a clearing. I gasped aloud as the utter enchantment of the place washed over me.

"Oh," I breathed, moving to the center of the clearing and turning in a slow circle. My tone was hushed, my body alight with wonder. "What is this?"

"This was Nan's special hideaway. Toward the end, she couldn't make it out here herself and asked me to take care of it for her."

He lifted a finger to twirl one of the dozens of windchimes hung from the branches above us. Suncatchers danced and glittered on the breeze, sending rainbow streaks of color across the ground. At the far edge of the clearing, the trees parted just enough to give a glimpse of the lake beyond.

"Oh, Henry," I said, my chest tight with emotion. "Thank you for bringing me here. This is perfect. I've never seen anything like it."

With a patient smile, he slipped the backpack from his shoulders and handed it to me, then sat on the ground with his back against a tall oak tree. There was a curved wrought-iron bench wrapped around a tree across the clearing, but I'd already zeroed in on it. I figured the ground was probably more comfortable anyway once I moved closer to inspect the bench.

"Take your time, Red, just let me know if you need me to move out of your shot."

I barely even heard the words, though I nodded absently. This was even better than the day he brought me to the lake. I couldn't stop smiling as I took it all in, as I basked in the beauty of this magical setting. Surrounded by nature, with the play of color from the suncatchers dancing over my skin, I felt like a wood nymph or a sprite of some kind.

I lost track of time as I tried to capture every nuance of the clearing, both in my mind and on camera. Henry had closed his eyes and leaned his head back against the tree, so I snapped a few covert photos of him as well. He looked scruffy and a little dangerous in his black tee and jeans, a fascinating contrast to the rainbows and windchimes dancing above him.

When I had at last absorbed my fill and gotten photos and sketches from every angle imaginable, I said as casually as possible, "You mentioned you'd pose nude for me, so I'm thinking that bench would be a good spot. Why don't you get undressed?"

As expected, Henry's eyes flew open in mock horror.

"You little imp," he growled as I laughed and danced out of reach. Instead of rising to his feet to chase after me, he held out a hand from where he sat. "Come here. I dare you."

Cocking a brow, I tucked the camera back into my bag and warily approached him. I took his outstretched hand and he tugged until I tumbled onto his lap, laughing breathlessly. When his arms locked around me and his lips feathered across my ear, my laughter faded into a whispered sigh. There was no mistaking the shiver that went through me.

"Someday, I'll bring you back here and make love to you right over there," he whispered, his voice husky with promise. "With all those rainbows dancing over your body and the chimes echoing every cry of pleasure."

Distracted as I was by both his words and his lips against my skin, I almost asked why not today—then I remembered my promise not to go out hiking alone, the events that led to that particular promise, and my mother's warning.

A matter of life and death.

No matter how calm he'd tried to sound the day before, Henry thought someone had been outside the cottage, watching. Waiting. He'd trusted my certainty that I heard a gunshot at Cooper's Point, and I trusted his belief there might be some danger out there. My head fell back against his shoulder.

"Someday better be soon," I grumbled.

He laughed softly and dropped his lips to the pulse below my jaw, which jumped beneath the caress. His teeth grazed my shoulder and I sighed, blinking up at him.

"It will be soon, if I have anything to say about it," he promised, "but in the meantime, what do you say we head back to my house? We can while away the afternoon, order some dinner, maybe track down some...dessert?"

"I'd say that sounds like heaven," I murmured.

I kissed him swiftly before I rose to my feet and offered him my hand. A slow, incandescent smile lit his face as he clasped it.

"Then let's go home."

Twenty-Seven

HENRY

WATCHING JULIET'S CAUTIOUS PROGRESS toward being comfortable with a serious relationship was far more rewarding than I ever expected. Day by day, she softened, opening up to me by slow degrees. Sometimes she would visit me at the inn, bringing a tote bag full of Nan's journals to peruse as she curled up in a chair in the corner of my office.

Those were some of my favorite afternoons—the quiet comfort of her company, the little smile that played across her lips at Nan's sharp commentary, the way her eyes lifted to meet mine over the top of a leatherbound book, twinkling with amusement whenever she caught me staring.

We talked about her plans to start painting in the garden next week, ventured into Mark's shop to sniff every bar of soap he had for sale, held hands as we wandered down Main Street with ice cream cones. I replaced the curtains in her bedroom, but it didn't matter much, since she spent her nights in my bed.

Even though she was no closer to uncovering her father's identity or her mother's reason for leaving town, Juliet seemed happy.

I knew I was—blissfully, exquisitely happy.

She was so easy to be with, such a startling contrast to our first couple meetings. Or maybe *because* it was such a contrast, it became a soothing balm against those sparks that had threatened to burn us both before they took on an entirely different kind of heat.

While she clearly enjoyed every moment we spent together, she confessed one night that she still worried. She blamed it on her mother's note, planting the prospect of danger in her mind, so she couldn't help but feel like she was waiting for the other shoe to drop.

Toward the end of the week, just after three-thirty in the morning, it finally did.

We awoke to the insistent buzzing of my phone, still tucked in the pocket of my jeans where they'd been thrown to the floor in a rush the night before. Juliet murmured sleepily against my shoulder and I pressed a kiss to her temple before slipping out of bed to locate the phone.

The buzzing stopped just as I read my grandfather's name on the screen, then started up again when he called back a second time. Expecting the worst, I answered it.

"Gramps, what is it?" I asked, my voice low.

Panic seeped through me, alleviated only slightly by the sound of his voice on the other end. My eyes shot to Juliet as I listened. She sat up, wrapping the sheet around her bare torso. With the phone tucked between my ear and shoulder, I pulled on my jeans, then knelt on the bed to cup her face in my hands.

"Yes, she's here with me. We'll be right over. Thanks, Gramps."

"What happened?" she asked, all trace of sleep replaced by sudden tension as her eyes widened with panic.

"There's a fire at the cottage," I said gently. "One of the guests at the inn saw the smoke. I don't know how much damage there is, but Gramps wanted to make sure you weren't inside. The fire department is already there."

Juliet drew back from my hands, her eyebrows angled down in confusion as she struggled to make sense of the words.

"The cottage," she whispered. "Oh, no."

In the next instant, she scrambled off the bed to pull on the clothes we'd scattered throughout the bedroom. All those boxes of memories, the old pictures on the mantle, Nan's beautiful painting in the bedroom—I saw Juliet fighting back waves of grief that had her hands trembling as she dressed.

I wasn't sure if any of it could be saved. My own heart broke at the potential loss.

"Maybe it isn't that bad," she ventured. The hopeful note in her voice gutted me. "Maybe they caught it fast enough."

I squeezed her hand and said nothing as I led her out to the truck. We made it to the cottage in record time, but I knew before we even turned up the driveway that it was, without a doubt, as bad as we feared.

Through the trees lining the driveway, the glow of the flames rose up behind them, the acrid tang of thick smoke hanging in the air. Juliet clasped a hand over her mouth to keep from crying out, even as her eyes filled with tears.

I pulled off into the grass, well away from the two fire trucks that were parked in front of the cottage. The cheerful wildflowers Blue loved to explore were blackened and trampled. Juliet slipped out of the truck and watched the scene with wide, horrified eyes while I spoke quietly with a police officer, then my grandfather.

When I returned to her side, I wrapped my arms around her, holding her tight through the tremors that wracked her body.

"I'm sorry, Red," I said against her hair. "I'm so sorry."

Those simple words caused the floodgates to open and she crumpled against me. All I could do was hold her as she wept. I rubbed my hands over her back, murmuring senseless, soothing words against her ear.

Never in my life had I felt so helpless.

The police would need to ask her some questions later about what had been inside, but for now, I simply tucked her against my chest and thanked all the forces of the universe that she'd been with me tonight instead of inside the devastation that was Nan's cottage.

With a shudder, my arms tightened around her.

She's safe, I reminded myself, but it didn't quiet my panicked thoughts.

It was nearly dawn by the time the fire was completely contained. Once Juliet finished talking to the police officers lingering on the property, I gently touched her cheek with my fingertips.

"Libby texted me as soon as she heard. She brought a bin of clothes for you over to the house. I know it's not—" I broke off, running my other hand through my hair. "I know what you've lost is so much more than just that, but it's a start."

"That's really sweet of her," she said, her voice thick with emotion.

Another car pulled in behind us and Chief Roberts stepped out onto the lawn. With the emergency lights blinking across his face, the man looked like an avenging angel as he met my eyes over her head. He grew up in Oakville, but like everyone else here in Spruce Hill, he had come to love Nan Montgomery like his own grandmother. His role was mostly administrative these days, but I wasn't surprised he'd shown up in person.

When we arrived, I'd told the Spruce Hill PD's senior detective, Rose Hanson, about everything that had happened so far, whether it seemed pertinent or not, including Melissa's warning to Juliet.

If the chief's stony expression was anything to go by, Detective Hanson had already relayed those details to him—and he believed it was all related.

"Chief," I said when he approached us. "This is Juliet Morrison. Juliet, this is Chief Roberts."

His expression was gentle, his voice low, but nothing could cover the fact that Juliet had experienced another loss, gained one more thing to mourn.

How much more could she take?

"Nothing I can say will give you back what was inside the cottage, Juliet, but I assure you both I'll keep you informed about the investigation."

I flinched at the shudder that trembled through Juliet's body and murmured, "Thanks, Chief."

"We will get to the bottom of this. I won't rest until we do."

All Juliet managed was a nod, her hair tickling my throat, as Roberts inclined his head and walked away. We watched in silence as the police cruiser pulled back down the gravel drive, followed by a parade of emergency vehicles.

Entering the cottage was strictly off-limits for now, but Juliet gestured to her little green sedan.

"Do you think I should leave it parked here?"

"Mark and I will come get it later," I replied.

We'd check over the car top to bottom before Juliet got anywhere near it. Maybe I'd seen too many movies, read too many thrillers, but I would protect Juliet from whatever threat was out there. I just hoped I was up for the job, because now that I'd found her, I absolutely would not risk losing her.

She gave another weary nod, so I bundled her into the truck, buckling the seatbelt around her still form.

As soon as we returned to the house, I tucked her back into my bed—she might not sleep with the images of the burning cottage seared into her mind, but the dark smudges under her eyes practically begged for rest. Though I wanted to stay, to hold her, shield her, she shook her head and whispered that she wanted to be alone, so I simply pressed my lips to her forehead before heading downstairs.

Sighing heavily, I sat down on the couch with my laptop to do some research. I needed to distract myself, to keep from thinking too long about what might've happened if Juliet had been asleep there when the cottage caught fire instead of safe in my bed.

It was all too easy to imagine a very different phone call. I forced myself to swallow down the tide of raw fear that threatened to choke me and dropped my face into my hands. Each breath that wheezed from my lungs was a revelation, not entirely unwelcome but still unexpected.

I'd fallen head over heels for this woman who'd swept into my world like a tornado.

The spectrum of emotions she inspired in me over that short period of time was impressive. As my pulse steadied, I rubbed my jaw and smiled a bit grimly. I'd told Juliet I didn't expect her to profess her undying love for me, and that was still true. I never promised not to fall in love with her, though.

With a tiny smile lingering at the corners of my mouth, I turned my focus to researching the information we'd found in

Nan's little lockbox, the news clippings that had assuredly been destroyed in the fire.

After sending a dozen articles to the printer, I checked my watch. It was almost noon, so I tracked down the phone number for Lewis Zoratti and set up a time to drop by after lunch. The Zorattis' oldest son was the same age as Aaron, so they knew me well enough to welcome a social call.

The sooner we got to the bottom of this, the better. If that meant talking to everyone in town who'd known Melissa Montgomery before she left Spruce Hill, so be it.

Juliet had come here for answers, and I'd be damned if I let her keep trudging along without them.

Twenty-Eight

JULIET

WHEN I AWOKE, I pawed half-heartedly through the bin of clothes from Libby, moved nearly to tears once again by the sweetness of the gesture. I pulled on a plain green shirt and leggings, then combed through my hair with my fingers and shoved it up into a bun.

Before going downstairs, I leaned against the cool porcelain of the bathroom sink and sucked in several deep, rasping breaths as I fought back a fresh wave of grief.

"It's going to be okay," I told my reflection, flinching at the hoarseness of my own voice.

I found Henry in the kitchen, slicing tomatoes. Numbness had set in, turning my insides as dry and dusty as they'd been before I set out for Spruce Hill. For a moment, I just stared at the back of his head, but he must've sensed my presence and turned toward me.

"Hey," he said gently, setting aside the knife and wiping his hands on a towel. "Did you sleep?"

As soon as he dropped the dishcloth, I moved into him, burying my face against his chest. His arms went around me, so steady and comfortable that something settled deep inside me. I breathed in the scent of his soap, letting it soothe my nerves as much as his embrace did, but it was another few minutes until I trusted myself to speak.

"Yes," I said. "A bit. Is it lunchtime already?"

Henry pressed his lips to the top of my head, then guided me to the table and brought over a tray of sandwich fixings.

"Just about. We're meeting Lewis Zoratti at two, if you're still up for it."

My head jerked up in surprise. "We are?"

"If anyone can tell us who the hell that other guy was, it's him," he said.

"You don't think the fire was an accident."

It didn't come out as a question, nor had I meant it as one. We were the only two people who'd been in that cottage recently and neither of us had left any appliances running that could have started a fire. Somehow I didn't think Nan had been the type to overlook outdated electrical wiring, either.

I watched the conscious effort he made to unclench his fists, then I wrapped my hand around his, rubbing my thumb absently across his palm. After a second, he rotated his wrist to twine his fingers through mine.

"I think," he began, "that there are too many unknowns for my comfort. This stuff doesn't happen in Spruce Hill."

"Until I came to town," I replied, horrified by the thought.

"Oh no," Henry said swiftly. "This is not your fault, not by a long shot. But something is going on, and we're going to figure it out."

His certainty reassured me to some small extent, enough that I was able to force myself to eat a sandwich, at least. Libby dropped by with one gift bag filled with toiletries, including my own bar of soap from Mark, and another bag containing a sketchbook and set of drawing pencils.

I burst into tears at her thoughtfulness. Henry looked on helplessly while Libby held me tight.

"You're not alone around here," Libby said when I finally drew back from the hug. "We look out for each other in this town, and you're one of us now. If you want to ditch this clown to go shop for underwear later, you just let me know." She shot Henry a look and added, "We'll keep Blue at our house until you're ready for her."

I gave a weak smile and thanked her again, then turned immediately into Henry's chest as she left, taking Blue home with her. Though my shoulders shuddered under his steady hands, no more tears came.

"When do we need to leave?" I asked. "I'd like to shower before we go, if there's time."

Henry kissed me gently and said, "Take all the time you need. The house isn't far."

I stood beneath the stream of hot water for several long minutes before finally shampooing my hair. When I lathered my body with Henry's soap, I realized the scent was different on its own.

Maybe he did have something to do with it.

Libby's bag of toiletries included a wide-tooth comb and a pack of hair elastics, so I sent a silent stream of thanks across the short distance between the houses. The shower had calmed me, washed away the lingering traces of smoke, and cleared my mind of the haunting image of flames leaping through the shattered windows at the cottage.

Instead of sorrow, I was filled with a rising surge of fury at the senselessness of it all.

There was probably nothing more to discover from any of the boxes we'd hauled down from storage, no answers to any of my questions about the past, but what a waste, destroying all those memories—photos and artwork and decades of hand-written journals, along with my painting for Henry.

And for what? To frighten me away? Send me packing back to Minnesota?

I allowed anger to comfort me in the face of loss.

When I came downstairs, Henry's eyes widened at the ex-pression on my face. I gripped the front of his shirt and pulled him against me.

"I take it the shower did you some good," he ventured.

"I'm pissed," I said in a low growl.

He lifted a brow as I claimed his mouth, pouring all of my raging emotions into the kiss, but he accepted everything I had to give, offering back something soft and sweet that I couldn't examine too carefully just yet.

After several long minutes, I released him. For the first time, he was the one to look a little dazed and off balance, but his resulting grin comforted me.

"Well then," he said lightly, "let's go."

The Zorattis lived in a tidy brick colonial about five miles from the inn. Lewis was a handsome, broad-shouldered man approaching fifty, sporting a full head of black hair peppered with silver. He clasped my hands in his as he gave me a warm, beautiful smile.

I was immediately charmed. It was easy to picture a young version of him with my mother—they would have been beautiful together.

"Oh, I'm sure everyone in town has been raving over your resemblance to Nan with that coloring," he said gently, "but you look just like your mother."

I jerked in surprise, but Lewis shook his head at my expression of disbelief and offered another sweet smile.

"Aside from the hair, you could've been her twin. Same big blue eyes, cute little nose, mouth made for smiling. She was a real beauty, just like you. I was truly sorry to hear about her passing, Juliet."

Though Henry looked ready to jump in at the first sign of tears, I felt calm, serene almost. That connection to my mother filled me with joy, despite the darkness in the day's beginnings.

"Thank you," I said softly. "That means a lot to me."

His wife, Anne, poured us all some lemonade as we sat down at a table on the patio. She echoed her husband's sentiments as she handed me a glass.

"You're a stunner, just like your mama," she said with a smile. "Melissa and I had a strained relationship, I'm sorry to say. Frenemies, you might have called us. But she was remarkable, so vivacious. This town was a little too quiet after she left."

"We heard there was a bit of trouble over at the inn last night, is everyone all right?" Lewis asked.

Henry squeezed my hand under the table. I bit my lip and let him answer for us both.

"There was a fire at Nan's cottage. No one was hurt, but we're not sure about the extent of the damage yet."

Both of our hosts looked horrified by the news.

"Oh, now that is a damn shame," Lewis said, shaking his head. "If you need any help with rebuilding, please let me know. I'm a contractor by trade. I'd be happy to help you with anything you need, anything at all. I have a lot of fond memories around the cottage and the inn—Missy and I were playmates long before we ever dated. That place means a lot to me."

I couldn't speak around the sudden lump in my throat, but I managed a wobbly smile and a nod of thanks.

We all sipped at our lemonade for a moment, then Henry drew a breath and bit the bullet, surging forth to get the real reason for our visit out into the open sooner instead of later.

"In Nan's journals, she mentioned someone by the initial T, someone who spent a lot of time with Melissa. Do either of you happen to know who she might have been referring to?" he asked them.

Lewis rubbed his jaw thoughtfully and shook his head. Anne, however, shot her husband an apologetic look before she answered.

"Yes," she said, dropping her voice a touch. "His name was Tom, I can't remember the last name. Started with an H. Heller? Holler? Something like that, I think. He wasn't from around here."

I leaned forward. "Does he still live in Spruce Hill?"

"Oh no, he left town not long after Missy did. Lewis and Missy were dating, but . . ." She waved a hand as though that explained everything.

"We weren't exactly exclusive," Lewis put in, seeing my baffled expression. "Missy wasn't the type to settle for one person, not back then anyway. We went to dances together, the movies on Friday nights, that kind of thing. I knew she was seeing other guys, but she never rubbed my face in it. I was half in love with her anyway, so I was willing to take what time she would spare for me. She even sent me a letter, right after she left town."

"She did? Do you still have it?"

Excitement flooded my veins until Lewis shook his head again. Before disappointment could take root, Anne cut in.

"Oh yes, it's in my dresser." At her husband's startled look, she smiled kindly. "When we got married, I found it tucked into one of our high school yearbooks. I showed it to Nan, because the whole town knew she'd been searching high and low for your mother. There was no return address."

"What did it say?"

"Not much, just that she was sorry she didn't get to say goodbye to Lewis, and that it was best for everybody if she didn't stick around. But she did mention…"

I straightened in my chair. "Mention what?"

"That she was pregnant. I don't think Nan knew until I showed her the letter. I've spent decades feeling guilty for invading Melissa's privacy like that, but it had been years since she left. I didn't know what else to do."

Lewis caught my gaze when it shot to him. "Much as I'd love a daughter like you, Juliet, Missy and I were never, uh, intimate."

"Right," I said softly, clearing my throat. "Anne, you shouldn't feel guilty. I don't know why my mom left town, but if that's how Nan knew I existed, I'm glad you told her. She wrote me letters over the years, even without a way to send them. I found them in the attic."

Henry squeezed my hand when my breath hitched—the likelihood of those letters surviving the fire was slim.

"I saved Missy's note. I'll go fetch it for you," Anne said, hurrying into the house.

Lewis eyed us both carefully now that his wife was gone, then said in a low voice, "I do remember Tom Heller. I didn't realize that's who Missy was seeing, but if so, it was probably a good thing she left. He wasn't a good man. Mid-twenties, maybe. Definitely some years older than us. He came into town on a construction job."

Construction job. I met Henry's eyes and saw he'd made the same connection to that newspaper clipping. An involuntary shiver slithered up my spine.

"Guy liked to park across from the high school, watch the girls from his truck. I wouldn't be surprised if she caught his eye. Missy could shine like the sun, when she wasn't storming like a thundercloud," Lewis finished.

"And you've never seen him since?" Henry asked.

I could feel the tension radiating from him and gripped his hand tightly, though whether I was hoping to give comfort or receive it, I wasn't sure. More puzzle pieces were coming together, even if we weren't finding answers yet to all of our questions.

Lewis shook his head just as Anne returned to the table and handed me the letter.

"You keep that," he said. "I know what it's like to lose a parent. Connections like that letter become priceless."

We stayed to finish our lemonade, but neither Lewis nor Anne could tell us much more than they already had. I impulsively hugged both of them before we left, ignoring Henry's muttered speculation about Libby rubbing off on me, and the couple looked delighted by the gesture.

Henry shook their hands instead, then laced his fingers with mine as we walked back to the truck. I stayed quiet until we were enclosed in the cab.

"So, my father might be Tom Heller, who might also be a serial killer, if those clippings Nan kept are any indication. Do you think he's responsible for the fire?"

Henry opened his mouth to respond, then snapped it shut for a moment while he thought it through. "If Heller left town, why would he come back now? It's been thirty years."

"Don't they say killers like to return to the scene of the crime?" I asked, then shivered again. "I can barely wrap my head around it all. My mom definitely knew Heller. She fought with him in public after a dance and again outside the inn, right before she suddenly left town. Why? Because he threatened her? Because she told him she was pregnant?"

"Or," Henry suggested quietly, "because she made the connection between Heller and those murders? She had quite a temper, from all I've heard. Maybe she said something that made him realize she knew the truth."

My blood ran cold, then my mind cleared of all but one thought. "So she might have left town to protect Nan."

"And you," Henry added.

"And me." My voice was barely a whisper as I processed that possibility.

I stared out the window as we drove home, caught on the idea that my mother disappeared to protect all of us, rather than to get away from Spruce Hill or Nan in particular. Stupidly, I'd assumed that she left town over something trivial. Whether it was some argument between Nan and my mom, or Mom and whoever my father might be, I figured it had been the result of a flare of my mother's famous temper.

Not because of a murderer. What the hell did you get yourself into, Mom?

Henry rubbed his jaw, mulling over the possibilities.

"I think we need to talk to Chief Roberts or Detective Hanson," he said finally. "If this guy is back in town, he's dangerous. Given the fire at the cottage, I'm inclined to think you've become his target."

As much as I wanted to protest that last statement, I had to accept that it was looking more and more likely. Henry's hand found mine and I leaned my head back against the seat.

"Okay," I said softly. "This is unreal."

"I know. But you're not alone in this."

There were those words again. I swallowed my tears as he squeezed my fingers reassuringly.

I reflected on clearing out my mother's house, finding her note, the long hours on the road, all alone. Somehow, this first true solo adventure of my life had resulted in gathering around myself a group of friends—friends who were becoming family, the big family I'd always wished for.

It seemed ridiculous to feel this warm, welling sense of affection in the midst of whatever this mess was.

Henry texted the chief a head's up with Heller's name, then drove us to Spruce Hill's very tiny police station. He smiled a little at my skeptical expression.

"Size isn't everything," he whispered in my ear as he held the door for me.

I hummed softly in response. "I mean, it sure helps."

He choked back his laughter as Chief Roberts greeted us and led us into his office at the back of the station. I'd barely noticed anything about the chief after the fire, but now I was able to appreciate his gentle green eyes, the softness of his voice when he asked how I was holding up. He was several inches shorter than Henry, a rotund but broad man with dark hair that had gone mostly gray.

Even in my distraction, I thought he looked like a man who probably had a lot of stories to tell.

Just as we settled into the two chairs in front of his desk, Detective Hanson joined us. She squeezed my shoulder reassuringly as she moved to stand at Roberts' shoulder behind the desk.

At my request, Henry did the talking. While he'd already informed the police about a possible gunshot during my trip out to Cooper's Point and given them the details about those news articles Nan had kept, he now added Lewis Zoratti's warning about Tom Heller and the entries that mentioned Melissa and T in Nan's journals.

After relaying that information, Henry drew some folded papers from his back pocket and passed them across the desk. Chief Roberts took the printouts, then leaned back in his chair.

"I printed these this morning. They're copies of the articles we found. The original clippings were at the cottage."

"Your mother left before my time," Roberts said to me, "but her departure had a way of coming up in conversation over the years. The sketch you found of this Heller guy, is it safe to assume that was inside the cottage at the time of the fire, too?"

I nodded, fighting back another wave of grief at the loss of Nan's artwork, but Henry straightened in his seat like an idea had just popped into his head.

"Juliet is an incredibly talented artist," he said slowly, turning to look at me. "Do you think you could recreate it?"

I cringed a little, more at the praise than at the prospect of drawing Heller. "I can try. I only saw it for a few minutes, though."

"That would be helpful, since I didn't find a single record of Tom Heller after he left Spruce Hill. It's like he disappeared, same as Melissa," Chief Roberts told us. "I found an old file from decades ago that mentioned him—an Officer Jameson broke up a fight outside a school dance involving one Tom Heller."

"That was in Nan's journal," I replied.

The thought of trying to recreate Nan's sketch after only seeing it for those few minutes initially caused a big ball of anxiety to settle in my stomach, but suddenly I was itching to get started.

"Do you have some paper? I'd like to try the sketch now, before I think about it for too long."

Hanson fetched me a pencil and a few sheets of blank paper from the printer. The three of them spoke in low tones while I worked, but I barely registered any of their conversation over the sound of the pencil scratching against the paper. These thin strokes were nothing like the sharp, dark lines of charcoal that Nan had laid out, but my memory of the image was clearer than I expected.

By the time I finished, the paper showed a fairly close rendition of Nan's artwork. I tried not to shudder at those malicious eyes staring back at me. When I slid the paper in front of Henry, his eyebrows shot upward.

"You're amazing, Red. That's him," he said, turning it around to show the chief.

I shrugged as I watched the chief for a reaction. He frowned slightly, then he tapped the image with one finger.

"Does he look familiar to either of you?" he asked. "Hanson?"

The detective shook her head. "I'm good with faces but I've never seen him."

"When I first saw Nan's sketch, I had a vague feeling of familiarity," I replied, though Henry also shook his head. "But then it evaporated, so I thought maybe I imagined it. Do *you* recognize him?"

Chief Roberts slowly cocked his head to one side, then the other. "I'm not sure. I should get this to a bigger department. The county sheriff's office has a sketch artist they call in sometimes. Maybe he could do up a picture, age it by about thirty years—unless you want to give it a go?"

I blew out a breath. "I'll take a picture of it so you can keep this copy. You should see if a professional can take a crack at it, but in the meantime, I'll try. I can't promise I'll be able to do it justice, though. Portraits aren't my specialty."

The chief promised us he'd have a patrol car outside Henry's house and another cruising by the inn at regular intervals, then suggested we go home and get some rest. None of it made me feel any less unsettled by this short visit, especially after letting the image of Heller's face take up so much space in my brain.

"This is an unusual situation for a place like Spruce Hill," Chief Roberts said somewhat apologetically, "but it's our top priority right now to get to the bottom of this."

Henry and I shook his proffered hand, then Hanson's, and left the station. The sunshine felt almost like an insult in light of my current mood.

Once we were seated in the truck, Henry asked, "Do you want to take Libby up on the underwear shopping offer? Not that I have a problem with you going commando, but if you want a dose of normal, I know she'd be happy to take you."

I grinned at his comment but shook my head. "I think I'd like to just go home and play with this sketch, if you don't mind."

I didn't miss the warm glow of pleasure in Henry's eyes when I referred to his house as *home*. At least, I assumed that was the reason for it, since I hadn't said anything else to warrant such an expression or the resultant rush of emotion along my limbs.

The memory of my own home engulfed in flames dampened it immediately, but I let the curl of belonging twine through me anyway.

"Home it is," he replied.

As he shifted the truck into gear, my heart whispered the word again.

Home.

Twenty-Nine

HENRY

Juliet stayed uncharacteristically quiet during the ride back to my house, but I resisted the urge to ask how she was doing, recognizing how idiotic it would sound. Her pain was palpable, coursing through my veins as surely as my own blood. As soon as we walked inside, she pulled the sketchbook from Libby out of its bag near the door and settled down at the kitchen table with her phone displaying the drawing from the station.

I kissed the top of her head and moved to the living room sofa to give her some space.

Muffled curses punctuated the silence, along with the occasional sound of paper crumpling. I fielded texts from not only Libby and Mark, but from my brother as well, who'd apparently been roped in and updated on the entire situation.

I wasn't sure whether my grandfather or my ex was to blame for that development, but I appreciated Aaron's concern, nonetheless. The more people looking out for Juliet, the better.

The inn was safe in the immensely capable hands of Mrs. Gregson, Sally, and Gramps, who were all shaken up after the fire but assured me they'd feel better if I stuck close to Juliet instead of coming in to help. They would hold down the fort as long as necessary, knowing one of their own was grieving.

Juliet was family—it hadn't taken long for them to recognize that, certainly less time than it had taken me. I had only my own stubborn pride to blame for that. The irony of my appreciation for her acceptance into the Lakeside Inn family didn't escape me, given that it was a source of annoyance for me before Juliet's arrival.

Now, I was simply grateful.

It was only a matter of time before my parents started blowing up my phone, too, now that my brother knew what was going on. I wondered if Juliet had updated her friend from Minnesota about any of this. If telling Sarah about her fall could have resulted in her friend rushing to her side, Juliet was probably even more hesitant to mention the fire.

Or the serial killer who could also be her father.

As far as I was concerned, she was much too used to fending for herself. Hopefully, with time, she'd come to accept the support of the people who loved her.

The doorbell rang and the scratch of Juliet's pencil abruptly halted. I glanced out through the glass pane at the top of the door, grinning despite the hell of the past eighteen hours, and swung the door open.

"Thought you might need a hearty meal," Sally said, shoving a wicker picnic basket into my hands, followed by a bottle of wine.

I stared down at them, so moved I had to take a moment to just breathe, which drew the scent of Sally's signature roast chicken into my lungs. After everything, all the ways I'd fucked up from the moment Juliet got to town, family—this family, *our* family—kept showing up for both of us.

"Thank you," I finally managed, just as Juliet slipped around me to greet the chef with a hug.

"Can't be living off pizza like you usually do." Sally's voice was gruffer than usual and a light sheen of tears glazed her eyes. "There's some things in there from Mrs. Gregson. Trinkets and photos Nan brought over from the cottage to keep in her office back when she was spending more time at the inn."

Juliet's breathing audibly hitched, but she managed a smile. "Thank you."

"You need anything else, you just call. Got it?"

"Got it," I confirmed, clasping her hand tightly when Juliet stepped back.

For a long, quiet moment, we stayed there by the door, watching as Sally got into her midnight blue Subaru and drove back toward the inn. Juliet took the wine from my hand and tucked herself under my arm.

"Doing okay?" I asked against the top of her head.

"As okay as can be expected, I guess. That smells heavenly, but I'd like to keep working on the sketch for a bit. I think I'm getting closer."

"Of course. I'll unpack everything and keep it warm."

Mark and Libby arrived just after five with Blue in tow. The dog raced past them into the house, ignoring me completely to dance circles around Juliet at the table.

"Damn, dude, you've been replaced," Mark said with a mournful shake of his head.

"I'll try to accept my fate," I joked.

Blue wagged her tail at me as I entered the kitchen but didn't move from Juliet's side. Almost unconsciously, Juliet set her hand on Blue's head, much as she had that day in the forest. I leveled a mock scowl in the dog's direction.

"Yeah, yeah, just remember who feeds you, silly mutt."

Juliet rubbed at her bleary eyes when I came to look down at her efforts. Only three sketches seemed to have made the cut as possibilities. They were arranged in an arc on the table before her.

"Portraits are not really my strength," she said wearily. With one finger, she tapped the sketch to her right. "This one looks a little familiar, the same way Nan's did when I first saw it, but I don't know if these are anywhere close to what Tom Heller would actually look like now."

Libby peered over Juliet's shoulder. She cocked her head thoughtfully as she studied the sketches. Mark and I looked at each other over their heads—if anyone would recognize the man from around town, it was likely to be Libby. Her clinic treated most of Spruce Hill's residents at one time or another.

"Can you give that one some facial hair?" Libby suggested, pointing to the sketch Juliet had indicated.

With the three of us clustered around her and Blue's head resting on her knee, Juliet added first a mustache, then a goatee, and finally a full beard.

"Oh, no," Juliet whispered, horror dawning on her face before she even finished shading. "I recognize him now. The beard changes his appearance dramatically. No wonder he only looked vaguely familiar before."

"I recognize him, too," Libby said. "I think he lives just outside of town. He came in for stitches back when I first opened the clinic. I've only seen him in town once or twice since."

Juliet's gaze met mine over her shoulder. "I ran into him at the grocery store when I first got here. He asked if he knew me from somewhere. Totally played up the harmless, small town guy routine, but he creeped me out. If he knew both my mother and Nan, there's no way he didn't recognize me right then and there. He's known I was here since the day after I arrived."

When she shuddered, I laid my hands on her shoulders and squeezed, fighting the urge to pull her into my arms—or to swoop her up and take her far away. I forced myself to think logically, lifting my hands away to take a picture of the sketch.

"I'm sending this to Roberts," I said.

Juliet dropped her attention back to the drawing, looking so damned fragile that it broke my heart. Over her head, I gave our friends a look and Libby immediately dropped into the chair next to her.

She started speaking to Juliet in the soft, quiet way she used with her younger patients, clearly trying to take her mind off the events of the past twenty-four hours. Mark gathered up the discarded papers on the table and set them in a tidy pile on the kitchen counter to make room for dinner.

Once the image had been passed along to Chief Roberts, I handed out plates of Sally's chicken and side dishes, which garnered unenthusiastic nibbling at best. I sat on the other side of Juliet and draped my arm over the back of her chair while we ate, occasionally stroking over her spine with my fingertips.

That physical contact between us, however slight, had a calming effect on us both.

"Do you think he's been here this whole time? All these years, I mean, since my mother left town?" she asked quietly.

My hand slid up the back of her neck and into her hair before I puffed out my cheeks on a long exhale.

"I don't think I've ever seen him around, but Anne Zoratti said he left the area when your mother did. Maybe he went looking for her, tried to follow her trail. Maybe he was hiding out, waiting for the uproar to die back down after Melissa's departure, which was a pretty big deal in this town. If he came back later on with that beard, older, a new name, I can see how he might have flown under the radar."

"Or maybe he came back after Nan died. Waiting for my mother to show up again." Her eyes lifted to mine. "And when he found out she wasn't coming, waiting for me."

When Chief Roberts arrived an hour later, his grim expression matched our somber moods. Without preamble, he said, "We got a hit on the sketch. Tom Heller is wanted for questioning about a string of missing girls outside of Rochester starting in 1987. The county sheriff's department is stepping in to help. If he was responsible for those murders here back in the eighties and nineties, I want that son of a bitch nailed to the wall as soon as possible."

"He must be using an alias," Libby said quietly. "I think he signed in at the clinic as Ted something or other. I'll check my records for the last name."

"That'd be much appreciated, Doc," Roberts replied.

He introduced the four of us to the officers who would be keeping an eye on the house, shook our hands, and left to go meet with the sheriff.

Though she looked pale enough that I worried she might collapse, Juliet seemed calmer and more focused after that conversation. It was like uncovering the identity of the boogeyman gave her something concrete to focus her energy toward, especially as the fury at this man for causing the rift between her mother and Nan—the chasm between *them* and Nan—began to fuel her.

The change came over her, bringing with it a new sharpness in her eyes, a stubborn set to her jaw. A mixture of relief and curiosity filled me, wondering what was going through her beautiful head.

Libby and Mark decided to head home as well, taking Blue with them. Each of them embraced both me and Juliet.

"You hang in there," Libby whispered in Juliet's ear as they hugged one another tightly. "They'll catch the bastard, I'm sure of it. And I'll be ready with champagne to celebrate."

A ghost of a smile lingered on Juliet's lips once I locked the door behind them and turned to her. When I opened my arms, she pressed her face to my chest and inhaled deeply, absorbing the calming scent of the soap she loved so much.

"What do we do now?" she asked quietly.

"Whatever you want, sweetheart," I murmured, brushing my lips across her forehead. "It's a waiting game now, I think."

She nodded and wrapped her arms around my waist, whispering, "I want to get my mind off Heller or whatever the hell his name is. I don't want to think about the past or my mother or the cottage."

"I have just the thing."

I guided her to the couch, positioned her so she was spooned in front of me as we stretched along its length, and found a romantic comedy for us to watch. It took longer than I would have liked, but eventually Juliet's body relaxed and she snuggled deeper in my arms.

By the time the movie ended, she was half-asleep, dozing with her head on my arm. It didn't take much coaxing to get her up to bed, where she burrowed into a cocoon of blankets around us and fell asleep curled against my body.

Just before dawn, I awoke to Juliet weeping into the pillow, her entire body wracked with sobs.

"Hey, hey," I said, drawing her close.

I opened my mouth to promise her everything would be okay, but the words caught in my throat. She deserved honesty. In the end, I simply held her and let her cry. Once her tears were finally spent, she sighed against my shoulder.

"I feel so selfish," she whispered. "I want him to pay for whatever he did to those missing girls, but I just can't stop thinking about what he took from my mother. Everything else feels so abstract to me still, everything except him splitting my family apart."

"That's not selfish, Red. You've lost so much. If he committed those crimes, the police will take care of it. We don't know who those victims were—hell, most of them were killed before you were even born. It's not selfish to grieve for what he took from your mother and Nan, for what he's taken from you."

My own chest twisted with pain, whether it was my place to grieve alongside her or not. I stroked her hair, wrapping a curl around my finger. We fell silent after that, tangled up in each other's arms, offering and accepting some small degree of comfort.

When she finally drifted back to sleep, I let myself doze, holding her tight against my chest. Several hours later, my eyelids peeled reluctantly open to late morning sunlight streaming through the open curtains. My arm was still wrapped around her soft, sleepy form, and I pressed a kiss to her forehead.

It felt like a lifetime had passed over the last forty-eight hours. Juliet stirred, grumbling sleepily before she clasped a hand over her eyes.

"What time is it?" She peeked out between her fingers, blinking at me dazedly. "What year is it?"

I laughed. "I was thinking the same thing. Then I figured, who cares? I could stay here forever with you."

In painful contrast to the words, my phone started buzzing on the bedside table and I groaned as I reached for it to read the series of texts.

Juliet's face drained of color. "What now?"

"No need to panic. Everyone is okay. The computer crashed over at the inn," I said, typing out a quick response and tossing the phone down so I could collapse back onto the bed.

"Stupid real world," Juliet muttered. "I was hoping you'd be up for providing some morning distraction."

With her hand still over her eyes, I couldn't see her full expression, but there was no hiding the tinge of pink creeping along her cheeks. That meant she wanted *distraction*, not another made-for-TV movie.

"They can wait another half hour," I said, then I grinned, stretched out along her body, and laid a fiery path of kisses across her collarbone.

A husky laugh escaped her lips, then a low moan as my mouth reached its destination.

"Yes, they can," she gasped, welcoming one last glorious interlude before the real world beckoned.

Thirty

JULIET

I QUICKLY AGREED WHEN Henry suggested I come with him to the inn. Even with an unmarked police car outside the house, I had no desire to be alone just yet.

We definitely missed the half hour window of Henry's estimate, but Mrs. Gregson greeted us with a broad smile that implied she understood the delay. Henry winked at me once we were alone in his office.

Covering my face with my hands, I whispered, "Do they all know that we're...?"

Another of my vague, embarrassed hand gestures had him grinning like a fool, though he tried for a look of innocence as he suggested, "Dating? Having nightly sleepovers? Making sweet, sweet love? Getting down and dirty?"

I pinched the bridge of my nose, certain my cheeks were growing pinker by the second. This was yet another facet of small town life I would need to get used to. Henry bent down to kiss me, then sat behind the desk to fire up the computer.

"Yes, thank you for that, Mr. Walker," I muttered as I sank into the chair in front of him. "I'll take that as a yes."

"Yes, Juliet, everyone knows we're together. Sneaking around in Spruce Hill is virtually impossible."

"Fantastic."

His gaze stroked over me, heating my cheeks further as memories of our morning flashed through my head. "Do you have any idea how sexy you are when you blush? Almost as good as when you—"

My outraged shriek cut him off, but he didn't lose the smirk until the monitor flashed a blue screen of death at him. He scowled at the computer as his fingers flew across the keyboard, though I was grateful for the distraction.

"Maybe I can convince the new owner to upgrade these damned computers sometime soon," he growled.

I laughed, thinking about all the ways he might convince me. Of course, he didn't *need* to—if Henry thought it necessary, I trusted him to make that decision for the inn. Still, I wouldn't mind seeing what tricks he had up his sleeve if he wanted to try to persuade me.

After a few minutes, however, I couldn't stop bouncing my knee with the nervous energy still pent up inside me. Watching

Henry growl at the computer was arguably more boring than him watching me sketch.

"If you don't mind, Mr. Computer Nerd, I'm going to take a very Victorian turn about the gardens. I saw Gerard out there weeding when we came in. I need some fresh air."

He leaned across the desk to cup my chin in his hand, studying me with an expression that made his concern abundantly clear.

"Sure, but stick close to Gramps, okay? I'll be as quick as I can with this. Will you tell Mrs. Gregson where you're going, pretty please? I've had my fill of panicked phone calls recently."

I caught his hand in mine and kissed the center of his palm. "Yes, I will. Good luck with the computer."

Though I felt his eyes on me as I left the office, he didn't say anything to stop me. I wandered into the sitting room, where Mrs. Gregson was arranging a vase of flowers. For a moment, I simply watched the older woman work, her capable hands and eye for perfection soothing my nerves.

The inn would probably never feel completely like home, not in the way the cottage had, but being surrounded by all that my grandmother had built soothed me as sweetly as a lullaby.

When Mrs. Gregson finished with the flowers, she glanced up and looked at me with such sympathy that it nearly unraveled the calm that had come over me. "How are you doing today, dearest?"

The endearment was all it took—such a little thing to pack such an emotional punch.

I covered my face with both hands and burst into tears. Mrs. Gregson's arms came around me barely a second later, along with the kind of motherly comfort that had been absent from my life for more than half a year now.

Without shame, I accepted every soft word and gentle pat until I'd cried myself dry.

"I'm sorry," I said with a shaky laugh as I rubbed my face with my palms.

Mrs. Gregson clucked, giving me a fond smile. "You have nothing to apologize for, darling girl. Can I get you some tea? I think there's a tray of cookies in the kitchen. Why don't you sit down for a bit?"

"No. Thank you for the sweet offer, but no. Henry's working on the computer, but I can't sit still. I'm going out to the gardens. Some exercise will help settle me down, I'm sure."

"Of course, dear. It's such a beautiful day. I'm sorry to interrupt your weekend with the computer problems, but I'm sure Henry will have it fixed in no time. When it rains, it pours, hmm?"

"You can say that again," I replied.

"If you need anything at all, Juliet, just say the word. We have a room here opening up tomorrow morning, if you want it. I can't say I'd blame you for choosing young Mr. Walker's house over a Lakeside suite, however."

I laughed at Mrs. Gregson's knowing smile, but she simply gave me another motherly embrace and told me to enjoy the sunshine. With a quick smile of thanks, I left through the heavy front door.

I didn't want to stay at the inn, no matter how kind the offer was. All I wanted was for this nightmare to be over, to paint every day without a care, to make love with Henry each night, and to focus on building the life I'd been laying a foundation for here in Spruce Hill.

The gardens were blooming with an overwhelming variety of flowers, far more than when I'd first arrived. Gerard was no longer kneeling by the roses, so I meandered, slow and aimless, between the rows as I looked for him.

I paused at the tiny plaque commemorating Nan and squatted down to kiss my fingertips before pressing them to the center of the cool metal circle.

"I'm sorry about the cottage, Nan," I whispered. "I'll make it up to you, somehow. I promise."

As I rose to my feet, I wondered how long it would take me to recreate the painting that had been lost in the fire, then a soft scuffing noise reached my ear. For a moment, I cocked my head, listening until it came again. I followed the sound to the far side of the garden and swallowed the lump in my throat as I remembered trailing after Gerard along this path on our way to the cottage that very first day.

When I reached the final row of flowers and still didn't see him, I frowned. Where the hell was he?

"Gerard?" I called, peering around a hedge.

Another few steps brought me to the source of the sound: Gerard, lying face down beside a bed of violets with blood trickling from a lump near his hairline. His eyes were open, imploring, while his left arm shifted helplessly against the stones beneath him. I gasped and started toward him, but I stopped short when cold, hard metal pressed into the small of my back.

Every muscle in my body froze.

This is it, I thought frantically. *This is the end, and I didn't even say goodbye to Henry. Or Sarah. Or Libby and Mark.*

My blood ran cold even as my mind raced a million miles per second, thinking of all the people I would never see again if this was the end. Those galloping thoughts were so overwhelming that I jerked in surprise when the assailant spoke against my ear.

"He'll be fine, assuming they find him in time," the man said, his voice strangely kind. "You, on the other hand, well. I've waited a long time for this. With your mother's pretty face and that red hair, I almost blew it that day at the grocery store. Can you believe my luck?"

He laughed softly behind me, nudging the gun against my spine to direct me toward the trees. The calm, polite tone he used contrasted sharply with my panic.

For an instant, I was struck silent. Where was he taking me?

Away from the inn. The realization filled me with a sinking sense of dread.

I knew I should keep him talking, try to buy myself some time until someone realized I was missing. Even though I wanted nothing more than to sink to my knees under the weight of my terror, I recognized that forcing his hand would only lead to death.

"Your luck?" I repeated, trying to inject a note of scorn into my voice to cover the tremor of fear.

When he responded with a cold laugh, I knew I hadn't succeeded.

"Keep walking, Juliet. I'd hate to have to finish the old man off to motivate you to do as I say."

My heart leapt into my throat. There was no way I would risk Gerard's life—I couldn't. I wanted to scream, cry, plead with him, but maybe I could get away from him once we reached the woods. If I tried to run while we were still out in the open, I was no match for him or the gun.

All I could do was keep him talking and hope for a distraction when I needed one.

"Where are we going?"

"A special little place I know," he said, guiding me with the barrel of the gun. "In fact, your boyfriend found it very special, as I recall. I would have taken your mother there, if only she hadn't ruined things. What a lovely circle this will make, her beautiful daughter taking her place."

He sounded so *normal*. The words curdled in my stomach, and I thought for one terrifying moment that I was going to be sick. If I doubled over to vomit, he might very well make good on his threat to kill Gerard.

"Did you—" I broke off, gripping my abdomen with both hands. "Are you my father?"

Heller laughed. That bizarrely normal façade evaporated into mist as a strange, high-pitched giggle burst from him.

"Oh no, that bitch ruined my plans for her when she got knocked up. I would never have pegged her for the maternal type, but I guess nature won out in the end."

I almost went limp with relief. I hadn't thought too deeply about sharing DNA with a murderer until that very minute. It didn't even matter now who my father was, as long as it wasn't this killer.

My toe caught on an uneven patch of grass and I stumbled, causing him to grab my arm in a wrenching, iron grip. This time, the cruelty of Nan's charcoal sketch was as evident in the harsh words as it was in the painful grasp of his fingers.

"One more day and I would've had her right where I wanted her, but she went and got pregnant. The bitch refused to do what she was told. So selfless, trying to protect everyone else, but I made sure every one of the girls I took afterward paid for her sins. You won't make that mistake, now, will you? I'd hate to have to take it out on your new little friends."

Henry.

I'd never forgive myself if this bastard hurt Henry. Though I wanted to scream his name, all I could manage was a gasping sob. He was probably still stuck behind that big old desk in his office, unable to hear me even if I managed to shout.

Tears blurred my vision when we reached the treeline and I struggled to drag enough oxygen into my lungs.

Just hold on, I told myself. *Your mother bested this son of a bitch, and so can you. Just hold on.*

Thirty-One

HENRY

I MANAGED TO GET the computer up and running again half an hour after Juliet left to visit my grandfather. No computer problem was distracting enough to quell the quick jab of fear in my gut when she mentioned going outside, but I'd seen Gramps out there as well. As much as I'd wanted to keep her beside me, I couldn't fault her for feeling restless.

Sally would be able to keep an eye on Juliet in the garden from where she was working in the kitchen. Hadn't the view from the kitchen windows gotten me in trouble that first day when Juliet stormed out of my office?

Now that things had worked out, I could smile at the memory.

The gardens would soothe her, I hoped. Being outside usually calmed her nerves—when she wasn't tumbling down hillsides, at least. With perfect clarity, I recalled the look in her eyes when she caught sight of the lake that day at the beach, those deep inhalations with her arms flung wide, the way she tipped her face up to the sun like a supplicant receiving a benediction.

My chest tightened with emotion as those images filled my head.

That was the way she should always look. She deserved to be carefree and utterly at peace, instead of pale and grieving and hanging on by a thread. Being cooped up didn't suit my beautiful artist.

It was funny, I could admit now, that I'd originally expected her to be too flighty for the good of the inn's future, too disinterested. Instead, here I was, wishing I could lighten the load she carried on those strong shoulders. Juliet had proven my stupid assumptions wrong time and again.

All I cared about now was keeping her happy and safe.

As I loaded the reservation software, a text from Libby came through on my phone. A name for the boogeyman.

Ted Holliston. Sent name and address from clinic records to Chief.

I blew out a breath, thanked her, and headed to the sitting room to tell Mrs. Gregson things were good to go on the computer front.

"I'm so sorry to drag you here on your day off, but thank you, Henry. I do appreciate you and Juliet stopping in."

"Not a problem, Mrs. G. Getting out of the house probably did Juliet some good. She loves the gardens almost as much as Nan did, I think."

Mrs. Gregson smiled fondly. "I think you're right. Enjoy the rest of your day."

I waved before making my way outside, but my limbs turned to stone when I got there and didn't see Juliet or my grandfather. Moving between the flower beds, my lungs tightened.

The absolute quiet caused an icy ball to form in my stomach.

"Red?" I called. "Gramps?"

A soft moan floated from the far edge of the garden.

Without a second thought, I ran toward the sound, dropping to my knees when I found my grandfather on the ground. That ball of ice in my gut exploded, sending shards of frozen terror through my limbs. Juliet was nowhere in sight, but as I gently rolled Gramps onto his back, it was clear he had been struck by something.

By *someone,* I realized with growing horror.

"Help!"

I shouted the word as loud as I could, over and over until Sally's face appeared at the kitchen window. She raised a finger to signal she was on her way, then disappeared from view.

If Gramps had been like this for long, Juliet would've found him when she came outside and called for help. There wasn't a chance in hell that she'd have left his side willingly.

Unless she was forced.

"You're okay, Gramps," I said, pulling out my phone to call Chief Roberts' cell. "Chief, it's Henry. I'm at the inn. We need an ambulance. Right now."

"Slow down, Henry. Tell me what happened."

The words tumbled from my lips. "I found Gramps in the garden. He's bleeding and Juliet is gone. She wouldn't have left the grounds on her own. Whoever did this took her."

Roberts sucked in a breath. "Heller?"

"It has to be him, but where the hell would he take Juliet?"

Think.

I knew this area better than anyone, had grown up playing on this property and spent hours exploring the woods with Aaron after school.

Where would a killer with a long-standing grudge against the family take her?

My grandfather locked a hand around my wrist just as Sally and Mrs. Gregson reached us, dropping to the ground beside me.

"Woods," he rasped. "To the woods. Go. I'll be...fine. Go."

The woods.

"He took her into the woods. Nan's clearing—that has to be where they went."

"Henry, I've got officers on their way. Stay where you are, do you hear me?"

I didn't bother to respond, just ended the call and looked at the women next to me. "The ambulance is on its way. I'm going after her. Will you stay with him?"

They nodded, their shock swiftly giving way to efficient action as they dabbed gently at my grandfather's bloody temple and began asking him questions.

I looked toward the woods as I rose to my feet, my mind racing. The police were on their way, but I was closer. Juliet couldn't have been gone more than a few minutes before I got outside.

Choking back the panic, I took off at a dead run. I slowed only once I reached the treeline behind the cottage, pausing to listen for anything beyond birds singing and leaves rustling in the breeze.

"I'm coming, Red," I whispered, wishing the vise grip on my heart would ease. "I'm on my way, just hang in there."

As I strode deeper into the trees, I forced myself to focus. Heller had Juliet, but I'd read those articles. He didn't kill his victims in a hurry. He must have something planned, some sick game in mind for her. But how the hell was I going to get her safely away from him?

I would find her. There was simply no alternative that I could live with.

Thirty-Two

JULIET

THE CHIMES AND DANCING colors in Nan's clearing lost their charm as I stumbled and fell to my knees beneath them.

My sketchbook, the one I lost at Cooper's Point, lay open on the grass to my left. I blinked away the haze of tears to see a sketch of my mother—the vivacious, healthy version of her from my childhood, before illness robbed her of that. It was the last drawing I did during my final day in her house, a farewell to everything I was leaving behind to come to Spruce Hill.

"I hoped you would come down the path to me that day," he said from behind me, "but the sketchbook was a nice consolation prize. It kept me company while I waited, along with her note to you."

The note. I hadn't accidentally thrown it out. He took it—the night I came home to find the door unlatched.

He'd been in the cottage.

A new rush of nausea washed over me at the thought of him in my home, touching my things.

"I had them with me the day I watched you through the window, you and your boyfriend, nothing but those useless curtains between you and my binoculars. I used to watch Missy up in her room from that very spot."

I nearly gagged again, closing my eyes as I fought down a surge of bile. The gun was no longer pressed to my back, but I wasn't stupid enough to think he didn't have it ready should I try to make a run for it.

"If that bitch wanted to protect you, she should've told you what was waiting for you here," he taunted. *A matter of life and death.* Leaving the old woman to explain? Even if she hadn't kicked the bucket, she had no clue. If she had, I'd have killed her the minute Missy ran."

I closed my eyes against a wave of grief, but I heard him moving over the leaves underfoot, circling me, and opened them again. This was no time to be caught off guard.

For the first time since learning his identity, I looked at Tom Heller head on as he came to stand in front of me. With a gleeful smile, he turned in a slow circle beneath the suncatchers, arms out wide in a macabre rendition of my first reaction to this sacred place.

"Perfect, isn't it?" he asked, his eyes strangely bright now as he smiled down at me. "An ending fit for an artist. I couldn't create the masterpiece I had in mind for Missy, but yours will honor you both. Mother and daughter, joined in death."

"Why are you doing this?" I asked hoarsely.

His expression twisted into something that might've been sympathy on any other person. He slid the gun into his waistband and reached out to touch my face. When I flinched away from his hand, he caught my hair in a painful twist, jerking my face up toward him. A sharp cry of pain slipped past my lips before I could stop it.

To my horror, the sound seemed to please him. He gently stroked my cheek with his other hand as bile rose in my throat.

If I puked on him, would he kill me any faster?

"This is the way it has to be, can't you see that? None of the others held a candle to Missy. Just poor, sad substitutes." A reminiscent smile lit his face. "She would have fought like a wildcat. I spent months planning it after I first saw her. I knew it would be beyond anything else I'd done."

"You're vile," I whispered.

"Oh yeah, you'll do just fine. The temper, the spirit. Just like her. Missy was worthy of being my masterpiece. I could have drawn it out for days, maybe even weeks. I told her how special it would be between us, but then she left. Stupid, sneaky little bitch!"

With the hand that had caressed my cheek, he drew back and struck me hard across the face. The sudden burst of pain sent tears sliding down my cheeks and stars dancing across my vision. When he yanked my head back up, I saw the twisted pleasure in his eyes. Every one of my fears was confirmed by that unholy glint.

He was going to kill me, and it wasn't going to be an easy death.

After all my mother had done to save my life and her own, this bastard was going to finish what he'd started before I was even born. There was no longer any doubt in my mind that he would succeed.

I'm sorry, Mom. You told me to protect myself, but I failed.

"Such a pretty thing you are, Juliet," he said softly, pressing the pad of his thumb so hard against the bruise blossoming on my cheek that I cried out. "We could have had such fun, if you weren't a meddling little whore like your mother. Still, it can't be helped. The clock is ticking. We'll just have to leave a pretty picture for your boyfriend to find, won't we?"

He reached for his belt and drew out a tiny pocket knife that filled me with a terror even more paralyzing than the gun had. Henry's name echoed in my head as I did the only thing I could think to do.

Fisting my hand, I punched upward between his legs, throwing all of my strength into the blow.

Heller let out a bloodcurdling scream and dropped the knife to the forest floor, doubling over as I shot to my feet. I bolted in the direction I prayed would lead me back toward the inn. With tears blurring my vision, the trees around me morphed into a hazy wall of green and brown.

My legs and lungs burned as I ran. With gasping sobs ripping from my chest, I wouldn't have been able to hear his footsteps behind me, but I didn't dare to assume he wasn't following me.

Don't look, don't look, don't look, I repeated over and over as I wove between the trees.

I didn't bother to wipe at the tears that soaked my cheeks, could think of nothing beyond getting as far away as fast as my feet would carry me.

When I collided with a rock-solid mass, I shrieked and drew my fists defensively upward. A whiff of sea salt and driftwood filtered through my terror even as I struggled against the arms that encircled me.

"Red, it's me. Look at me, Juliet. It's me, I've got you," Henry said in a frantic whisper.

"Henry," I gasped, throwing my arms around him.

I clung to him so tightly he probably couldn't manage a deep breath, but his hands fisted in the back of my shirt and he buried his face in my hair. My entire body trembled in his embrace. I gave myself only the span of a few seconds to hold onto him before insisting we get moving.

A few seconds, however, was too long.

"Ah, young love. How adorable."

The words came in a sing-song voice from a few yards away. Henry shifted to position me partially behind him as he looked toward Heller. I peered around his shoulder, unwilling to let him shield me from this. His presence had flipped a switch in my mind from panic to determination.

This monster would not get the best of us, not now that we were together in facing him down.

From this distance, Heller looked so benign, so harmless in his faded jeans and red flannel shirt, that his malicious sneer alone would have taken me aback, even if he hadn't also been pointing a gun straight at us.

"Star-crossed lovers, aren't you? So precious, really, but destined to part. Maybe it's even better this way, a true homage to Melissa fucking Montgomery. Come on down, folks! Let's have a volunteer. Which one of you should I kill first? I wanted to leave her butchered in the clearing for you, boy, but making her watch while I put a bullet in your brain might heighten the emotion a bit, know what I mean? I love the smell of fear on a woman."

The shudder that wracked my body caused Henry to flinch in front of me.

"At least let me say goodbye," he pleaded.

He sounded so desperate to buy at least one more moment with me, I thought my body might tremble into pieces. I knew what he was trying to do, to buy time for me to escape while he sacrificed himself.

There wasn't a chance in hell that I would let that happen.

Heller waved the gun magnanimously. "Make it quick."

Henry turned, taking me in his arms as he murmured, "I need you to run. Run as fast as you can toward the inn. Roberts is on his way. You have to run."

He kissed my forehead, looking so earnest that my heart shattered, then peeled my arms from his neck even as his eyes shimmered gold beneath the sheen of tears.

I shook my head frantically, but Henry hadn't even managed to step away from me when another voice shouted from somewhere behind us. We both turned and I almost wept with relief when I saw the ring of police officers emerging from the trees around Heller, weapons drawn and trained on the man who wanted to kill us both.

"Drop your weapon! We have you surrounded!"

Then Heller smiled—that broad, cruel smile Nan had captured so perfectly in stark charcoal strokes—and winked at Henry as he pulled the trigger.

I screamed, throwing myself against Henry's chest as fire burst through my shoulder.

We both hit the ground hard enough to knock us breathless as a volley of gunfire broke through the quiet forest. The sound reverberated through the trees, causing a raucous exodus of birds from the branches overhead.

When silence fell once again, Henry dragged in a breath as he rolled over to look down at me.

"Juliet? Look at me. We're okay. It's over now."

My face tipped toward his and I stared up at him, watching his gaze settle on my cheek, where I could tell a bruise had already formed. I felt strange, like I wasn't present inside my own body.

"We're alive," I whispered.

A joyous smile split his face as he nodded, but I didn't smile back, couldn't quite get those muscles to move. Instead, I took in all the warmth of his expression, hoping it would fill me up enough to regain control.

"Yes, we are. We're alive, Red."

"My arm feels funny," I said thickly.

My tongue became awkward in my mouth and my body seemed weighed down, like I was made of concrete. Henry's hands grasped my arms as he scrambled to his knees. I stared up at him, thinking I must be in shock, until he squeezed my left shoulder. Dizzying spirals of pain permeated the numbness, shooting along my limbs as I cried out.

"She's been shot!" Henry shouted, but to my ears, it sounded like his words were coming from a great distance.

The forest overhead went starkly white, then darkness swam across my vision as I slipped from consciousness.

THE SOUNDS THAT FINALLY wove their way through the fog were disjointed, incoherent, tweaking at the corners of my mind from across time and distance. I struggled to open my eyes, to put names to the voices that seemed so close and yet so far away, but my eyelids were so very heavy.

Even with them closed, the room was too bright for me to bear. With a soft sigh, I let sleep overtake me once more.

When consciousness finally pricked at me again, the room seemed darker and my eyelids cooperated after only a momentary struggle. As I blinked away the haze, I saw Henry slouched in a chair beside me, his eyes closed, his face shadowed with stubble now thick enough to be considered a beard.

One of his hands clasped mine on the bed, and with no small effort, I managed to squeeze it. Those hazel eyes I'd come to adore shot wide.

"Juliet." My name caught in his throat as he leaned forward. "Hey."

I watched drowsily as his gaze traveled over every inch of my face, like he was searching for any sign of pain or fear. Though he looked utterly exhausted, he was blessedly, beautifully alive.

Emotion welled up in my chest and I squeezed his hand tighter. I tried to reach for him with my other hand, but it was trapped close against my rib cage. I watched him for a minute before I tried to speak.

"Hey," I replied, startled when the word came out a hoarse croak.

Henry flinched slightly at the sound, but he reached out to stroke my cheek with his other hand. It was a moment before I realized he was avoiding the bruise where Heller hit me, coasting his fingertips across my skin like his affection could erase the mark of violence.

I cleared my throat and spoke again, mollified a bit when the second attempt sounded more like myself. "Hey. Where are we?"

Even in the dimness, the room looked wrong.

"At the hospital. You—" His voice broke and he lifted our entwined fingers to press his lips to my knuckles. "You were shot. Left shoulder, not too much damage, but the bullet was lodged in the muscle there and you needed surgery to remove it. The doctors said you were damn lucky."

At that, I smiled. "I feel lucky."

"Jesus, Red, you took a bullet for me. Pretty sure that makes me the lucky one."

He gave me an unreadable look, but my vision wasn't so bleary that I couldn't catch the shimmer of tears in his eyes.

"I guess I did. Gerard, is he okay? He was bleeding."

Panic flooded me just as swiftly as it had when I found his grandfather on the ground. The details of what happened in the forest started coming back to me in a rush of sound and color that left me dizzy.

"Gramps is fine, just a little banged up. He was released this morning. My brother came up to get him, so he'll stay with Aaron and Lee for a few days until he's back on his feet. You're the one everyone's been worried about. You lost a lot of blood."

"What happened with...him?" I asked.

Henry sighed softly and lifted his free hand to stroke the tangled curls back from my face. I leaned into his touch, more grateful than ever that he was there to give it.

"After he shot you, he opened fire. The cops tried to disarm him, but he kept shooting until they finally took him out." He paused, then said quietly, "He's dead, Juliet. Chief Roberts said they found enough evidence at the cabin he'd been staying in, over by Cooper's Point, to pin over a dozen unsolved murders on him."

My eyelids fluttered slightly under the weight of exhaustion and relief, but I forced them upward again to smile weakly at him. His lips brushed across my forehead as my eyes closed once more.

"Rest now. I'll be right here when you wake up."

I let his reassurance drape over me like a cloak and drifted back off to sleep.

Thirty-Three

HENRY

WHEN JULIET'S EYES FINALLY fluttered open again, she smiled faintly at me. As promised, I was still seated by her side, but when her gaze caught on her friends Sarah and Andre hovering near the foot of the bed, she blinked several times, like she was afraid she might be dreaming.

"What are you doing here?" she whispered.

"Jules," Sarah cried, flying to her side.

Since Juliet's left arm was strapped tightly against her side with a black sling, Sarah very carefully slipped hers around Juliet in an awkward embrace.

"I'm so glad you're okay," Sarah whispered into her hair before drawing back.

"You're supposed to be in Europe. What are you guys doing here?"

As Juliet's focus shifted from Sarah to me, a smile spread across my face at the delight shining in her eyes. Even injured and wan under the harsh fluorescent lights overhead, she looked radiant.

"Henry called us," Sarah said, shooting me a grateful look as she stood again, "and we got on the next flight back to the States. We have a suite at the inn, actually—it's the most adorable place I've ever seen."

I'd found her number in Juliet's phone as soon as Libby got word Juliet was out of surgery and managed to arrange for their stay thanks to a last-minute cancellation, but even if there hadn't been room, I would've made sure they knew they were welcome to a guest room at my house for as long as they wanted.

Andre nodded in agreement as he came over to kiss Juliet's cheek. "And the bathrooms are much better than our last hotel," he said with a grin, but it faded as he wrapped his arm around his wife. "We were worried about you, Jules. Henry told us about everything that's happened, I can't even believe it. We would have come home sooner, you know."

"I know," she whispered, "but you've been planning your trip for so long and I didn't want to screw it up for you."

Sarah gave Juliet a ferocious scowl which quickly melted into a sweet smile as she said, "You couldn't screw anything up if you tried. We love you. I'm just glad Henry was here for you when we couldn't be."

Juliet's head fell back against the pillows, her hand still clinging tightly to mine. "I'm so happy to see you both. Tell me all about your trip."

As Sarah rambled on about their travels, I sat back and watched the three of them together. My worry, an unceasing companion these past two days, eased bit by bit as her friend described the cathedrals and museums they had visited. I'd never been to Europe, but the prospect of vacationing with Juliet to soak up as much beautiful artwork as she could handle filled me with a warm surge of hope for the future.

Whatever it took, I would make it happen. We had the rest of our lives before us, after all.

Nearly an hour had passed by the time Libby popped her head into the room. The way she beamed when she saw Juliet awake and upright mirrored my feelings perfectly.

Juliet had captured so many hearts here in Spruce Hill. I was humbled to be among that number.

"How's our patient?" Libby asked as she approached the bed.

"Happy to be alive," Juliet said softly, "but I'd be even happier to go home. How long do I have to stay here?"

When I saw the blush and sideways glance she shot at me after using the word *home*, I squeezed her hand in mine.

I didn't think I'd ever get tired of hearing it.

"I'll see if I can pull some strings. That is, if you've got someone to keep an eye on you this time around?" she asked, her teasing glance landing on me.

"I might never take my eyes off her again," I vowed.

With the way Juliet was looking at me, I didn't think she would find any cause to complain about that.

Several long hours later, after discussions with the surgeon who'd removed the bullet from her arm and with Chief Roberts himself, Juliet was cleared to leave the hospital. I kept my arm firmly around her waist from the minute she stood up out of the policy-mandated wheelchair until she was safely ensconced in my truck, then again until she was tucked into my bed.

Though she said she appreciated my concern, her tolerance for being coddled ran out first thing the next morning, when I tried to serve her breakfast in bed.

"Henry," she snapped, "I promise you, I am fine. I have two perfectly good legs. I'm not spending another minute in this bed unless it's to get naked with you."

I didn't take the outburst personally. In fact, I was pleased she was finally well enough to speak her mind again. Those days spent hovering over her pale, lifeless form, connected to sensors and machines, had been the stuff of nightmares.

Instead of arguing, I tugged the covers off her and held out a hand, then grinned when she stared at me.

"Oh, I'm sorry. Was that an invitation for me to get naked? I assumed you meant you wanted to get out of bed, but if I was wrong, I'll gladly join you," I told her.

Juliet grabbed my hand and rose carefully to her feet, then studied me for a moment.

"Yes," she said finally. "I mean, yes, I want to get out of bed now, but also yes to getting naked. Later. Always. Forever. I thought you were going to give me the 'Juliet, you almost died' speech."

I lifted my other hand to her cheek. The bruise had mostly faded, leaving just a hint of shadow behind. I'd never be able to erase what she had endured, but I would do my best to support her through healing from it.

"Always. I like the sound of that. And you did almost die, but I'm trying my damnedest to focus on the fact that you didn't. I need to tell you something, though."

"What?"

Her expression filled with dread, but she must have seen the softness in my eyes as I gazed down at her. That seemed to ease her tension before I even spoke.

"I love you," I whispered. "You don't have to say it back, but I need you to believe it's true. The thought that I could have lost you without ever saying it, without you knowing, I can't risk that happening. I love you, Juliet."

She released my hand only to throw her good arm around me, then buried her face in the crook of my neck as I wrapped both of mine around her, clasping her to me. I rubbed one hand soothingly along her spine and cupped the back of her neck with the other.

Even though the breath shuddered from her lungs, no tears dampened my skin, which seemed like a good sign. Still, I asked, "You don't hate me for saying it, do you?"

Her nose brushed against my throat as she shook her head. I kissed her temple, content just to hold her again. After a few minutes, she drew back and tangled her fingers in the front of my shirt. The fierceness of her gaze made me want to kiss her, but I forced myself to wait patiently instead.

"I love you," she said finally, firmly, a declaration that came without hesitation or doubt. "I need you to know that, too."

A tremor ran through her just before my lips met hers. There, in the warm circle of my arms, I knew Juliet had finally come home.

Epilogue

Juliet

As spring blossomed into a hot, beautiful summer, I worked hard with the physical therapist Libby recommended—and also with Lewis Zoratti, who swiftly came to appreciate my visions for renovating the cottage into something new. I sometimes suspected he might've had a moment or two of regret over offering to help once he finally understood the scope of my plans, but the man was a godsend and I desperately enjoyed fostering a friendship with someone who'd known my mother so well.

Every tiny connection to her and Nan was a blessing in itself, each one of them worth far more than the journals and notebooks that had been lost in the fire.

In the early weeks of my recovery, I ventured once or twice to mention that I could find an apartment if I needed to, but

Henry had pinned me with his intense hazel gaze and made sure I knew just how much he wanted me there with him at his house.

The memory of his efforts to convince me to stay still brought a rush of heat to my cheeks.

With my project to keep me busy and Henry's renewed focus on updating the inn's website and reservation systems, the summer passed in a flurry of activity. Though I didn't think I'd ever get used to being the topic of small town gossip, I did finally start to feel like I was no longer an outsider, thanks in large part to the continual stream of well-wishes from everyone in town after our final confrontation with Heller. Henry's house was swiftly filled with flowers, gift baskets, and enough prepared meals to keep an army fed for months.

By the final week of August, I looked forward to Nan's memorial. The arrangements would all be carried out by Mr. Escobar and the staff at the inn, leaving me with little to do as far as preparation.

I did, however, decide to use the occasion to unveil my official plans for the cottage, which added an edge of nervous excitement to the days leading up to the event.

The day of the memorial dawned bright and sunny. With a cloudless blue sky overhead and the promise of a gentle breeze along the lake, I didn't think I could have orchestrated more perfect weather.

When I came downstairs in a gauzy, flowing sundress of pale yellow, Henry drew a sharp breath as his expression heated. I paused in front of the lighthouse painting I'd gifted him with—I'd started it from scratch for him as soon as I was able after my surgery. It was the only painting of mine to hang in the house rather than the inn, at Henry's insistence.

He held out his hand to usher me down the last few steps and drew me in for a kiss. "You look absolutely ravishing."

The scar on my left shoulder was only partially covered by the thin strap of the dress, and Henry brushed his fingers over it as he kissed me again. It had become something of a habit, as though he needed to reassure himself that I was really there in his arms, that I'd survived the nightmare.

When I questioned him about it, he confessed it was more like an act of reverence, a reminder of what I'd risked for his sake and how much I meant to him.

Though the area was neither tender nor ticklish, the way my skin shivered under his fingertips reminded us both of other, more pleasurable things.

In pressed khaki pants and a short-sleeved linen dress shirt, he cut an impressive figure himself. Henry drove us over to the inn in my car, with Blue in the back seat to keep her hair off my dress as she stuck her furry face out the window.

I clasped my mother's ring in one hand, the other toying nervously with my skirt until Henry covered it with his own. The gentle stroke of his thumb across my knuckles gradually drained some of the tension from my body.

"Do you think many people will show up?" I asked.

"Whether they do or not, it'll be perfect."

Henry lifted my hand to his lips and smiled over at me. I tucked his simple reassurance around me like a blanket.

The parking lot was nearly empty when we arrived, but there was an hour still to go before the memorial was scheduled to begin. Though I'd been at the cottage regularly over the months that had passed, neither Henry nor I had been back out to Nan's clearing since that fateful day.

We were both ready to lay the ghosts of the past to rest, even if it had taken some encouragement from him to convince me I could handle it.

Leaving the car in the lot, we strolled together through the gardens on our way to the woods. Blue danced excitedly around us, pausing here and there to sniff at the flower beds. I laughed at the dog's antics, but I gripped Henry's hand a bit more tightly than usual.

He leaned down to murmur against my ear, "Sure you're ready for this?"

My sigh was barely audible. "As ready as I'll ever be. Besides, if I pass out, I figure you've proven you can carry me a pretty good distance through the woods."

"I'll carry you anywhere, Red," he assured me, grinning.

Though my tension returned the minute the faint tinkle of windchimes met our ears, we continued walking, hand in hand. I fought hard to keep the images of that day from flooding my mind, focusing instead on the warmth of Henry's hand in mine, the brush of my dress against his pants, the scent of his soap wafting over to tease my senses.

As the trees opened to Nan's clearing, the two of us paused to hover just outside the circle of dancing colors. I sucked in a deep breath and propelled us both forward until we were standing in the middle of the clearing, right where I'd stumbled to my knees.

I closed my eyes, turned into his embrace, and willed myself to think only of us, now, in this moment. Eventually, the tension ebbed once more and I peeked up at Henry.

He cupped my face in his hands and mouthed, "I love you."

My heart fluttered wildly against my ribs as I mouthed the words back to him.

When his lips covered mine, the clearing fell away, taking with it every memory of terror that had flashed through my head. Even with my eyes closed, the warm rays of sunlight settled against my skin, a rainbow caress imbued with all the love Nan had poured into this special place.

When at last we drew apart, Henry trailed his lips across my forehead.

"This is what she would've wanted," he said softly, "for this to be a place of love and hope and comfort. She loved you, even if she never got the chance to tell you in person."

"I wish I could have known her."

"I do, too."

A tremor wriggled up my spine as I let my gaze travel over the streaks of color across the grass.

"I don't want that bastard to taint what she left here. He took too much from all three of you. Right now, we're taking it back."

I rested my head against his chest, listening to the steady rhythm of his heartbeat under my ear. For several long moments, I simply stood there with my arms wrapped around his waist. I believed it, the truth of his words, as they settled in my heart.

When Henry's fingers traced gentle circles across the skin of my upper back, I recalled other words he had spoken here. He felt the resulting shiver run through me and laughed softly.

"Someday," he murmured, "but not yet. We've got all the time in the world."

At that, my hand slipped around to the back of his neck so I could kiss him again.

"Yes, we do."

After a few slightly more heated minutes under the tinkling chimes, we took one final look around the clearing and set off toward the inn. I couldn't be certain that memories of Tom Heller wouldn't haunt this beautiful place for the foreseeable future, but with time—and, more importantly, with Henry's reassuring presence at my side—I hoped that I'd someday replace those memories with better ones.

Once we returned to the gardens, the sheer number of people mingling among the flowers with punch and daintily decorated cookies in hand startled me. My stride faltered and my courage wavered.

Henry turned me to face him instead of the crowd, smiling down at me in that heartbreakingly gentle way of his.

"This is your day, Red. They're here as much to support you as to remember Nan. I won't let you stumble, I promise."

I forced a deep breath into my lungs and nodded. "Let's do this, then."

We wound our way through the crowd, shaking hands and chatting, until I caught sight of Sarah. The two of us threw ourselves into each other's arms. Even our daily text exchanges hadn't kept me from missing my best friend fiercely.

"You look beautiful, Jules," Sarah said, dabbing at her eyes with a crumpled tissue. "God, I'm so emotional these days."

I leaned back a little and cocked a brow. "Oh? And why is that, might I ask?"

Sarah's face burst into a huge smile as her gaze drifted to Andre, who stood several feet away with Henry, Mark, and the two men who'd been introduced as Mark's brothers. "We weren't going to tell anyone yet," she whispered, "but you're not just anyone. Will you be my baby's godmother? Oh, Jules, I miss you so much."

"I miss you, too, and of course I will. I'm so happy for you both."

My heart grew lighter as I linked my arm through Sarah's. It was strange to think the two of us were old enough for things like marriage and babies—and inn ownership, I supposed—but the promise of new life as we celebrated Nan filled me with joy.

I tugged Sarah into another tight hug just as Mrs. Gregson took the microphone from Mr. Escobar's hands and urged us all to find a seat.

With Henry on one side and Sarah on the other, I laughed, cried, and everything in between as the speakers who'd been enlisted stood before the staggering number of townspeople who had shown up. When the stories of Nan's wonderfully full and beautiful life finally came to an end, I rose and rubbed my hands nervously against my skirt before I stepped up to the podium.

"Thank you all so much for being here today. Through each of you, Nan's memory has come to life for me, and that has been a truly priceless gift. We can't change the past, no matter how much I might wish to sometimes, but together, we can look to the future."

My eyes caught Henry's across the short distance between us and I had to pause for a second as the impact of his smile hit me. After a deep breath, I went on with my speech.

"And since I'm not nearly as eloquent as the rest of you, I'm going to stop babbling and simply show you what I've been working on these last few months. After the fire, I couldn't imagine trying to recreate everything Nan had left, but I couldn't bear to tear down any piece of her history, either."

I stepped over to the easel Henry had set up for me and lifted the sheet to reveal my own artwork, a poster-sized color sketch of Nan's cottage. When I lifted away the top image, the one below showed a depiction of the inside of the cottage—not as a home, but as an intimate art gallery.

A hushed murmur of approval swept over the crowd.

"The Lakeside Gallery will feature work from local artists, including a number of Nan's own pieces. Through the inn, Nan's legacy lives on—and through the gallery, so will her heart."

Applause echoed across the gardens. I swallowed hard and blinked back tears at the enthusiastic show of support.

A moment later, I was surrounded by well-wishers offering congratulations on such a beautiful tribute to Nan, by friends who had become family, by love, acceptance, and that sweet sense of belonging that had eluded me until I set foot in Spruce Hill.

Long after the crowd moved on, the glow of it lingered deep inside of me.

As most of the others filtered away, Henry's brother Aaron and his husband, Lee, approached me and Henry. Behind them was a tall man with a ruddy complexion and sandy brown hair. I smiled politely at him even as I noticed the streaks of copper in his goatee.

"Juliet, this is our neighbor, Matthew Callahan. He grew up next door to our house in Oakville. We were talking about the memorial yesterday while we were working in the yard, and, well . . ." Aaron trailed off, gesturing for Callahan to come closer.

The man had a shy smile and warm blue eyes several shades darker than my own. He shook my hand, then suddenly he was blinking back tears.

"I was a very close friend of your mother, Juliet. Well, that's not quite true—I was head over heels in love with her. I gave her a promise ring not long before she left town. We were going to get married after graduation," he said softly.

"You were?" My heart tripped in my chest as the implications sank in.

Callahan drew an old Polaroid photograph from his pocket and handed it to me. There was my mother, young and carefree in a way I'd never seen, her blonde hair crimped and teased. Beside her stood a baby-faced Matthew Callahan, gazing over at my mother with such love that I could feel it, even across the decades that had passed. My mother held up her left hand for the camera, revealing a dainty opal ring.

"She wore that ring every day of my life. She always said my father gave it to her, that it was all she had left of him," I said softly, when at last I was able to drag my gaze from the photo.

Drawing the ring on its silver chain from under the neckline of my dress, I stared at the man standing before me, dimly aware of Aaron dabbing at his eyes with a tissue. Callahan gave a wobbly smile.

"I didn't know she was pregnant when she left or I would've followed her, no matter what arguments she gave. I had her take my car the night she came to say goodbye. She made me promise not to look for her, she said it was a matter of life and death for both of us."

I closed my eyes for a beat, then whispered, "It was."

"I didn't understand at the time, but I knew she wasn't the frivolous party girl everyone made her out to be. She was every bit as shrewd and clever as her mother. I always thought she'd come back home eventually. I didn't realize that would be the last time I ever saw her, but she refused to let me come with her."

"She was a stubborn woman," I said with a teary laugh.

"I've never loved anyone the way I loved Missy. We might be strangers, Juliet, but now that I see you, I feel like I've known you my whole life. You're all grown up and probably don't need a father figure around, but maybe we can be friends?"

I swallowed twice, then threw my arms around him. Even Henry looked a little misty-eyed when I caught sight of him smiling at me over Callahan's shoulder.

"Yes, yes to all of it," I whispered.

When I finally let go of him, Callahan insisted I keep the picture. We exchanged phone numbers and another fierce hug before he departed. I stared down at the photo for a long time as the rest of the crowd dispersed, until Henry came up behind me and slipped his arms around my waist.

"That was unexpected," he said softly, "but what a perfect ending to a perfect day."

"Yes, it was."

I turned in his arms and held him tight. I wasn't sure whether to laugh or cry or both. Even though the conflicting emotions threatened to bubble up out of me, the strength of Henry's embrace helped me to hold it together.

A few stragglers came up to offer their congratulations on the cottage project and Henry reluctantly let go of me so I could thank them for coming. I wasn't an outsider, not anymore—the town had claimed me as one of their own, a beloved granddaughter finally welcomed back to the hometown where she belonged.

My heart swelled with love for the man beside me and for the friends who'd helped me make a place for myself in Spruce Hill.

When Henry at last had me to himself, he took my hand and led me past the gardens, all the way down to the lake. He knew about my project, but I'd insisted he wait to see the big reveal along with everyone else. His arm looped around my waist, tugging me tight against his side, and I laid my head against his shoulder.

For a long time, we stood there together, enjoying the view of the water almost as much as we enjoyed the quiet companionship we'd found in one another.

"You were incredible today, Red. You *are* incredible. How'd I get so lucky?"

"It wasn't luck," I replied, "but I think it might be just what Nan would have wanted."

He pressed his lips to the top of my head. "Then I guess we better not let her down."

With the lake stretching before us, the inn at our backs, and the future in our hands, I wholeheartedly agreed.

Also by

Rachel Fitzjames

Keep in touch! Sign up for Rachel's newsletter at https://rac helfitzjames.com/ for FREE bonus content, sneak peeks, sales, and news about upcoming releases!

Spruce Hill Series

Unpacking Secrets

A Lonely Road

Canvas of Lies

Crumbling Truth

Playing for Paradise

Sinister Returns

Treasured Legacy

Lucky Save

Wrenching Hearts

Flash of Danger

Acknowledgements

I never expected to be here, sending a whole series out into the world, but to the little baby version of Rachel who dreamed of being an author—thank you for setting us on this path (we would have made a terrible fashion designer, so this was the right choice). And to my family, I would never have made it happen without your support, from forcing my pantser self to at least try to plot on occasion to helping me name my characters (and their pets) to being endlessly patient when I beg for just another minute to finish writing this chapter. Every failure cake, every Pinterest fashion inspo board, every piece of artwork, and every moment of telling me this dream would someday come true—you're my favorite and my best. I love you guys.

Melissa Rotert, I would absolutely not have made it to this point without you. I'd still be sitting on my dragon hoard of crappy, head-hopping manuscripts with only redheaded heroines, too afraid to even attempt a query letter, if not for your steadfast support. I'm so immensely glad you chose my introvert self to be your friend, and I love you everything.

To my CP group—Christie Curry, Christina Brennan, and Briana Newstead—you guys have made these books into what they are, and I cannot thank you enough! Having you with me through every up and down of this process has meant the world to me. I will be eternally grateful that my desperate plea for readers (thank you, Christie!) resulted in connecting with you all!

To Tara Ryan, Shelby Holt, Erin Rose, and Heather Frances, thank you so much for taking the time to read this book (sometimes more than once!). Tobie Carter and Lindsay Barrett, thank you so much for being my indie gurus along this path!

To the friends and family and members of the romance writing community who read this book in various stages, I appreciate you all and hope you find this version far better than the old ones! And lastly, to everyone on SF 2.0 for answering my often-panicked questions and talking me down, you're all amazing and I'm so glad I found my way to your doorstep like a sad little feral kitten waiting to learn from your experiences.

About the author

Rachel Fitzjames is the author of a contemporary romantic suspense series set in the fictional town of Spruce Hill, NY. She started writing on her brother's ancient computer back in the early 90s and never looked back, though her first short story about an underground cat thievery ring was sadly lost. With a degree in geography inspired by wanderlust, Rachel has a keen appreciation for the escape that the romance genre allows. She is a lifelong resident of Western NY and created Spruce Hill in order to give a little bit of home to all of her characters.

Connect with Rachel at her website, https://rachelfitzjames.com/, or on Instagram and Threads at @rachelfitzjames.